LAWN HOUSE BLUES

PHILIPPA HAWLEY

In memory of Dorothy and Philip, my dear parents.

Philippa Hawley

I'd like to thank my writing tutors, old and new, as well as the members of my two supportive writing groups. Thanks particularly go to the readers of multiple drafts along the way, especially Clinton Hale, Jane Canfer, Helen Chambers, Pauline Rendall, Sue Dawes, Clare Hawkins and Eleanor Young. I am most grateful to Kimberley for her editing skills, Stefan for the lovely cover and Gabriel for looking after me at SpiffingCovers.

I

LAWN HOUSE

September 2013

A jolt from the past and hopes for the future enhanced the thrill he felt on coming through these wrought iron gates. When visiting Oliver and the children at Lawn House, Max loved to proceed sedately up the drive, pretending he was rich enough to own the impressive red brick house with its tall chimneys. He'd take in the view of the manicured, formal gardens and the well-established trees in the distance and think how lucky he was to have a friend with a place like this. He'd heard a number of Oliver's stories about the house, but probably not quite all of them – it must be like living in a history book.

'Be quick, Max,' Jenny said sharply.

He reached over and touched his wife's hand, which was resting on her huge bump.

'You all right?'

'He's jumping on my bladder. I really need the loo,' Jenny answered.

'Okay, I'll park right by the door,' Max said.

She pushed his hand away and adjusted her seat. 'That's better. Well, there's certainly no room for him to turn now is there, so I'll just have to accept the idea of a Caesarean section.'

'It's out of our control, darling. At least your mother can

plan her diary and be here to help you next week once you're home from hospital.'

'Hey ho, another joy to look forward to!' Jenny sighed.

The heavy, oak door of Lawn House opened and their two godchildren rushed out.

'They're here, Daddy,' called Issy, the larger of the two four-year-olds.

'Hello, lovely girl,' said Max, jumping out of the driving seat to hug her.

Willow, the other twin, ran around to Jenny, who was hauling herself out of her side of the car.

'Careful, Auntie Jenny needs the bathroom,' Max said, extricating himself from Issy's clutches.

'I'll take her. We don't want an accident,' Willow said with the wisdom of someone soon to be five.

'It's fine, I think I know the way by now thanks.' Jenny managed a weary smile and flicked one of Willow's plaits.

'This baby is making her tired Willow, but she'll be okay. Where's that father of yours?'

Oliver appeared in the doorway. He was wearing his best gardening gear of long brown boots, baggy corduroy trousers and a thick green jumper with holes at the elbows.

'See you in a minute,' Jenny said as she swept past him. 'Call of nature.'

'Come inside you lot. Mrs Hall's got a roast in the Aga for lunch, but we've time for a beer first.'

'Not for me, I'm driving, but I could handle a cup of tea. Jenny's just on water with a slice of lemon at the moment, everything else gives her heartburn.'

'Ha, I remember Alexis was like that when she was having the twins. I'm so glad you two could make it this weekend,' Oliver said. He was trying hard, but his expression was flat, and Max knew why.

'We wouldn't have missed it for anything, other than maybe premature labour. We know how important this anniversary is to you,' Max said. He followed Oliver in to the drawing room.

Oliver didn't talk a great deal about his late wife. He would just drop her name into conversations from time to time, as if testing that he could do so without falling apart. However, each year, on the anniversary of her death, he made an exception and she briefly became centre stage, as if she'd re-joined the family for the day.

The men were settled in the drawing room, recalling memories of Alexis, when Jenny reappeared. Issy and Willow rushed about getting cushions to make her comfortable on the couch, while Oliver fetched the drinks. The twins sat their dolls on yet more cushions, then snuggled themselves in next to Jenny.

'No Celine today?' Jenny asked.

'It's her day off,' Issy announced. 'We don't need her as much now we're older.'

'Oh, I expect you do, but it's nice she can have time off sometimes,' Max said, remembering how in the first year after Alexis's death Celine, the nanny, and Mrs Hall, the housekeeper, had kept the sad house going. He looked at the happy faces on the couch today and thought what a good job they'd done. If only dear Alexis could see them now.

Oliver appeared with a tray. 'Mrs Hall says twenty minutes until lunch. Careful girls, don't squash Jenny.'

'I'm fine, don't worry,' Jenny said.

Oliver gave out the drinks and raised his glass. 'To absent friends and family,' he said, and Max and Jenny murmured the same.

'Can we do a toast?' Issy said. Both girls jumped up and found their glasses of juice. 'To babies and dollies,' she said, and the sombre moment was gone.

'All set for next week then?' Oliver asked.

'I'm trying not to think about it too much. Just want it over and done with and the baby out safely.'

'Celine says he's going to be cut out,' Issy said.

Max heard Willow say 'urgh'. He understood her feelings perfectly; his own anxiety had been building up as they neared the due date.

'I will be having an operation in my tummy, but it won't hurt because they'll give me a special injection. They'll be very careful,' Jenny explained.

'Oh, that's all right then,' Willow said. She picked up her doll and gave it a cuddle. 'What shall we call your baby? Can we call him Tiger?'

'I don't think that'll go with our surname. Tiger Brown would sound weird. No, we've got an idea, but we're keeping it secret until he's born,' Jenny replied.

'Let's talk about something else,' said Max with a smile. 'The gardens are looking good, Oliver. Many visitors last month?'

'Yes, and the trees are in good nick, especially Alexis's oak. The gardening team are working hard and it's paying off. Numbers are up and the shop's doing well. Trouble is, the damned taxman's chasing me, and the solicitor is still battling with the accountant. All this time and I still don't have Father's final probate sorted out.'

Max saw how the wrinkles on Oliver's face had increased in the four years since he'd lost his wife. Alexis had been Max's friend from student days, and he and Jenny had absorbed Oliver into their circle much later. Poor Oliver then had to deal with losing his parents and inheriting the house, while he was still grieving for Alexis. Having an expensive estate to run couldn't be easy in today's world. It was certainly brave of him to allow a recording studio to be built in the stable block, and although that brought in revenue, Max knew it also brought worries. In reality, Max wouldn't actually want to own this place, however much he loved to be entertained here. And he did enjoy coming over for therapeutic runs in the beautiful grounds too. When he ran at Lawn House, he would pass by Alexis's tree on his circuit. The tree took pride of place within the fenced off arboretum and Max always nodded at the brass memorial plaque Oliver had put at its base.

Max's thoughts and the general chit-chat were interrupted by a knock at the door. As Della Hall pushed it open, she straightened her apron and smiled, moving grey wisps of fringe to one side with the back of her hand. Her flushed face suggested it was hard work in the kitchen, and it was clear she wasn't getting any younger.

'Lunch is ready in the main dining room, Mr Oliver,' she announced, and then she smiled at Jenny. 'We thought we'd treat you this weekend, my dear, because you might not be able to get over here for a while.'

'Thank you, Mrs Hall, that's so thoughtful,' Jenny said.

'Not quite the last supper, more like the last lunch,' Jenny whispered to Max as he helped heave her up off the sofa.

'Oh, Mr Oliver, not outdoor boots in the dining room if you don't mind,' Mrs Hall said quietly as Max slipped past her on his way to the cloakroom to wash his hands.

Max looked round and saw the housekeeper nod down at the boss's feet in much the way as Celine would have done to the children.

2

Fifty Years Earlier

Della's diary, Saturday 22nd February 1964

Mum, I'm writing this for you. I wish you could see this amazing place I've come to. It's a far cry from our semi in Hertfordshire and I don't know if I'm excited or terrified. I've had a guided tour from the housekeeper – Old Mrs Hall they call her – and it's so huge I'm sure I'll get still get lost about these corridors.

I have a room on the top floor. I wish the window were bigger so I could see more of the lovely gardens. Most of the other staff live out in the village so I have a bathroom and kitchenette to myself. I should be grateful, but it does seem awfully quiet up here. I hope I make some friends soon.

I've met Mr and Mrs Trelawney-Smythe. I'm to be her lady's maid and do whatever she wants, apparently. He seems older than her, handsome in a distinguished sort of way, and rather serious. She looks beautiful but haughty, and I'm wondering if I did the right thing answering that advert in 'The Lady' knowing so little about the position. As you would have said, Mum, only time will tell. I can't believe you've gone – I do miss you so very much.

3

NEAR MISS

March 2014

Six months after Jenny had the baby, Max was working at his desk when the phone rang. All he remembered hearing was the name "Oliver Trelawney" and the words "urgent" and "emergency" before his secretary transferred the incoming call. Until that day he'd always thought of her as being so calm; however, this morning, her voice was anything but and he sensed her genuine alarm.

There was a click, then Max heard Oliver's voice tremble down the line: 'I'm at the hospital in Ipswich. You need to get here as soon as you can.'

'Is it Jacob? What's happened?' Max let out a breath and the words rushed out with it. Why did he suspect Jacob was in trouble? He'd only been a parent for a few months, yet the connection with his son was already deeply entrenched.

'Jacob and Jenny, they're both here, and you need to come.'

'What –' Max said.

'Listen, Max, just get here as soon as you can,' Oliver said.

'Why? What's happened?' Max asked again, and the word "urgent" suddenly made sense.

'An accident. I'll tell you more when you get here,' Oliver said.

'Jesus Christ! Are they –'

'Everything's going to be all right. Don't waste time asking questions, just drive, but be careful.'

He checked his mobile – shit, it was on silent. His secretary had poured him a glass of water from the cooler, and he saw she was now getting his jacket and laptop case ready for him to depart. In her hurry, she knocked the glass and water spread all over a file on his desk, labelled "Maxwell Brown, IT Director". (He hated it that at work they called him Maxwell.) He saw the watery ink run like escaped tears over the edge and onto the floor. How could Oliver possibly say everything would be all right when his six-month-old baby was in hospital? This was beyond belief. His thoughts were madly jumping. He had to go.

Max drove at a steady 70mph once out of London. He knew there was no point in risking a speeding ticket or another accident. His brain still raced, even if the car didn't, and he tried to understand why they were both in Ipswich, when Jenny should have been at work in Norwich and Jacob with his nanny. A familiar chant came into his head and he repeated it to prevent his mind from diving into an abyss of anxiety: *All will be well, all will be well, all manner of things will be well.* Over and over he said it as he drove through the flat fields of Essex and Suffolk. When bad thoughts slipped in though the mantra he switched to the calming exercises he'd learned from a counsellor he once knew. Now he practised her breathing patterns as he concentrated on the road. He used every tool at his disposal to stay calm and reach his family safely. He even prayed to the god he didn't believe in and, with an intensity which surprised him, he asked for his wife and baby son to be well.

The roads were kind to him and progress was, thankfully, good. Max did well for a natural worrier, whose family were in the midst of potential disaster. He thought about how he'd left the office without a moment of hesitation. At school he'd picked up the nickname "Instant" after a certain branded coffee, even though he was anything but instant. In fact, his classmates had thought him a cautious ditherer. On this day, however, when life took a swerve in a scary direction, his departure from the office had been about as instant as it got. Once road signs saying Ipswich started to appear, though, anxiety stirred up again, like a dormant parasite coming back to life, gripping his innards.

The hospital car park was full, and on the second circuit he gave up and parked in a space marked Consultants Only. *Sod it, sue me*, he thought as he rushed to A&E. A nurse pointed him towards a container of hand sanitizer, then showed him to some blue plastic curtains, through which he was relieved to hear Oliver's cultured voice, not now trembling but speaking gently. When the nurse drew back the curtains, Max found Oliver perched on a stool, next to Jenny's trolley in the pokey cubicle. Jenny's eyes were shut in semi-conscious sleep – heavy painkillers were at work in the battered body. The pervading odour of the hospital, disinfectant and illness was nearly too much for Max. The alcohol-based hand sanitizer added to the smell, and he gulped to control the acid rising in his gullet. Oliver stood up and put a steadying arm round his friend's shoulders.

'What the hell's happened?' The words caught in Max's constricted throat.

'She's okay. She's had a brain scan and there's no sign of damage,' Oliver said. 'Jacob's in the children's unit.'

'But ...?' Max said. 'What ...?'

'Jacob was taken ill at Lawn House. It was his breathing. They called Jenny. I'm so sorry, Max, she ... was almost here when she collided with a lorry on her way back from Norwich,' Oliver said.

Max leaned over his wife and stroked her brow. 'Oh, Jenny, what's happened to you, darling girl? I'm here now. I'll check on Jacob too.'

'Jacob's quite poorly, Max. The doctors want to talk to you,' Oliver said.

'Oh God. I need to go to him. What about Jen, though?'

'I can stay a while – Celine's at home with my girls. Jenny is going to be okay. The doctor told me she has two un-displaced fractures of the pelvis – they'll heal in time – but her right leg is broken just above the ankle and that'll need surgery.'

Jenny parted her hooded eyelids and spoke with a woolly voice. It didn't sound a bit like her. 'An operation?' the voice said.

'It's all right, I'm here.' Max held her hand and stroked it.

'Where's Jacob?' she said. 'I want to see Jacob.' She grasped Max's hand and grunted in pain as she tried to move her body. She fell back onto the pillow and closed her eyes as if to shut out the despair.

Max, who at that moment would have gladly swapped places with her, leaned across with the gentlest of hugs, and kissed her dry lips. He dabbed away the tears, which leaked onto her pale cheeks, and made calming noises, and uttered those meaningless words often used in times of crisis: 'Don't worry, it'll be all right, I'm here for you.' The words really said nothing at all, but somehow soothed.

'J-Jacob,' Jenny said, sounding even more slurred as she struggled to stay awake.

Max was close to being back to Max the ditherer, uncertain how to be with his wife and, at the same time, go and find Jacob. Inside the blue-curtained cubicle he understood what was happening, but when he went to his son he knew he'd have to face something of greater uncertainty.

Terror beckoned.

'I'm going to go and see him now. I'll be back quite soon.' He turned to his friend. 'Thanks, Oliver.'

Just then a nurse appeared to tell them Jenny's ankle would be pinned the following morning and until then she'd be transferred to a bed on the orthopaedic ward. 'I've ordered a porter,' the nurse said. 'I'll be going with her. She'll be on Charnley Ward on the first floor.'

Max followed the yellow signs to Paediatrics, which proved to be miles away at the opposite end of the hospital. He trudged, and muttered as he went. 'Bloody typical! Who designed this place? *All will be well ... all manner of things will be well.*'

His strides were long and became more purposeful as he counted the footsteps in runs of fifty. He wasn't sure his counsellor would have approved of the counting, but now was not the time to address that habit. He didn't know what he'd find at the end of those long straight corridors, with grey floor tiles, marked with black streaks from the soles of previous passing shoes. His anxiety seemed to heighten his awareness of everything around him. The walls were clad with white tiles, and different coloured signs showed which departments he walked past. There was a background smell of cheap cleaning agents, and every now and then the heavier stink of disinfectant as he walked past the visitors' toilets. Max could have done with using the loo himself but dared not delay. He passed a cafeteria and the pong of soup and coffee mixed together made him feel nauseous. He then turned a corner and ran up the stairs, following the yellow arrow to Paediatrics. There was no time to wait for a lift and, anyway, Max didn't do lifts.

Before he could ring the buzzer at the entrance to the paediatric unit, the swing doors opened and he recognised Tricia being escorted out by a bustling, middle-aged woman whom Max later discovered was a social worker. Tricia looked wild, and her long copper-coloured curls fell bedraggled over her face. She turned to Max but was pulled away.

'That's Tricia, Jacob's nanny,' Max said to no one in particular.

'Max, I need to speak to you. I love Jacob. I saved him. I need to see he's all right!' Tricia shouted.

'Tricia?'

Max tried to go to the distressed woman but the ward

sister appeared, took his arm, having gathered who he was, and firmly steered him through the double doors to an inner lobby saying, 'It's this way, Mr Brown.'

'Where are they taking Tricia?'

'We'll tell you later. Your son is safe here with us.'

'Is he breathing?'

'He's settling,' was all she said whilst she showed him where to wash his hands. His patience was being challenged, and she seemed quite brusque when she insisted he don a green gown before entering Special Care.

'Special Care, that sounds serious,' Max said. 'Will someone please tell me what's happened to Jacob?'

Once on the ward, in the presence of the children, the sister softened her tone. 'We're still piecing it together, but yes, his breathing was causing problems,' she said. 'He's improving already, but the nanny seems rather agitated and we can't have her upsetting these babies. Now come and see Jacob for yourself, and please don't be alarmed by the machines.'

She took Max to the side of a little clear plastic cot, in which lay his darling, with a tube up his nose and another in his mouth. His hair, which had just begun to give a hint of the Brown family curls, had been flattened down. He had a drip held in place by a thick bandage on his tiny left arm. On the other side of the cot, machines blinked and beeped like robots in a science fiction film, and a young doctor leaned over, placing his stethoscope, which surely was too big for the job, on Jacob's chest. Max watched Jacob's ribcage pulse in time with the robots and felt his own ribs grip in sympathy.

The doctor looked up and spoke. 'Mr Brown, hello, I'm Dr Mercer and I work for Dr Singh, Jacob's lead consultant. Jacob's doing well.'

'Can I touch him? What's wrong with him?' Max asked.

'Sure, just mind the tubes. We're ventilating him until we get some test results back. His breathing was very irregular when he first arrived and his oxygen levels were low.'

'But why?' Max asked. His boy was breathing normally when he'd left for work this morning; he couldn't imagine what could have changed that.

'We're treating it as a near miss cot death. I know that sounds bad, but the quick actions of his nanny saved it from being ... worse. We're hoping he'll be breathing for himself again soon.'

'But why was Tricia being marched away?' Max said.

'We have to get all the facts before we can confirm what's happened, but in the meantime, we have to stick to protocol. You see ... we're just a bit worried about a bruise on Jacob's right arm.'

'What bruise? Can I see it?' Max said.

'Yes, sure. Now did you or your wife notice a bruise this morning? Does he bruise easily?' Dr Mercer asked.

'No, never has. Let me see it?' Max demanded.

Dr Mercer called a nurse and they carefully moved the light sheet which covered the top of Jacob's right arm, revealing a livid bruise, red, mottled and angry, just as Max himself felt at the very thought of it. He'd never before seen anything like it on Jacob's skin.

Sister joined the inspection and commented that the pale centre that had developed in the bruise was most unusual. She produced a small magnifying glass and peered more closely before passing the lens to the doctor for his thoughts.

'You're right, sister. Is that a small puncture wound? Surely this can't have been due to a needle, we'd have seen a spot of blood on such fair skin?'

'Have you seen this kind of thing before? What could it be?' Max asked.

'We're just exploring all the possibilities, Mr Brown. I'll bleep Dr Singh immediately. We might need to do a toxicity screen,' the sister said. She rushed off to her office, leaving the staff nurse to stand guard.

Max sat and watched his son, who was eerily still, apart

from the metronome-like movement of his chest. He listened to the machines helping Jacob to breathe, until he himself was almost hypnotised. Max couldn't believe how bonny Jacob looked, despite the indignity of all the tubes. He told the nurse what a little wriggler Jacob normally was, and she explained that they'd temporarily sedated him to allow the ventilation of his lungs. His limbs weren't moving at the moment, but they'd wriggle again once he was off the ventilator. Max allowed himself to smile, grateful for the reassurance. He suddenly got to his feet.

'I need to make some calls,' he told the nurse and she pointed to the parents' room. Max was desperate to speak to his own parents, but knew he first had to steel himself to call Jenny's. They would want to be with their daughter and, by the time they arrived from Bromley, they might have a better idea of Jacob's condition.

'Mike Best speaking,' said a deep voice. Max perched on the couch, with a brief sense of relief at being spared a potentially hysterical conversation with his mother-in-law Carol.

When he finally got through to his own parents, that Thursday afternoon, he knew his in-laws would be on the road. After much debate he persuaded his mum and dad to wait until the weekend to travel, and until then he promised to stay in touch by phone.

When Dr Singh arrived, he suggested Max return to Jenny while they ran some more tests and spoke to the social worker. Jacob's condition was stable and he was safe, in the best place possible, and being closely monitored. Max was given little choice and, after another peep at Jacob, he blew him a kiss and set off, slowly and thoughtfully through the maze of hospital corridors, following the red signs to Orthopaedics. The hospital smells no longer seemed to bother him, but the thought that someone could have harmed Jacob most certainly did.

4

WALKING AND THINKING

On the long walk back to Jenny, Max couldn't stop thinking how they had come to employ Tricia as Jacob's nanny. It had fallen into place rather too easily when he came to think about it. The right person seemed to be there at just the right time, when Jacob was six-months old, and Jenny's maternity leave came to an end. Perhaps they should have advertised the post more widely and interviewed more candidates. Perhaps they should have taken more time.

With each step he mulled it over, trying to justify their decision to allow Tricia to take Jacob to visit Lawn House, where she rented one of the many spare rooms. Max and Jenny both loved the manor house. It seemed entirely reasonable for Tricia to drive Jacob over to the estate once a week to go and play with their godchildren. He and Jenny treated Issy and Willow as if they were family, and they both wanted the twins to be close to Jacob, so why did he feel so guilty?

Each turn on the route towards Charnley Ward brought another thought with it. Max's brow puckered and his footsteps faltered. He was used to doing his thinking on his run, processing questions far less serious than these. A long and pensive walk along those wretched corridors was not as therapeutic, as good, adrenaline-burning exercise on

Oliver's parkland. Max remembered he had started running as a bet, raising money for charity, but then he got hooked. Having never been an athletic child, he was rather shocked at the effect running had on him. He wasn't strong enough for rugby, or sufficiently skilled for cricket; and much to his disappointment he'd never quite made six-foot, so basketball was out. He wasn't a sprinter but a steady runner who now ran for fun, and to control his thirty-year-old waistline. He was convinced it also helped his tendency to overthink things. He'd often count his steps as a distraction, but at times he'd still worry about work, and Jacob, and Jenny, and their work-life balance.

Before they had Jacob, Max used to try to get Jenny to run with him. 'You've got the legs for it,' he'd say. 'You physios are supposed to be fit, aren't you?' he'd tease her, and Jenny would reply that she preferred walking and that kept her fit enough.

'Walking and talking, you mean? I don't think you'd be able to chit-chat and run at the same time,' he'd add. She rarely rose to the bait, other than perhaps by giving him one of her playful punches, which is what he deserved then.

Now he longed for Jenny to be up and about again, on those long, shapely legs; to be fit to walk and talk in the local park near their cottage in Stowmarket, or in the grounds of Lawn House. Sometimes he asked Oliver to join him for a run, thinking running would help his friend with the awful grief of becoming a widower, but Oliver didn't take to it any more than Jenny, and the grief continued regardless.

Max and Jenny had supported Oliver by being the best godparents possible to the motherless girls, and he remembered taking Jacob to visit as soon as they could. The first time they went, the girls treated him like a little doll, stroking his baby-hair, and cooing and fussing him. As the visits continued, Jenny started to comment that Issy simply wasn't as gentle with the baby as Willow, and Celine repeatedly had to tell Issy to take care.

'Keep an eye on the girls, Max,' Jenny had said. 'Don't ever leave them alone with Jacob, will you?'

'I'm hardly likely to leave a new baby with a pair of four-year-olds in charge, am I?' Max said, and together they'd laughed at the very idea.

That conversation hung in Max's memory and, he recalled, the day at Lawn House, when Jenny was breastfeeding Jacob. Max watched as Issy put her best doll, Lulu, to her own pale girlish nipple. As she held the doll, Issy pulled strands of nylon hair from the plastic skull, exposing shiny, bald patches. Jenny had seen it too and it made her shiver. In the car on the way home, with Jacob asleep, snoring like a baby hedgehog in his car seat, she'd brought the subject up.

'I am still worried about the girls, well, Issy actually,' she said. 'If I'm on my own with the children Issy gives me really odd looks, especially if I'm feeding Jacob. It freaks me out.'

'Jenny, she's only four for goodness sake. How freaky can a four-year-old be? It's probably the feeding. She might just be intrigued. I expect neither of them have seen a mother breastfeed before,' Max said.

'Perhaps, but have you seen the state of Issy's precious doll Lulu? Poor Lulu, who was, after all, her bridesmaid's present from us, now looks like a victim of child abuse. Willow loves her doll Tallulah. Tallulah still looks brand new,' she said.

'Ooh, that's harsh! They're just dolls, not babies. The girls may be twins but they are very different little people. Just think about their bedroom: Willow's side is all tidy and Issy's is a tip,' Max commented.

'A bit like our dressing table, you mean, with my side cluttered and your things perfectly lined up like soldiers on the other side,' Jenny said.

'Ha-ha! Touché. You see, some people just like things in order.'

'Well, I'm surprised Celine allows it. Even a four-year-old can learn to put her things away. I might even have expected Mrs Hall to step in and say something. She is the housekeeper as well as the cook, and aren't housekeepers supposed to oversee everything?'

'Can't say I've ever had one. I guess she is a bit of a grandma figure in the household, though,' Max added.

'Exactly.'

Max had heard the note of exhaustion in Jenny's voice but at the time felt obliged to stand up for Mrs Hall as well as Celine.

'Mrs Hall's has had her hands full, and you know jolly well Celine's done a great job with those girls. It can't have been easy holding the fort after Alexis died. Remember, neither of them stopped working that first year or two, when Oliver was drowning in sorrow.'

'I know, sorry – I'm just a bit tired – but I do worry about the girls,' she said. 'We're supposed to be concerned about them if they're our god-daughters, aren't we? We did say we'd take it seriously when we took the job on.'

'And we do. It's not really a job, though, is it? On the whole, it's more of a joy,' Max said, successfully softening the tone of the conversation.

'You're right. Do you remember we were worried the twins might miss out on hugs and kisses when Alexis was so ill? Celine must have thought that, too, and that's why she relaxed her super-nanny image. She must have swapped tidying for hugs,' Jenny said.

'Nice thought. I must say these days I like the slightly more relaxed Celine – much nicer to see her in normal clothes, rather than that ridiculous nurse-like uniform she used to wear. She's quite attractive in a homely sort of way, now she's literally let her hair down,' Max said.

'For goodness sake, Max! She's almost old enough to be your mother.' Jenny flicked his shoulder with the back of her hand and Max laughed.

'Only if she was a teenage mum,' he said. He certainly liked Celine, she wasn't that old, and he had always hoped she and Jenny might be good friends. They were quite similar; both practical, capable women with big, forgiving hearts.

'As you well know, I don't mean attractive like *that*. I only have eyes for you, light of my life and mother to my son-and-heir.'

'Glad to hear it,' Jenny had said with a little smile.

'Mind you, that younger sister of hers who's come to stay, Tricia, now she's a head-turner ...' he remembered saying.

'Max!' Jenny shrieked, and Jacob had saved the day by waking up at that very moment and joining in with a howl of his own – such a vivid memory that he could almost hear Jacob's howl in these hospital corridors.

Now Jacob was seriously ill, and Jenny was broken and in pieces, Max just hoped he could step up and be the practical, capable one. Jenny always seemed so much more resilient than he was, and thrived on his teasing and a bit of banter before Jacob was born. She used to give as good as she got, too, but this parenthood thing sure did change things, Max thought. Change is always difficult, whatever the reason – bereavement, a new job, a new home or a new baby.

5

Della's diary, Sunday 29th March 1964

This is my first Easter without an Easter egg. I'm still missing you, Mum, even if you used to scrounge my chocolate. I think I've lost weight and my jeans feel baggy! Today I've walked in the grounds – the daffodils are out and the sun is shining. I shouldn't be sad but I have no one to talk to. The rest of the staff are older than me and dash off home as soon as the work's done. Apparently, it's different being a lady's maid and they seem to think I'm 'not one of them'.

Mrs T is as haughty as she looks, Mr T is always in his study, and Mrs Hall is just bossy. I feel I don't belong here in this remote house. There, I've said it. I've made a mistake and I'm stuck with it. At least I can listen to the cleaners' gossip. They call the housekeeper 'Old Mrs Hall' – she can't be much over sixty. They're rude about Reg, her son, too. He's a gardener and they say he's a bit slow. Lady Muck's last maid left in a hurry and nobody really knows why. They think she was sacked for being too pretty! Wonder if I'll be sacked – you always said I was pretty, Mum. I need this job. Dad's made it clear I can't go back to an empty house while he's away at sea.

Reg has lent me a transistor radio and set it to a new station called Radio Caroline. He seems kind and at least someone is. I'm listening to 'Please Please Me' and I feel like crying. Maybe I shouldn't address my diary to you, Mum, it makes me too sad.

6

SAFEGUARDING

March 2014

Jenny looked a bit more comfortable when Max got back to her. She was now in a side room on a proper ward, tucked up in a real bed with crisp, white sheets instead of being balanced on a hard hospital trolley covered by a nasty, blue woven blanket. Max gave Oliver a hug of thanks and let him get back to his girls.

The nurse had brushed Jenny's tangled, fair hair and wiped the mascara from her puffy, panda-eyes, leaving her with a pale and vulnerable face. She woke up when Max kissed her and squeezed her free hand – the other bore the portal for an intravenous line, which was allowing tiny drops of clear liquid to plop into her veins. Once more she uttered just one word, 'Jacob.'

'I've seen him. He's hanging on in there. He's in a sort of intensive care unit for babies and they're looking after him really well.'

'Is he awake?' she asked, seeming more alert.

'I've spoken to him and stroked him, so he knows he's not alone,' Max replied.

'What happened? Why won't anyone tell me anything, Max?' she pleaded.

'He stopped breathing,' Max said. 'We'd agreed Tricia

could take him to the big house for an outing, hadn't we? Well, he was down for his afternoon nap and the baby alarm went off. Tricia found him and did CPR until the ambulance crew took over. Now he's being ventilated while they do tests. We'll know more soon.'

'Oh God! How long?' she said. 'If he was starved of oxygen for too long he might have brain damage.' She started to shudder and Max tried to tuck the sheets round her shoulders to warm and comfort her. Brain damage was not something he'd even considered at that stage, just having him alive was more important. But then there was that bruise to worry about.

'It's too soon to say anything more, my darling. You must stay strong and get better, then we can both help him. Are you in great pain?'

'Oh, Max, how can this have happened to us? Never mind me, the morphine's helping, even though my mouth feels lined with felt. Do I sound odd? It's hard to speak.'

'You don't need to speak,' said Max. 'Just try to rest.'

But he couldn't stop her. With the voice of a slurred alien she made an announcement: 'Surgery tomorrow morning, but today, I've got to see Jacob.'

'I don't think you can, love. You'll not manage a wheelchair with a broken leg and your pelvis in bits.'

'Max, I need to see him.' She closed her eyes and a line of tears collected along her lashes.

'I'll go and see what I can do,' Max said and kissed her forehead. 'Your parents are on their way, and mine will come soon. Until they arrive I'll run backwards and forwards between the two of you, so he'll not be left alone.'

'I have to see Jacob for myself or I'll simply refuse surgery. What if I don't wake up?' she said.

'Of course you'll wake up.' Max knew his wife, still determined despite being smashed to pieces, meant what she'd said. For the first time since they'd met, he longed for the arrival of Carol and Mike to help him through this feeling of being torn in two.

The ward sister insisted Jenny could not be moved that day. She was, however, second on the surgeon's morning list, so an early porter was booked to wheel her to theatre via the paediatric department. Jenny could have a quick peep at Jacob on the way, and that was the best they could do. Jenny wept at the news, and her determination faded when sister told her that even that detour would require a considerable rearrangement of machinery to get her mobile bed into the special care unit. Max wiped Jenny's tears before dabbing away his own.

'We need to settle your wife down a little, Mr Brown. She's due for more pain relief, then she must rest,' the sister said.

'It's Max, call me Max, and thanks for everything. I do understand. I need to go back to see Jacob now, but you know where I am if you need me. Jenny's parents should be here soon.'

When he got back to the paediatric department, Max wasn't allowed into the special care unit. Why did hospitals make things so difficult? His head pounded, and he felt he might explode with frustration. How could he help Jacob if he wasn't allowed in? Sister came to the rescue and sat him down in the corridor outside, while an orderly brought him a cup of tea. The cup rattled on the saucer as he took it and brown droplets of hot liquid dappled his trousers.

'The police have been called. I'm sorry, Mr Brown, but Jacob is our priority at the moment, and no one is allowed in to see him until the forensic specialist has completed her checks.'

'I don't understand what's going on,' Max said. He ran his a hand through his tousled hair.

'We'll know soon, but first the police will want to interview you and your wife. They've asked you not to leave the hospital.'

'I'm hardly likely to bloody leave, am I, with the two people I love most in the world stuck here. Sorry – this is really hard.'

'I know it is Mr Brown – Maxwell, isn't it? Can we call you that?'

'Max'll do.'

'I'm sorry, Max. Why don't you go and be with your wife and we'll call you when we're ready for you to return? One thing though – please don't discuss the bruise. Do you think you can manage that?'

'I haven't mentioned it yet. I wouldn't know what to say. Surely you don't think we've harmed him? We love him. He was fine this morning when I left for work. He was changed and dressed and my wife Jenny was just waiting for Tricia, our nanny, to come and get him before she left for work too.'

Max knew he was going on a bit, but he was trying to piece the morning together. He knew a bit about child protection, he worked for a children's charity for goodness sake – okay in IT rather than on the safeguarding side of things, but he knew the score. He certainly never envisaged being involved in a case personally. Jesus, if he lost his job on top of everything else, how would they cope? His parents would be distraught, and he couldn't begin to imagine Carol and Mike's reaction. No doubt they would blame him for everything. *Hang on a second*, he thought, *I haven't done anything wrong*. He plodded back to Charnley Ward.

He looked at the people he passed on the way; they must have thought he was a patient himself, staggering along with heavy feet and hunched shoulders. His mouth was dry, despite the tea, and he held his arms across his stomach to try to still the jagged rock he felt in his gut.

Max was relieved to find Jenny deep in sleep when he got to her room, with no sign of any grandparents yet. He worked out they must still be stuck in the tea-time traffic around London and up the A12. It might be some time before he had to face them, so he tapped out an email to Ed, his best mate, who along with Oliver, had been chosen as Jacob's godfather. Ed would want to know what was going on. Even though he was so often away, travelling the world with his music, he was still Max's closest friend, and knew him better than anyone, apart from Jenny.

Max saw the battery signal on his phone indicating low so he quietly dug around for the charger in his laptop case, which he'd pushed into Jenny's locker. He saw her handbag on the shelf below and felt sick. She was so proud of the designer bag he'd bought for her from a fancy store in Bond Street. It went everywhere with her, and now the tan leather was torn and it bore an oily smear across its front. The handle was stained, dark brown, and he wondered if it was mud or blood. Max shut the locker door quickly and went to wash his hands at the basin in the corner. He returned to sit on the plastic chair by Jenny's bed, and even though it was as uncomfortable as sitting in a bucket, he closed his eyes, blocking out the reality of the accident and substituting it with other thoughts.

He had known Jenny was dreading the thought of leaving Jacob when she had to return to work after her maternity leave. The two of them had debated the options long and hard, often in the car at weekends on their visits to and from Lawn House. They did some of their best talking in the car. Max wished now he could have spent more time just being at home, playing with Jacob and chatting with his wife about everything and anything. He spent too much time away, or travelling, and imagined most working parents felt that way. In the car their conversations about childcare seemed recurrent and endless, dominating their journeys. Now Max ran over them again, appreciating how crucial they'd been, and they played out like a film in his head.

'All the local childminders are full, but the little nursery down the road seems to have improved since I last visited,'

Jenny had said. 'I think it's more homely than the big one at the hospital.'

'What does "improved" mean?' Max had asked.

'More staff around, and they seemed more attentive. The atmosphere just felt better.'

'But the problem remains that they aren't open late enough in the evenings for us to get back to collect him. Isn't that why we ruled them out before?' Max said.

'I know, don't get grumpy with me,' Jenny replied.

'We've been over and over this – if you're busy in Norwich, he's in nursery in Stowmarket, and I'm at the office in Colchester, or Ipswich or London, we're all too spread out. At least he'll be near you if he's at the hospital nursery in Norwich.'

'I'm still worried he'll think he lives in a car. It's not going to work. We need to rethink the whole thing.'

'We're going round in circles, Jenny,' Max said, lowering his tone – Jenny never responded well to grumpy.

Then, one day, Jenny said she'd come up with another idea, but she wasn't entirely sure about it because of a careless comment Max had made a few weeks earlier.

'Oh God, what did I say? You'd better just tell me what this idea is,' he'd said.

'Right, here goes,' Jenny started. 'I only have to return to The Norfolk and Norwich for a few months to maximise my maternity benefit, and they say they'll let me reduce my hours a bit and leave early.'

'Like a mini-flexitime?' Max said. 'That sounds good, but we'll still need help.'

'Exactly, so I wondered if, just for a while, we could call in a favour and ask Celine or her sister Tricia to help out – but then you made that daft comment about Tricia being very attractive and I went off the idea,' Jenny said.

'You twit, surely you've not been worrying about that? It was just a joke,' Max replied.

'I know, but she is a bit of a flirty piece.'

'That's really not an issue, and I promise she's never flirted with me. It's not a bad idea. Tricia has worked with children in the past, and we've helped the Lawn House tribe enough in recent years. I can't believe we've not thought of it before,' Max said.

'The Tricia comment didn't help, I suppose, and also things at the manor have changed such a lot lately – the estate has only just recovered from the death of Oliver's parents – and you've been busy at work and I didn't want to add to your stress. I know you get tired, too, so I thought I'd work it out in my own mind first,' Jenny said.

'And I thought when we got married we said we'd share everything; that means stress and worry as well as the good things. Tell me how this plan works. Look, Jacob's awake and listening too.' Max had nodded his head towards the baby seat and Jenny looked over and smiled her proud, new-mum-smile, while Jacob dribbled like a hungry puppy, clutching his giraffe-shaped teething ring.

'My poor postnatal brain is trying to work out the logistics and decide whether it's the right thing to ask them. Do you think Celine or Tricia would look after Jacob as well as we would?'

'What do you mean? Would they be able to protect him from the mischievous twins?' Max said, with a smile.

'That's a point, but no, it's more than that. Oliver runs the place like a commune rather than a grand house these days, and there seem to be lots of weird people around.'

'What, you mean the guys in the music studio and the lodgers Oliver's taken in? They don't go into the house much, and Mrs Hall still keeps an eye on things.'

'Okay, but have you noticed Oliver's stopped wearing his nice tweed jacket and cords? He dresses like a hired hand. I think Mrs Hall spends more time in the kitchen than seeing to the house, and Gus the gardener looks more like the lord of the manor than Oliver does these days.'

'Do you think Oliver's tweeds were a pretence?' Max said.

'Yes, probably a charade, putting on a show, but now the old guard has passed on, the show is over. Jacob's gone back to sleep. Go around the block again and we'll have a few more minutes peace before we get home,' Jenny said.

'Dropping the charade is a good thing, surely, more honest? Didn't you know Gus Hall has been made head groundsman? He's just showing off his position with some new clothes,' Max said.

'Oh, I suppose some things have improved. I like new name – Lawn House sounds so much better than Trelawney Manor. That was way too pretentious, and rather Cornish,' Jenny said.

'Probably had Cornish ancestors; anyway, what's wrong with Cornwall? We had great holidays there as kids.' Max had loved his holidays Cornwall, playing in rock-pools, fishing for mackerel and eating pasties.

'Nothing's wrong, but this is rural Suffolk.'

'Fair comment. It's good they've been able to take on more staff though, with the money coming in from the new recording studio,' Max said.

'Thanks to Ed,' Jenny said.

'Yes okay, Ed's money, but also Gus's hard work. Gus is just reaping the benefits and enjoying his managerial status,' Max said.

'And his new home,' added Jenny. 'He and Sandra have done well moving into Oak Lodge.'

'It's not like you to sound jealous, Jenny. What's really up? You don't want to live in the lodge, do you?'

'Course not. Don't mind me, I've just got a lot on my mind. The practicalities of returning to work are getting to me.'

Jenny was picking anxiously at the skin of her thumbs with the nail of her forefinger. Max read the warning sign: Jenny was disturbed by something.

'We'll work something out, my love. Other families survive the minefield of childcare, and so will we.'

The soul-searching continued until, eventually, Max and Jenny spoke to Celine. Celine said that once Issy and Willow started school she would have a little more free time, but not enough to take on a six-month-old baby. And besides, she hoped to do a few hours in the garden centre shop with Gus's girlfriend Sandra, and then be free for the girls after school.

It was Celine however, who then echoed their idea about Tricia. 'You know Tricia's been visiting a lot? Well, she wants to stay on in Suffolk. We want to spend a bit more time together, if we can, and get to know each other again, as sisters. You know we grew up apart, don't you? Anyway, she's job-hunting at the moment, so why don't you talk to her? She has got a diploma in childcare.'

Max nodded in agreement – and hoped Jenny didn't think his smile meant he preferred the idea of Tricia's help rather than her plainer, older sister. Neither of them wanted to have anyone living with them – Tricia, or anyone else for that matter, as that would make their cottage far too crowded. Tricia was bright and seemed nice enough, and Jenny knew she mustn't be put off by her tight jeans and threatening fingernails, painted in a red so dark it was almost black.

'We'd need to interview her and see her references, do it all properly, after all, she might not want to work for us,' Jenny said. 'And you know we don't want a live-in nanny.'

'That wouldn't be a problem. Tricia could drive over to Stowmarket each day,' Celine said. 'Oliver has been letting her stay at the house in the blue bedroom. He might rent it to her on a permanent basis if she has a job. No one ever stays in that room and he told me it's good to give it an airing.'

Celine's approval seemed to calm some of Jenny's doubts, so Tricia was invited to Stowmarket for an interview. She brought details of two referees, a police check certificate and an impressive testimonial from her previous employer. She happily produced a clean driving licence, as well as intelligent answers to every question put to her. Jenny was pleased to see she had swapped her red nail varnish for a paler shade of pink, and wore better fitting trousers for the meeting. Max and Jenny both noticed how quickly she took to Jacob, and he to her. When the formalities were over, and Jenny went to make tea – calling Max into the kitchen to "help" – Tricia got down on the floor and played with Jacob, ignoring the beige carpet fluff that stuck to her black trousers.

Max thought Jenny had warmed to Tricia when they discussed her interview. She accepted Tricia was better than she thought, and she could tell he didn't actually fancy her. She admitted to being embarrassed she'd even thought it. They decided the plan might suit everyone and would fall nicely into place – probably too nicely in retrospect – and now Max was here struggling to decide if Tricia was a hero or a villain. Could she have bruised Jacob's arm or been careless with him ... this did all happen on her watch, after all?

At the time Tricia was appointed, Max was happy it would give Jenny a few months to weigh up whether to continue as a full-time hospital physiotherapist or to pursue her other option of looking for a private practice nearer to home. He wondered if her parents might need some convincing if Jenny's career changed track. Her mum was particularly ambitious for her elder daughter, and loved boasting to friends that she worked at a respected teaching hospital, and was engaged in a major research project before she had Jacob. Who knew, perhaps they could brag about her being a private physiotherapist just as easily?

As for Max, he'd once nearly prompted a row with Jenny saying that private health care might fit in better with her parents' politics. They certainly leaned more to the right than he did. He also suspected they didn't brag much about their only son-in-law being the IT director for a children's charity. But after a slow start, they had eventually cottoned on that his love for Jenny was permanent, and they allowed themselves to grow a little fonder of him. Helping provide them with dear little Jacob had finally won them over.

A police officer knocked on Jenny's door and interrupted Max's rambling thoughts. He beckoned for Max to join him in a nearby private room, where a second officer and a social worker were waiting. He answered their questions in a kind of haze; the adrenaline and shock of the day had worn off somewhat, only to be replaced by despair and exhaustion, and he struggled not to cry in front of them. They were gentle enough with him and seemed to trust his answers: yes, Tricia was Jacob's nanny and had been with them for just over three weeks; yes, she had permission to take Jacob to Lawn House and they knew the house well; and yes, most important of all, Max was able to assure them the child was fit and well when he last saw him.

By the time they all returned to Jenny's room she was awake, but still dozy. Max was grateful her emotions were cushioned by morphine, but that she was able to clearly state she'd seen no bruise that morning when she got Jacob dressed.

'It must be from when they resuscitated him,' she said.

Max nodded vigorously, wondering why he hadn't suggested that.

'Possibly,' said the senior of the two policemen.

Max was feeling calmer by the time the in-laws arrived – a calmness that was unlikely to last long. Carol and Mike fussed over their daughter for a while before Max could tell them about Jacob's condition. He avoided the issue of the mystery bruise, telling Jenny had been hard enough.

Tiger-mum Carol got her claws out almost at once, ready to sharpen them on Max, who fought to banish the image of a large, striped cat from his mind. He hoped Jenny was too zoned out after another dose of morphine to hear the hissing conversation that followed.

'I was never happy about that woman taking Jacob over

to Lawn House. A baby that age should be in his own home, not gadding about the countryside in a stranger's car. You should have put your foot down about that, Max.'

'It was a joint decision, Carol. He's only been going there once a week to play with the girls. It was a nice outing, going to the lovely gardens. And Tricia is an excellent driver – we did check.'

'Once a week proved once too many,' Carol snapped. 'And the driving is the least of my concerns. There's something odd about that house. I felt the troubled atmosphere the moment I stepped through the gate. I'm very sensitive to these things.'

Thankfully Mike interjected. 'You've only visited once, Carol, and that was soon after Alexis had died. It was bound to feel odd in the circumstances. I thought it was a lovely house, old-fashioned but charming.'

Max flinched – fancy calling an early eighteenth-century manor house "old-fashioned". If Carol was sensitive to atmosphere, Mike certainly wasn't sensitive to history. 'Perhaps we could just concentrate on Jacob,' Max said.

'Absolutely,' Mike said. 'Can we see him soon?'

Jenny must have heard more than they realised. Even though her eyes were closed, she spoke, saying, 'Please stop. I need you to help each other, not bicker.'

'We're not bickering, darling, just making a point.' Carol patted her daughter's hand.

'Of course, we'll help each other. We're all a bit tense, that's all. Everything will be fine.' Max gave Carol a conciliatory smile, even though at that moment part of him wanted to strangle her.

'Mum, if I can't see Jacob until the morning can you and Dad go on my behalf? That'll help, won't it, Max?'

'Yes, of course. They're running a few more tests, so I'll have to check when we can go over to the unit, and then I'll show you the way. They only allow two visitors in at a time but we can swap about.'

Carol raised her eyes to the ceiling, making little pleats across her forehead. 'That'll be a problem when your parents come, Max. Where are Eleanor and Richard, anyway?'

Mike made a low hushing sound, directed at Carol, but before she could say anything else, Max suggested they might make a visiting rota, ready for when his parents got here. He didn't bother to justify their delayed arrival to Carol, but they were GPs, and Max knew how hard it was for them to leave fully booked surgeries at short notice.

'That's a good idea, isn't it, Carol? A rota.' Mike said. 'We can take it in turns.'

He seemed to have the knack of switching Carol off at just the right time, and Max realised Jenny had picked up a similar skill, shutting him up if the occasion required. Thank goodness she wasn't like her mother in other ways. Jenny was funny and witty and kind, as well as strong and capable. Now Max realised he was beginning to step up and be the capable one.

Word came that the forensic examination was complete and Jacob was able to receive visitors. Carol and Mike didn't even question this delay, and as Max escorted them to the special care unit he noticed in astonishment that they were actually holding hands. Carol hesitated before using the handwash. She then used it with only the slightest hint of a sneer, before Mike patiently helped her into her gown. Perhaps she wasn't as tough as she made out, but Mike was undoubtedly a saint. Once inside, the two of them sat gazing at their only grandson while Max went to speak to Dr Mercer.

'Any news?' Max's tone had already become more familiar now he was seen as a regular feature on the ward. The doctor must have been about his age, and in a different life they could have been friends, shared a pint. They even had the same scruffy curls and unshaven chins.

'They're still interviewing the nanny, but the forensic

expert doesn't think it's a needle mark, more likely to be an insect bite. She wants to go to Lawn House to see the nursery herself. We've just phoned the owner – Oliver Trelawney-Smythe I believe – to arrange a time.'

'Actually, he just calls himself Oliver Trelawney. His late father was the only one who used the double-barrelled bit. Why on earth does she need to go to the house?' Max said.

'Gathering information, checking things out,' Dr Mercer replied.

'What, like looking for a wasp's nest or a giant mosquito? This is as surreal as a Dali painting,' Max said.

Max went to sit on a bench outside the special care unit, needing to distance himself from Carol's edgy presence. He could have wept again. He longed to briefly hand over some of the responsibility to his parents – people with more medical knowledge than he possessed – when they came at the weekend.

At the end of a long evening watching over Jacob, Max persuaded Carol and Mike to book into a nearby B&B for the night. (He was as pleased as he could be, under the circumstances, that they agreed to stay.) Until sunrise he dozed fitfully in the parents' room and then ate digestive biscuits from a tin for breakfast. Mike would go back home soon – he had work to do – but there was little doubt Carol would stay.

7

DR GREY

It was two days before Mothering Sunday and Jenny clutched a special card, chosen by Max on behalf of Jacob, as she was given her pre-med. The injection was meant to relax her, but even so she shook and looked like a ghost on a detox program. Witnessing Jenny's early morning nil-by-mouth visit to the side of Jacob's cot would have melted the heart of the sternest of ward sisters. After much shunting of furniture, Jenny calmed herself and was able to reach over and touch Jacob's head for a brief time. She tried to fluff his hair up into a little crown, before the porter returned and took her off to theatre. The escorting nurse distracted herself from the emotions of the scene by fiddling with Jenny's drip as they left. Max stayed at the cot-side, hardly able to move, while another nurse checked on Jacob.

'His temperature has gone up a bit, Max, and the arm is looking more inflamed,' she said. 'I'm calling the doctor.'

Dr Mercer looked almost as wrung out as Max when he arrived. 'Long night for both of us by the looks of it,' he said. 'Let me have a look at this little chap. Do you mind stepping outside?'

Max sat on his familiar bench in the corridor. There was a sudden flurry of activity, phones rang and bleepers beeped as two doctors Max had never seen before swept past them into the special care unit.

Max's first thought was, *he's arrested, I know it, oh God, what'll I do?* He jumped up to peer through the window in the double doors. Time seemed to stand still and the world went quiet. *What'll I tell Jenny*, was his next thought as he tried to open the doors.

The ward sister emerged, looking flushed.

'Is he alright?' Max took hold of her arm, fearing the worst.

She glared at his hand and he dropped it quickly. 'Jacob's improving. We've started him on something to reduce the inflammation. You can go in and see him now,' she said, as if nothing had happened.

'What was the alarm for? Did he stop breathing again?' Max asked. He coughed, almost choking due to the tightness in his throat.

'No, he's fine,' she smiled. 'The little one in the next bay gave us a bit of a scare but he's okay now. In you go, after you.'

She followed Max into Jacob's bay. 'Good news,' she said. 'We think we have the answer to Jacob's bruise. The forensic team have phoned from Lawn House and they've found a rather large spider in Jacob's cot. They've trapped it and it's being sent over to the path lab for identification. It may be a Brazilian wandering spider.'

'I've read about those in the paper – brought in by bananas, aren't they? What's the treatment?' Max asked.

'I think we need confirmation first,' the sister interjected. 'Someone will be over from Pathology soon. Now, if you'll excuse me.'

Max couldn't believe that the sister seemed pleased at the idea of a bite from a giant arachnid. It was like a horror film, and Max was having trouble believing it was good news. He imagined his dad saying, 'Knowledge is power, Max.'

Whilst awaiting the arrival of the pathologist, Max's gut was churning with the extra worry of a poisonous spider.

Once again, he'd been tussling with the thought of what on earth to tell Jenny – a spider in the cot was one thing they couldn't have prepared themselves for with their carefully considered childcare arrangements.

Max walked up the corridor to stretch his legs and saw a short man in a white coat, shuffling files of notes as he approached. The man pushed his horn-rimmed glasses up his nose and peered through the thick lenses at Max with small, dark eyes.

'I'm Grey,' he said, 'D-Dr Grey from Pathology, here about your spider.'

'I'm Jacob's father, Max Brown.' Max went to extend hand in greeting. It was met by a blank stare from Dr Grey, whom Max immediately judged as being as pale and dull as his name, and in need of a hearty meal. He smiled ironically to himself – not a bad analysis from a guy called Brown who hadn't had a meal for nearly twenty-four hours. He wondered if low blood sugar was making him intolerant, addling his brain.

'I'm sure it's a j-juvenile male Brazilian wandering spider,' Dr Grey said.

'So, does Jacob need anti-venom? Where do we get it from?' Max sounded as if he was an expert on spiders after all of five minutes searching on the World Wide Web.

Dr Grey's focus was directed to the floor. He started to mumble and quote statistics and medical jargon with his annoying stutter so Max could neither keep up nor fully understand.

'Are you telling me there is no anti-venom?' Max interrupted.

'Ah, w-well ... the nearest available in the UK at the m-moment is in London, but it's not always needed.'

'I don't believe this,' Max snapped.

'As a juvenile the bite might not be too toxic. It could just be sh-shock that stopped Jacob breathing. Treatment is often just s-supportive and nature sorts it out.'

'Not always needed – that sounds ridiculous. This was more than shock! Jacob nearly died!'

'Sh-shock is a medical term, Mr Brown,' the man replied.

'And what if nature doesn't sort it out? What if he has brain damage through lack of oxygen?'

'Are you a d-doctor, Mr Brown?'

'No, I'm not, but I'm worried. What if Jacob can't ever breathe for himself again? We need to do something – he's only six months old for Christ's sake. When can we get the stuff from London?' Max realised his voice was raised but couldn't contain himself.

'Steady on, Mr Brown. Do calm down. There's no need for histrionics. We can discuss the risks and benefits of anti-venom with Dr Singh shortly.' A sheet of paper slipped from Dr Grey's file onto the floor.

Part of him wanted to punch Dr Grey, even though he'd never hit anyone in anger in his life, let alone someone wearing NHS specs. *This won't do,* Max thought, *this won't help Jacob.* 'Forget it – I'm going to find Dr Singh,' he said.

Instant Max, no longer the ditherer, turned angrily and shoved the door to go back into Special Care, just as Dr Grey bent to pick up his escaped document. Max's elbow caught Dr Grey's nose and his horn-rimmed glasses fell to the floor. Then there was a crunching sound followed by a screech from Dr Grey, as Max then accidentally stepped on the glasses.

Dr Mercer rushed out to investigate the commotion and almost tripped over Dr Grey, who was kneeling on the floor clutching his nose. Blood, red as printer-ink, dripped onto the tiled floor. Fragments of the broken glasses littered the corridor.

'Oh my god, are you alright?' Max gasped.

'N-no,' whimpered Dr Grey.

A staff nurse ran up the corridor, closely followed by the sister, who calmly restored order as if these things happened all the time.

'Gentlemen, enough, this is a hospital, not a bar for brawling in. Nurse, take Dr Grey to the treatment room and get him cleaned up. Mr Brown, you'd better come to my office.'

As the nurse helped Dr Grey up Max heard him mutter, 'He hit me. I'll s-sue.'

She replied, 'Do be quiet, Dr Grey, it was obviously accidental. You'll live.'

Max sat in the ward sister's office with his head down, feeling ashamed at having lost his cool, and in despair at the whole situation. He was running on empty, with no clear idea of whether Jacob needed anti-venom or not. The ward clerk brought him a cup of sweetened tea and another digestive biscuit, which he nibbled at until Dr Singh appeared.

Dr Singh seemed under the impression that Max had assaulted Dr Grey on purpose and started to speak as if to a naughty child. It was the way Max's father might have spoken to him when he was a kid, making him feel his dad was not angry but ashamed of him.

'You do realise it was an accident,' Max said. 'Of course, I'm sorry. I may have disliked Dr Grey's attitude, I may have stormed off, but I didn't hit him.'

'If you say so,' said Dr Singh. He sounded unconvinced and looked down at his notes.

'That staff nurse must have seen it all — you only need to check with her,' Max said.

'I intend to, but I also have work to do. Let's just concentrate on Jacob for now, Mr Brown. I do, however, suggest you write a convincing letter of apology to Dr Grey as soon as possible,' Dr Singh said.

'Yes, of course, I will, and I'll pay for his glasses. As I've said, I am truly sorry.'

'Enough,' Dr Singh said. 'Now, Jacob's doing well. The antibiotics will kick in soon and the inflammation should settle. We'll support his breathing for the next few hours, then try to wean him off the ventilator. The anti-venom is on its way from London by courier, but we may not even need it now.'

'Are you sure?'

'I've consulted my colleagues in London and we're doing all the right things. The first few hours are the most dangerous and Jacob has coped well with those.'

'Do you really think so?' Max said, finding it hard to believe that still being ventilated was classified as coping well.'

'I do. He's going to be all right. I'm sure you'll have him home before too long. Any other questions?' Dr Singh seemed a kind and empathetic man, unlike Dr Grey. Max realised he needed as many people as possible on his side at that moment, and especially Dr Singh.

'I'm a bit bothered by the child protection issue. Why is Tricia being kept away from us and questioned in so much detail?' Max asked.

'When we thought the mark on Jacob's shoulder was a bruise we had to follow safeguarding guidelines. Of course, now we know it was a spider's bite, things have changed somewhat,' Dr Singh replied.

'And I'm still puzzled how a spider got into the house and up to the first floor, where Jacob was having his nap.' Max was thinking out loud, trying to put the pieces together.

'I hear it's an old house,' Dr Singh commented. 'Perhaps the spider had been lurking for a while. Environmental Health are onto it already, because I gather there are other children in the house.'

'My god-daughters, Issy and Willow. They're nearly five. And Tricia Bird's sister, Celine, is their nanny.'

'Oh, I see – it's all slotting into place now. I think we'll end up thanking Tricia Bird for her early resuscitation. Now, I'm off to check on the patient.' Dr Singh stood up and looked Max in the eye, reading the younger man's character. 'Join me?' he said.

Max managed a smile. 'I'll be in to see Jacob soon. I just need to go to Jenny first. She should be awake after her surgery now.'

Dr Singh gave Max a fatherly pat on the back as they parted. The doctor headed into the ward, and Max set off back to find Jenny in Recovery. Max looked down to his right elbow and saw a spot of Dr Grey's blood on his pale blue shirt. He washed it off and scrubbed his hands in the visitors' loo on his way past. He counted the steps back to Jenny, feeling very alone.

8

Della's diary, Thursday 9th April 1964

I can't believe Mrs T goes away on her own every weekend and I have to stay here doing her washing – lovely silk underwear and blouses that need washing by hand. I wonder if I'll ever get to wear such lovely things. It makes my cotton draws look like a schoolgirl's.

Mrs Hall must think I'm scruffy. She sent me to Ipswich by bus to buy a dress I can wear with my special cream apron. She was unimpressed when I laughed at the 'not too short' instruction. Still, it means I can help when there are guests to entertain. The old battle-axe insists on a navy apron for everyday wear, and special cream ones embroidered with the family crest for best. At least I'm allowed to wear jeans on navy apron days, and she's letting me help out in the kitchen more now – she obviously thinks I'm not such an idiot after all. I can even serve Mr T his tea and coffee sometimes. I might have liked to go to catering college if things had been different.

Would you believe there are only three buses per day to the town and it took me over half an hour to get there? I'm pleased with my new cotton dress and smart new jeans. I treated myself to a fashion magazine too – might as well try to cheer myself up spending the money I've earned.

It's a good job I like reading – that helps the loneliness. Mr T has a stack of DH Lawrence novels in the library room and I'm working my way through those. Do you remember I read 'The Virgin and the Gypsy' to you when you were trapped indoors by your illness?

9

GODFATHER

March 2014

Soon Jenny was able to make short trips to Jacob in a padded wheelchair pushed by Max. When she needed a rest, Max dozed by Jacob's cot or camped out in the parents' room, existing on coffee, catnaps and snacks. When he couldn't be persuaded to eat in the hospital canteen or pop out to a local restaurant with Carol, she brought takeaway food for him to pick at. She stayed on alone at the B&B for those early days, once Mike had gone back to work, and Max's relationship with his mother-in-law was not as strained as he thought it might be. She did like to meddle but, on the whole, was being supportive without getting in the way, thanks to the visiting rota. (She was often at opposite ends of the hospital to him, which helped!). For both Carol and Max one day merged into the next in an insulated bubble far removed from any sense of the real world. In fact, they both became institutionalised, and only Carol's daily phone calls to Mike and Max's regular calls to his own parents, between their short visits, kept them in touch with life outside.

Max knew Jenny was getting better when, after a few days, she invited her mother to go home. She also tried to convince Carol there'd be a greater need for her help when she was discharged from hospital and, with a jolt of reality,

Max could see that was true. But Carol insisted on staying a couple more days, suggesting she'd come back in a couple of weeks, before Easter. She took a trip to the town centre to get some shopping for Jenny, and made a big show of telling the nursing staff where they could contact her. Max was astonished when she gave him a warm farewell hug when he put her on the train back to London.

Now Jenny was fit to receive non-family visitors, Max called Ed, who was top of the list of those queuing up to come. He knew Ed would make both him and Jenny feel human again, and cheer them up with his jokes and dodgy anecdotes, maybe even a little music.

The master showman turned up with a sumptuous goody box for Jenny, packed with aromatherapy oils, fragrant soap, and a luscious handcream to combat the hand sanitizer found at every door of the hospital. On top of the box, wrapped in tissue, was a silk bed jacket with a matching eye mask.

'I see your lovely Lucy has been busy shopping,' Max said, noticing colour and light returning to Jenny's pale cheeks and sunken eyes.

'I don't know what you mean?' Ed said.

'Well, it doesn't really look your style, Ed,' Jenny said. 'You're more a chocolates and champagne kind of man.'

'Fair cop. Lucy sends her love, by the way. She's busy at work today, but I'm sure she'll come with me next time.'

'Say a big thank you to her, this is so thoughtful. Perhaps by next time I'll be home,' Jenny said. 'You can bring me champagne then.'

'It won't be too long by the looks of you,' Ed said.

'Yes, I'm more comfortable every day, and the physio is getting me up on crutches. This ankle boot is a pain, but at least I can get myself out of bed now to go to the loo.'

'Bet that's a relief!' Ed pulled a comedy face.

Max raised sarcastic eyebrows. 'Anyway, she can get to see Jacob more easily, and that's the main thing.' He'd forgotten how easily a tiny spark of jealousy arose when Ed and Jenny connected.

'Am I allowed to see my favourite boy?' Ed asked.

'Check the rota, Max,' Jenny ordered.

'We don't need it now your mum's gone,' Max said.

'I suppose not,' Jenny laughed.

'Are you two kidding me?' Ed asked.

'It was the only workable option – a visiting rota – especially on the odd day when all the grandparents were here. Once Jenny was well enough to spend time with Jacob, the children's ward got a bit crowded.' Max explained.

'You see, they restrict the number of visitors on the children's ward and it's at opposite ends of the hospital,' Jenny added.

'I always said you two would organise yourselves to obscurity when you got together, and how right I was.' Ed snatched the rota from Max and sniggered.

'We thought it'd stop the mother-in-law and me getting in each other's way, as well as helping the nurses,' Max explained.

'And it helped me to know where people were when I was stuck in bed,' Jenny said.

'Oh my god, it's happened, you've morphed into the same person. You finish each other's sentences. I said you would when you stole her away from me, Max!' Ed exclaimed.

'I am here!' Jenny said.

'Shut up, Ed, she was never yours to steal. I know you mean well, but we're not quite ready for your sense of humour at the moment.' Max noticed Jenny was looking tired. They still had a long way to go before she was back to full strength, and he hoped they wouldn't discharge her too soon. He leaned over and kissed her.

'Ah, what was that for?' she asked.

'Just felt like it,' Max said. 'Come on, Ed, let's go and see Jacob and give the girl some peace.'

'I thought you'd never ask,' Ed said. 'He's doing okay, isn't he?'

'Yes, he's on the main kids' ward now and off the ventilator. He eventually got the anti-venom I told you about, although the consultant thought it was hardly necessary once it arrived. So, Spiderman is suddenly looking livelier, and I think we'll soon be getting him home, too,' Max said, more bravely than he felt.

'I've asked you not to call him that. Stop showing off in front of Ed,' Jenny warned. 'You owe me another kiss now.'

Walking through the hospital Max lapped up a bit of normal, non-illness-based conversation. The corridors seemed lighter and the smell more tolerable with Ed at his side. Ed even commented it didn't seem a bad place, then said, 'But you look rough, mate. When did you last shave? That stubble makes you look fifty and you need a haircut.'

'Thanks. Not top of my priority list. I do manage a daily shower,' Max replied, and sniffed his armpits.

'Fair enough, at least you don't smell.'

'Drop it, Ed. Tell me about you. How's things?' Max found himself ready for news of the outside world.

'Hectic. The new album's nearly finished. I've had to travel up from London quite a bit to sort out the studio, ready for the final recording.'

'I heard Oliver's offered you a room to stay in at Lawn House. That's pretty cool.'

'It's not long-term, just while we finish this album. It means I can work late, or even through the night if I need to.'

'What do the others do, sleep in the stables and live on beer and fags?'

'Almost. No, actually Della Hall cooks for us if we want. She's a great cook. It's no wonder Gus grew up to be such a solid lad. She runs that kitchen like a twenty-four-hour bistro.'

'You're kidding? I never knew that. I thought she was the housekeeper who just cooked on special occasions. I presumed Celine cooked for the kids, and Oliver fended for himself unless he was entertaining,'

'Oliver can't boil an egg. He's a nice chap, and it's really good he's letting me develop the studio my way, but he's a bit of a soft touch. He'd rather have his nose in an art book than check the contracts. Can't make a decision to save his life, either. That's why I keep such a close eye on my investment – I don't want people taking advantage.'

'I knew business wasn't his thing, but I thought by now he'd learnt by experience. The estate certainly seems on a better financial footing these days,' Max said.

'That's mostly down to my financial input and Gus's hard work. Gus Hall sorts the outside, and his mum runs the inside of the house.'

'I'm amazed. I must have had my head in a bucket of sand,' Max responded. Oliver, Gus and Ed were all his friends and he'd got the pecking order wrong. He'd been dipping in and out of life at Lawn House with his trusting eyes half-closed, and if ever life settled down he thought he might take a bit more notice on behalf of his god-daughters.

'You've been busy at work and nest-making with the gorgeous Jenny,' Ed said. 'You don't see the whole picture if you're only there at weekends. It's midweek when the work gets done, and it's then you can see who's in charge. The balance of power has shifted since Oliver's parents died, and when it changed from being Trelawney Manor to Lawn House.'

'Yes, that was odd, they died within weeks of each other and he changed things as soon as he could. Unlikely couple, his parents,' Max said. 'Sad, though.'

'That's one word for it,' Ed replied. 'I bet there's more to it than we know. I think it must have been quite an unhappy house.'

'I know he didn't like his father much.'

'Pretty extreme altering his surname, though. I mean, I didn't like my dad much but I didn't need to change my name to make the point.'

Max wished he'd asked Ed what else he knew about Oliver's parents and the house but, at that very moment, as they arrived at the main door of Paediatrics, Dr Mercer dashed out.

'In a hurry, Max, sorry, have a word with sister. They want a meeting to discuss Jacob's discharge and follow-up. The ulcer at the bite site is healing, so he'll be able to have physio at home now.'

A wave of nausea rose in Max's stomach, but whether from excitement or terror he could not tell. The safety he felt with the nurses watching over Jacob suddenly felt fragile. As it melted away, he wondered how he and Jenny would cope at home. With a forced smile on his face, he led Ed in to see Jacob.

IO

Della's diary, Thursday 23rd April 1964

I'm at a bit of a loose end. Today is Mrs Hall's day off and Mrs T's weekends seem to start on Thursdays now. I had to pack three long gowns for her this week for dinners with old friends from her modelling days. Actually, I think she looks a bit like Jean Shrimpton in my magazine. Mum, you should see the jewellery Mr T got out of the safe for her to take! It must be worth a fortune! I should ask for a pay rise. I wonder why he looked so strange when I asked him why he wasn't going to the dinners too?

He seemed to want to talk though, and asked me about myself. Did I like it here? Was my room comfortable? He didn't even know how old I was but he already knew I liked books. He likes talking books and so do I. Perhaps he's not so bad, after all. I've decided he's lonely too.

He lent me a book called 'Brighton Rock' and asked me if I'd ever been to Brighton. I told him we had no money for holidays, especially once you got ill, Mum, and that I'd nursed you for the last two years so missed out on college. Just talking about you brought tears to my eyes and he gave me his white handkerchief. I think he was sorry for me when he realised I was only eighteen.

He's nice when he smiles. His brown eyes look soft and warm so you could almost imagine he was handsome once. I think he must be about forty-five, and I've heard his wife is just thirty-three. They're an odd couple. I wonder if they'll ever have children. He asked what I would have wanted to be if I'd gone to college and I said a librarian or a chef in a bistro. He laughed and thought that was very modern, then offered to look up cookery courses for me. Too good to be true.

II

ARTWORK

April 2014

For a while the spare room at the cottage in Stowmarket became "the granny room", with the Carol and Eleanor staying alternate weeks. They also took on a female cleaner, and Max felt the house was taken over by women. Easter was extra special this year for Max and his family, even though Jacob was too young for an Easter egg. He bought a huge and very expensive one for Jenny and a smaller one for Carol, whose turn it was to be with them. He filled the house with daffodils, which were only slightly overshadowed by an enormous and exotic bouquet from Mike for Carol. (He'd gone off on a golfing holiday with some colleagues and was obviously feeling guilty.) Max was surprised how satisfied Carol seemed by this easy gesture – one to remember for the future, he thought.

Soon after Easter, a letter arrived for him, marked "Private, addressee only", and he almost opened it at breakfast, sitting across the table from Jenny and his mother, but something stopped him.

'What's that, Max, another appointment for Jacob?' Jenny asked. Jacob was sitting up nicely in his high chair and she held up a thin crust of toast for him to chew on.

'Oh, nothing, just a satisfaction survey about the hospital,

I think. I'll deal with it later.' Max shoved it in his pocket and finished his coffee.

He read the letter in the car and felt a flush rise from his chest to his freshly shaved face. It wasn't a satisfaction survey. Dr Grey had made a complaint to the hospital administrator. *Shit*, he thought, *I forgot to send him a cheque for his glasses.* He was relieved he hadn't opened it in front of Jenny and Carol, who knew nothing about Dr Grey. The letter said the hospital had made enquiries and, from their perspective, no further action was required; however, if he didn't pay the £480 Dr Grey had requested for his glasses, the doctor was in his rights to take things further. A cheque could be made payable to Dr Grey via the hospital administrator.

His gut cramped at the thought that an enquiry had to take place. Even though Jenny was used to him dashing to the bathroom, he couldn't go back into the house now to use the loo or to get his chequebook. (They hadn't given him Dr Grey's bank details to enable an online transfer.) Max regretted his decision to keep Jenny in the dark. He had started to see the funny side of it, but now the Dr Grey episode was becoming a nuisance again. He tucked the letter into the side pocket of his briefcase to deal with later, and tried to relax through his diminishing gastrointestinal spasms.

Max knew he'd done nothing wrong, but he felt a niggling guilt that Dr Grey had got hurt. His current account was a bit low this month, however, so maybe Dr Grey could wait a little longer? The belt of his trousers felt tight as he drove off to work. He really needed a good run and couldn't remember when he'd last managed more than a little jog around the local park. It just wasn't the same as running in the grounds of Lawn House, and he had gained a couple of pounds. He knew he needed to break the ice and get that first return visit over and done with.

Tricia and Celine had paid a subdued visit to see Jacob at home, and they'd wondered why it had been so strained as

Tricia had been given the all-clear by social services. She had probably saved Jacob's life, but she still seemed fidgety and uncomfortable, and Celine had to do most of the talking. Not one of them addressed the issue of whether Tricia would be able to return to her job of looking after Jacob, and the subject disappeared in a mist of uncertainty.

That evening Jenny agreed that normal relations needed to be restored, at least with Oliver and the girls, so with her blessing, Max arranged to go over on his own at the weekend for an afternoon run.

Issy and Willow rushed to greet him at the door, with Celine watching them closely from behind. Issy's hair was tied up in a high ponytail, which flicked Max's cheek when he hugged her. Willow hung back a little and tugged at one of the blue ribbons on her plaits while she waited her turn. They both spoke at once, so Max could hardly keep track of who said what.

'Uncle Max, look at the scab on my knee. Issy pushed me over.'

'Uncle Max, I'm much taller than Willow now, look.'

'Poor knee. I hope Issy said sorry. My goodness Issy, you have grown tall.'

'I think you might have to delay your run, Max. The girls have got so excited waiting for you, they won't let you escape just yet,' Celine said. 'Come and have a cup of tea and some cake.'

'Something in here smells good,' Max said as they settled round the kitchen table. Willow crept up and slowly climbed onto Max's lap like a naughty puppy that wasn't allowed at the table. Issy had her own chair and sat, straight-backed, like a debutante at deportment class.

'Mrs Hall has been teaching us to bake, hasn't she, girls?' Celine pointed to the flour-dusted floor.

'Well, I hear she's the best cook in the area,' Max said.

'Yes, she is,' Willow said. 'We can do Victoria cake.'

'Sponge,' Issy said sharply.

'Sandwich?' suggested Celine.

'And chocolate cake, and lemon drizzle, oh, and banana bread.' Willow counted the cake names on her stubby fingers. 'Four.'

'Banana bread was ages ago,' snapped Issy.

'We don't do that one any more do we, girls?' Celine looked at Max to see if he'd reacted. 'How do you have your tea, Max? It's been so long that I've forgotten.'

'Milk, no sugar, thanks.'

'No, we don't have bananas any more,' Issy said. 'It's not fair, I love bananas.'

'Now, Issy, why don't you tell Uncle Max about school?' Celine said.

'I'm the best at writing and sports, aren't I, Celine? Willow's the best at drawing.'

'Can Jacob draw yet?' Willow asked. She then wriggled off Max's lap and ran to the playroom to find her sketchpad, which she plonked in front of him.

'We can't stop Willow. She'll be a famous artist one day,' Celine said.

'And I'll be a famous explorer and climb mountains,' Issy said.

'You probably will, my little adventurer.' Celine poured Max's tea, and he thought he heard a tired sigh as she added the milk. 'Who wants coconut cake?'

'Me. After tea can we show Uncle Max where Daddy and Gus are going to build my treehouse?'

'Only if you say please.' Celine frowned at Issy, who gave an unconvincing "please" in return.

'*Our* treehouse, not just yours,' Willow said.

'Of course, the treehouse is for both of you, we've talked about sharing, haven't we? Now run and find your anoraks while Max finishes his tea. I'll come and help,' Celine said.

Max turned the leaves of Willow's drawing book while

he waited for their return. There were pages and pages of lovely nature drawings – flowers, trees, and colourful shapes he took to be butterflies. But the last two pages seemed quite different, and when he looked closer, his breath caught in his throat. One picture showed a baby in a cot with a person standing next to it. The person was a little girl with yellow hair, tied in a high ponytail, and in her hand was a black splodge. Could it be a spider? A small face was peeping round the blue door of the room. Max tried to think if Jacob's nursery at Lawn House had a blue door. A chill ran through him.

The last picture in the book was of two bigger people lying side by side on a blue rectangle, which Max thought could have been a bed. One figure was a chubby man with brown hair, and next to him was a woman with orange curls. She had two circles drawn on her front – boobs! The same little face was peeping round the door of this room and twisty plaits of yellow hair had been drawn down either side of the face.

It must be her imagination; after all, Willow had a great imagination.

Max heard voices shouting in the hallway.

'Come on, Uncle Max, Celine's just changing her shoes.'

Willow came and took his hand as he walked from the kitchen. 'Do you like my pictures? Would you like to show them to Auntie Jenny and Jacob?' she asked.

'I don't know, you still have some blank pages to fill. I'll ask Celine.' Max wasn't sure Jenny would like those pictures very much.

'Celine won't mind. She doesn't like the last two, anyway. She says they're silly, so I haven't shown anyone else. They're what I call my special pictures – secret.'

'Why's that? What do you mean by secret?' Max asked.

Issy and Celine had gone ahead into the garden by now, and he wanted to ask Willow more questions, but thought it might be unwise. She was only just five, and he could hardly subject her to an inquisition, or risk putting words into her mouth for that matter. He decided the pictures couldn't possibly be telling a real story. She must have heard the adults talking and made up her own story in pictures.

'Daddy has a book of special pictures we're not allowed to see, so I thought I'd have some of my own,' Willow announced. Max simply winced.

'But you say I can show Auntie Jenny, can I?' Max asked.

'Oh, yes, because you are special people, and we have to be nice to you because your baby has been very poorly. Pictures make people happy,' she said.

Max wasn't sure she'd got that right, but couldn't fail to be impressed by her powers of communication, be it through pictures or words. But his first trip back to Lawn House had been more of a challenge than he'd expected, and he was already keen to return home to his nice, safe, semi-detached cottage in Stowmarket. He didn't want to over-analyse the pictures, but couldn't just forget about them. The people on the blue bed must have been Gus and Sandra, but Sandra's hair wasn't red and curly. The little faces must be Issy and Willow, and the baby just had to be Jacob ...

'Come on, Uncle Max, slowcoach.' Willow nudged him.

'Who are you calling slowcoach?' he replied. 'Race you to the tree.'

The chosen trunk had already been marked with chalk and the smaller branches trimmed back to leave big, strong arms on which to build a platform. Max managed to look impressed, and patted the bark as if checking its condition. Next Issy led him to the nearby play area where a squelchy surface of black rubber had been laid – *all the better to fall on*, thought Max. The girls took turns being pushed on the swing before moving to the seesaw. After a while, Max made his excuses and left Celine to control the bounces. Their whoops of laughter as he walked away would normally have made him smile, but not today, not with worry growling in his sensitive gut.

Oliver had texted to say he was in the house and would meet Max in the first-floor study, so he tramped up the staircase, rattling the brass poles which held the dark red carpet in place at every rise. He had to decide whether to ask Oliver about the picture book before or after running it by Jenny. Was it extreme to think Social Services might even need to be involved? No, the girls weren't actually at risk, and he needed more information, so he'd hand the problem over to Oliver.

He ran his hands up the highly polished curve of the handrail and thought how as a child he'd have loved to slide down it. (He had a feeling Oliver wouldn't have been allowed to do so!) Max then looked up and saw Oliver waiting for him at the door of his study. Oliver was taller than he was, but at this moment he looked positively statuesque. Max was in his trainers and tracksuit bottoms and felt like a scruff.

'Hi, come and take a seat,' Oliver said.

Max thought today he looked every bit the lord of the manor – weird because that was a phrase he'd only previously used in jest to describe his friend, whom he'd thought until now to be the least lordly person he knew. Oliver's late father looked down on the two men from a statesman-like portrait hanging behind the desk. His painted eyes stared at Max as he sat to face Oliver, across the leather-topped desk. Yes, today Oliver had a look of his father that Max hadn't seen before. He was dressed in the tweed jacket Jenny so admired, and sported the brushed back quiff of sandy hair that she thought made him look handsome. Max had been inclined to disagree, thinking Oliver's looks were too pretty, even slightly weak, and not manly in the traditional sense. He wasn't used to seeing Oliver looking as authoritative as he did now, sitting on his throne – actually a rather nice padded leather office chair, surrounded by books – and it occurred to him what a long way Oliver had come since his days as a hippy, when he'd travelled the world and found Alexis. Oliver had always been on the eccentric side, but being widowed so soon after becoming a father had changed him. Then inheriting the estate, a couple of years later, took its toll.

'Thanks, how are you?' Max said.

'Been better. And you? It seems ages since you were here.'

'Yes, it's time we caught up properly,' Max said. It dawned on him this wasn't quite like talking to a well-established old friend, as Alexis had been his real friend, and he'd acquired Oliver's friendship much later and only by association.

'How's Jacob doing?' Oliver asked.

'Making progress, thanks.'

'I'm so glad. You know how sorry we all are.' Oliver was saying the right things, but Max sensed he had his guard up.

'I still need to ask you a few things, Oliver.' Finding a strong voice, Max was determined to ask about the things that still troubled him about Jacob's accident. He felt as if Willow's pictures had unlocked a box, and the words now came tumbling out in a random flow. 'How is Tricia these days? Do she and Celine get on well? What's Tricia like with Issy and Willow? Does she have a boyfriend? Who is she friendly with, the guys at the studio perhaps? Where is her room? Is it near the room where Jacob took his nap? What colour is her bedspread?'

'Hey, keep your voice down, Max. You've got a serious obsession with Tricia. You need to get a grip. Think of Jenny and Jacob,' Oliver said.

Max raked his hands through his hair and gripped the curls at his temples. 'I *am* thinking of Jacob. I can think of nothing else. I'm not obsessed by Tricia, and I certainly *don't* fancy her,' he stressed. 'I just feel we haven't really resolved what happened the day Jacob was taken ill. People aren't asking the right questions. I just want to know how a spider, however big it was, climbed upstairs from the scullery and into Jacob's cot. We need an explanation, and Tricia might have the answer.'

'Max, I promise you I have spoken to everyone concerned and there's nothing more to say. Mrs Hall was making banana bread with the girls while Celine popped to the village shop. Tricia was in her room, where, if you must know, the bedcovers are blue.'

'And how do you know that? Do you spend a lot of time in there with her?'

'I shouldn't even grace that with an answer but I know because it's my house; besides which, we always call it The Blue Room, you fool.'

'Please don't call me a fool. I have reasons for these questions,' Max replied.

'Okay, I know the colours of all the rooms in my house, and if you must know, mine is grey, the twins' room is pink, Celine's is sort of peach-coloured, and the one where Jacob takes his naps has blue with striped wallpaper and a connecting door through to Tricia's. I can go on ... as you know, there are many more rooms.'

'I'm sorry.' Max had quietened down, but was still dissatisfied.

'Listen to me. Tricia was in her room, reading apparently, but with the baby monitor on. You know that already. She was alerted by the sound of Jacob choking and went to him straight away. He was dusky and blue and seemed not to be breathing, so she started to resuscitate him while screaming for help. She saved his life, Max, so why does it sound as if you're on some sort of witch hunt?'

'Who dialled 999 if she was doing CPR? There must have been a delay she's not told us about?'

'Gus did. He was upstairs, doing some odd jobs. He told me the ambulance came very quickly and the paramedics took over. They gave Jacob oxygen before they shipped him off to hospital. Gus called me and I followed in the car with

Tricia, who was, of course, distraught. I know you've heard all this before.'

'And no one saw the spider? Was it just bad luck that it climbed the stairs and chose Jacob's room when there were about ten others to choose from?'

'Environmental Health seem to think so. Incidentally, they have got onto the supermarket's fruit supplier,' Oliver said.

'Good. Now what happened after the ambulance left? Where were the girls?'

'Oh, Max, can't you let it go. Jacob's getting better and that's the main thing.'

'No, not until I can visualise the whole scene. Tell me about the girls.'

Oliver sighed. 'Right. Mrs Hall stayed with the girls until Celine got back. She wasn't gone long. Said she passed the ambulance on her way back from the village. She went straight to the nursery to switch off the baby alarm, because it sounded like a bleating lamb and was upsetting everyone. She said she didn't touch anything else. She went quickly to see the girls, who were in their bedroom being comforted by Mrs Hall.'

'Both in their bedroom?' Max asked. 'How upset were they?'

'Very upset – and what an odd question! What do you expect?' Oliver's patience was wearing thin. 'Enough now.'

Max twitched as Oliver's phone rang.

'Sorry, Max, I need to get this. I'm expecting an important call.'

Max stood up, feeling frustrated he hadn't talked about Willow's pictures yet. Oliver swivelled his chair sideways and waved his hand as if dismissing Max, who hovered for a minute then stomped out.

He didn't want to go back to Jenny feeling so unsettled. He was cross at having achieved nothing with his stupid questions. All he did was get Oliver worked up. He was also annoyed that he hadn't even managed to tell him about Willow's drawing book. He felt useless, and hoped the run he'd planned might help burn off the feeling of uncertainty that was lurking. He set off on his usual route, planning to return to Oliver later.

He circled the rose garden before heading for the arboretum. The trees were in full leaf and, from a distance, through the greenery, Max saw flashes of colour that looked like blossom. A row of evergreens drew his eye in to where the trunk of the largest of the oak trees stood proud, and as he got closer he saw the familiar brass plaque at its base, bearing Alexis's name.

Max tripped and nearly fell. He recovered and looked up to see the tree was not in bloom – oak trees do not bear blossom – and dangling on coloured threads from the lower branches was a collection of sinister dolls and old toys. The disfigured artefacts twisted in the wind, and a lone silver bell tinkled eerily as it brushed on a twig. A deep gash daubed with red paint was carved into the bark, like a bleeding scar. Max bent to get his breath, taken from him by shock more than exertion.

He knew Oliver and Gus were the only key-holders to this protected place, and the tree was Alexis's sacred memorial. Max couldn't believe Gus or Oliver had allowed anyone else near enough to do such damage. Even when Max had visited in the past, carrying his own sadness, he stayed outside the railings that had been erected around the tree. Max almost wept with the memory from five years ago, when it was he who'd found Alexis hanging there from a high branch, dressed in the diaphanous blue of a pale butterfly, while a wooden ladder lay on the grass below. He hadn't known how severe postnatal depression could be until that day. Everyone knew Alexis was ill, but just thought she'd get better with time, not kill herself and leave her husband with two small babies to care for.

The arboretum had become a place of peaceful reflection. That peace was now ruined, and it looked as if a satanic ritual had taken place. Despite his robust appearance in the study that afternoon, Max knew how stressed Oliver had been. Could he have lost his mind and trashed the tree in a fit of madness and never-ending grief? Surely Gus had no reason to harm the tree he cared for? Max reversed his run, and went straight back to Oliver's study.

He almost knocked the door down as he entered. Oliver took one look at his face, made an excuse to the caller and put the phone down.

'What's happened to the tree? Was it you? Have you gone crazy?' Max demanded.

'What the fuck? Max, stop! You're the crazy one. What tree, what about it?' Oliver moved round his desk and grabbed Max by the shoulders. 'I'm getting really worried about you. You need help, man.'

'Alexis's tree – how could you?'

'How could I what? I don't know what you're saying. I haven't been near it for days.'

'It's covered in crap! Hanging monsters on strings. It looks awful, like Satan's Christmas t-tree.' Max choked on his words.

'Are you hallucinating? ...' Oliver hesitated. 'God, you're serious, aren't you? Show me. Let me see for myself.'

They briskly walked out into the grounds, and Oliver yelped when he saw the tree in the distance. He ran towards the gate, which had been left ajar, with the open brass padlock discarded on the ground.

'Jesus Christ, Max. What's going on? This wasn't here when I came last weekend,' he said.

'I thought you came every day?'

'Tricia suggested I didn't. She thought it was stopping me moving on, and making me more depressed ... thought once a week might be better for my mental health. In a way she was right, I was starting to feel a bit brighter,' Oliver replied.

'I don't think there's a timetable for these things. You come when you want to or when you feel the need – there are no rules.'

'I realise that now. I don't know why I agreed with her. She seemed quite convincing at the time. I'm just an idiot.'

'Go easy, we're both stressed out. You'd better talk to Gus. He's the only other person with a key, isn't he?'

'Yes, but he and Sandra have had a couple of days away. They needed some time together. Things have been a bit tense between them recently. I'll see if they're back yet. Are you coming?'

Max checked his watch. 'I really need to get back to Jenny. Give me a ring when you've spoken to Gus. And Oliver, I'm sorry I went off on one. Thinking about what happened to Jacob makes me tip over the edge sometimes. I don't think I'll settle until he's fully recovered and I know all the details.'

<hr />

That evening Oliver phoned. He said Gus knew nothing about the damage to the tree, but admitted the gate had been unlocked for a few days. He'd mislaid his key and because of going away he hadn't got around to replacing it. He couldn't stop apologising and promised he'd sort everything out: the padlock would be replaced first thing, and all the rubbish removed. He also promised to interrogate all the gardeners, but he really thought it was just some village kids playing a prank.

'Pretty pathetic prank,' said Max. 'Are you calling the police?'

'No, I don't think so. I don't want them tramping all over my land and scaring off the paying visitors. We're expecting a large walking group tomorrow, and Gus has promised it'll be ship-shape by then.'

When Max told Jenny she said, 'Oh dear, it's all about

money with Oliver at the moment. Mind you, a walking group might be good.'

'You could join?' Max said, but his suggestion slipped away, unheard.

'I bet Oliver was scared of what the police might find,' she then said with a sly smile.

Max liked it when Jenny's wicked side slipped through her sensible exterior. He decided to encourage it. 'What, you mean magic mushrooms or the occasional discarded spliff hanging round the office?'

Jenny's smile broadened. 'More like falsification of records, lost documents, tax evasion, the employment of illegal immigrants ... The list could be endless. I know! A secret gambling den!'

'You don't get gambling dens in a place like that, you twit. I'd say stolen antiques were more likely, or forged artwork,' Max said.

Jenny put on a theatrical voice, full of intrigue, and continued the list of possibilities. 'How about prostitutes in the stable block, prisoners in the basement, dead bodies in the grounds, and a witches' coven in the garages?'

They started to giggle, then laugh, like fools. The emotional release was cathartic as they invented even more devilish crimes that, in all innocence, they believed their friends were not even remotely capable of. It felt good to laugh again after weeks of worry and Max didn't want to break the mood. Now was not the time to talk about Willow's pictures. He was perfectly capable of putting his head in the sand when he wanted to.

He tucked the drawing book into his sock drawer as he went to bed, then lay for a while listening to Jenny's relaxed breathing as she fell asleep. He wondered if the tree had really been vandalised by kids from the village.

12

Della's diary, Thursday 14th May 1964

The second week on my evening cookery course went really well. Mum, you'd be so pleased with my short pastry. Mr T's paying for the course and Reg takes me in his green Hillman Minx. Reg is not very exciting but pleasant enough and we travel in comfortable silence. The other students are fun, especially a boy called Bill – he's exciting. He has to tie his long hair up for the class. His workbench is next to mine and he chats and tells jokes and we flirt. I look forward to Wednesdays now, and I quite like Thursdays when Mrs Hall's off too.

Thursday 21st May 1964

I took Brighton Rock and the washed and ironed handkerchief back to Mr T's study last night, and when I was choosing another book he briefly put his arm round me, just like Dad might have done. I stayed for ages and we talked books. It felt a normal, a nice way to spend the evening.

Oh my god, though, I can hardly write this, but when I went to go he pulled me towards him and kissed me. It wasn't a Dad-kiss, it was long and hard, the sort of kiss I'd been imagining from Bill, but have never had. I don't know what to do now, who can I talk to? I let it go on for ages before I made him stop. I knew it was wrong but it felt wonderful to be held and I was no longer alone. I'll not do it again but I'll never forget it. It really wasn't my fault, Mum.

13

MUSIC THERAPY

June 2014

Jenny's sick notes came to an end and she handed her notice in at the hospital. She told Max she felt unable to leave Jacob again, and Max had to admit to being relieved. He tried not to worry about the money, and just decided they'd budget more efficiently; after all, other families could manage on one income. He had a small savings account to fall back on, and was due a pay rise at his next appraisal, and at least they would save on childcare costs. Childcare issues remained an undercurrent rippling beneath their solid ground, however, as Jenny and Max both wanted the grandparents to get back to their normal lives, and longer-term, Jenny wasn't ready to entrust Jacob to a nursery yet. For Jenny to be a stay-at-home mum for a while was the best solution.

'He's still not moving his right arm very well,' she'd say. 'Do you think his eyes move equally?'

'He doesn't make as many sounds as he should. He should be babbling at ten months,' she then said one day.

'He's fine. Look how happy he is,' Max said.

He knew how much Jenny talked to the health visitor, and he reminded her that all Jacob's hospital checks were satisfactory.

But Jenny just accused him of belittling her concerns.

'Satisfactory isn't enough,' she said. 'I want Jacob to be more than just "fine". I want him to be perfect. We need to be doing more to boost his progress.'

'I try to stimulate him when we play,' Max said, and at once he realised how weak that sounded as a contribution.

He did some soul-searching and knew he couldn't cope with the idea that Jacob might have special needs as a result of his illness. He'd convinced himself that his role was to work hard and provide materially for his family, while Jenny was in charge of the home-front. His mum would not be impressed – this gender stereotyping wasn't how he'd been brought up – but it was all too easy to fall into, and somehow prevented him from facing his fears.

Max often cooked and did the washing-up, but when Jenny set about cleaning the house, he escaped to do the garden or have a run. In other words, he did the jobs he liked, when it suited him. He had a choice and Jenny picked up the pieces if he didn't. He decided to make more effort about the house, but still realised he was in denial and avoided dealing directly with Jacob's problems. It wasn't him, but Jenny who faced up to things and challenged the health visitor, the speech therapist, the physios or the doctors at follow-up appointments. It was Jenny who kept a close eye on Jacob's developmental milestones. Max's contribution was to provide hours of exciting play for his son – or as Jenny would say, he got the "fun bits".

He had to be pleased, though, as his creative play seemed to be paying off. Jacob ate well, smiled a lot and grew. He made Max laugh by becoming a bottom-shuffler rather than a crawler. They both thought Jacob's eyes seemed to focus better, and he followed brightly coloured balls rolled across the floor with glee. He grasped things well with his left hand but still rarely used his right.

'He might just be left-handed,' Max said and Jenny shrugged her shoulders. She was more worried about his lack of baby babble. There was certainly no "mama" yet, no "dada". She arranged to have his hearing rechecked, and it was fine.

Then Ed came and brought Jacob a book of nursery rhymes. Jacob's bright blue eyes lit up when he heard Ed sing, and he started to hum along.

'That's good, humming needs to be encouraged,' Ed said. 'Fill the house with music. Hum back at him and sing your sentences. Jacob seems to love music.'

Next time Ed came he brought a little wooden glockenspiel and played it with Jacob all afternoon.

'The boy's sure got rhythm! Look how he bashes that glockenspiel. He's even holding a stick in each hand. I'll buy him his first drum kit when he's old enough. You'll have me to thank when he's a famous drummer,' he said.

So, for a while, the Browns became the family that sang. When they were in the house Jenny and Max sang their sentences – Max thought it too embarrassing in public – and Jacob slowly discovered how to make more sounds, and even the odd word popped out. When Celine, Issy and Willow visited, the girls joined in the singing therapy and made games of it. One afternoon Willow made up a song of her own. Jenny sang it to Max when he got home from work and Jacob tried to join in.

Do-re-me,
Can Jacob come to tea?
Can he visit our house?
Come and play with me?
We have a treehouse,
He can climb our tree.

'Ah! How did you answer that?' Max said.

'In song,' Jenny replied.

'I didn't mean that. You've not taken him to Lawn House

since he left hospital, so what did you say? Is it time?'

'I think it is. The girls seem to miss our visits and want to see us all together as a family again, however much they like seeing you alone in your Lycra.'

'I don't wear Lycra, I wear purpose-made therma-cool clothing.'

'If you say so. Go on, phone Oliver and ask if we can all go for tea this weekend.'

Max gave Jenny a hug and then a kiss. 'You are the most wonderful woman.'

'I know,' she said. 'We're moving forward. We can't change what happened but we can change how we deal with it.'

'I'll phone before you wimp out.'

'I won't, don't worry,' Jenny said. 'I think it's time we unwrapped some of the cotton wool we've put round him.'

'That might be easier said than done, but we can try. We're bound to be a bit overprotective after all that's happened.' He picked Jacob up and pretended to throw him up in the air.

'Another thing – the health visitor called and she's found a specialist nursery that takes children with his sort of problems,' Jenny said.

'Problems?' Max looked worried.

'Yes, you know, learning difficulties, special needs, minor degrees of brain damage, things like that,' Jenny tried to explain.

'He's not got brain damage, don't say that,' Max said. He knew he wasn't coping as well as Jenny and that's why he still sometimes shied away from the issue. He just couldn't bear the thought of his bonny boy having permanent problems. Jenny could talk to the health visitor, friends and the other mums she met at clinic. Max just had his own busy family, and Ed, to talk to and, on the whole, he just put on a brave face. Quite frankly, Ed didn't know much about babies, even if his music therapy sessions were great.

'Okay, slightly delayed milestones and in need of a little extra help. Anyway, she thinks she might be able to get Jacob a place, soon after his first birthday. It will be more expensive, but she thinks it's worth it and he'll benefit from the socialisation.'

'You sound enthusiastic.' Max wondered how much more expensive.

'We need to learn to let him out of our sight occasionally, or else we'll burn out,' Jenny said.

'I suppose so. Shall we go and look at it together, then? I can take a morning off, one day next week, if you arrange it.'

'Deal. You phone Oliver and I'll phone the nursery,' Jenny said.

14

Della's diary, Thursday 4th June 1964

Bill didn't come to cookery last week or this and I feel miserable. Our tutor says he's not coming back because he's got a new job. The workbench next to me is empty and so am I.

Mr T's been extra nice recently, though, smiling at me in the corridors and reassuring me if he thinks I look sad. He can't even know about Bill. He must just be embarrassed about the kiss.

He invited me to his study this evening, to pick another book, and before I knew it he was kissing me again. Then he took me by the hand and led me across the landing to an empty bedroom, where he said we could relax more. He called me his Thursday Girl and said I was lovely. I went in to the blue bedroom with him, where we stayed for hours. Just before midnight I had to change the sheets before returning to my own room. What on earth have I done?

15

KITCHEN TALK

September 2014

Jenny and Max tried to control their tendency to jump to Jacob's every demand. Just before his first birthday, he tried to pull himself up on his chubby little legs to stand by the side of the sofa, and after that they let him stumble and fall while he continued to try.

'Hey, he's doing so well,' Max said. 'I told you he'd be fine.'

But Jenny knew he might almost be walking but he still wasn't trying to talk. She told Max the expensive new nursery would help, and without telling her, Max transferred some money from his savings account to help pay the fees. He wondered if his parents might help out, too, with an early birthday present. Jenny took some money from her own savings account, without telling Max, to pay for a weekly Pilates class, which helped restore her mobility and strength, lost since the accident.

Albeit with a few secrets, but a new attitude of mind, that September they got back to having family outings to Lawn House, and noticed Oliver was renting out more rooms on the top floor in what used to be the servants' quarters. With some amusement, Jenny and Max called them "the paying guests" – at least they hoped they were paying, but you never quite knew with Oliver, as he was quite capable of forgetting to charge rent, even if he needed the money. Any passing stray might be offered a bed – random pretty girls, friends of friends of the estate workers, or visiting musicians – and Jenny spotted a fair number of them were described as "distant relatives" of the Hall family, and Max joked that the Halls were taking over.

Mrs Hall had set up what amounted to a canteen in the back scullery and, one day, in search of chilled water after a run, Max found her there on her own. Always rather fond of a chat, she let him interrupt her baking.

'Hello, Max. Do you want tea?'

'No thanks, just water. How are you? Not too busy with all those mouths to feed?'

'Oh, I love it. Having all these young folk around livens the place up a treat,' she replied, with genuine joy. 'I like to keep busy. I expect Gus has told you Reg isn't so good these days.'

Max and Gus hadn't been on personal sharing terms recently. 'Yes, I'm sorry to hear that,' Max pretended.

'And it had become so stuffy round here after Arthur, I mean Mr Trelawney-Smythe, had his strokes. The first was only minor, but something dragged him down and it wasn't just his wife's car accident.'

'It was all very sad, wasn't it? He must have felt miserable, having to stop driving,' Max responded.

'Yes, frustrated, I'd say. It made him restless and, to be honest, rather cranky. Of course, I was fond of him. I've been with the family forty years, you know, Reg even longer. You get to know people's ways, but as an old man Arthur got more and more awkward. The responsibility of the place seemed to get him down.'

'So, he was always difficult, was he? I hardly met him,' Max asked.

'It depended how you handled him. His wife found her own way, but he and Oliver clashed when he was a young man. Then there was poor Miss Alexis, she was such a sensitive soul. Even before the twins she struggled.'

Mrs Hall checked the timer. A lovely smell of baking bread was emerging from the oven, making Max's stomach rumble. 'Ten more minutes,' she said, settling herself at the table.

'And then she got postnatal depression, poor Alexis,' Max said, and sat himself down opposite Mrs Hall. He swigged his water, thinking some buttered bread, fresh from the oven, would go down well, and worth risking gut ache for.

'Yes, but there were problems before that. She wasn't happy in this house, and Arthur and Diana didn't help. They felt she wasn't good enough for their Oliver. Arthur could be very controlling, I'm afraid, especially if he saw a weakness.'

Mrs Hall hitched her apron up over her matronly bosom and pushed her grey hair off her face. Max observed a note of bitterness he'd never heard before in her normally calm, Suffolk voice. And her tongue was so loose he wondered if she'd been at the cooking sherry.

'Don't you miss the old boy and his wife?' he asked, rather enjoying the airing of confidences.

'A bit, but it's a blessed relief he's gone. As I said, I was fond of him, quite close at times, but we had a strange relationship. I was more than just a housekeeper, but not quite a friend.'

'What about his wife?'

'Diana wasn't too bad. She just switched off if he got belligerent. She never really stood up to him, just waltzed off to London when she'd had enough. She had her own life there, you see, with the smart city set, and Arthur was terribly jealous. She was quite a bit younger than him and very beautiful. Used to be a catwalk model before they married. The tighter rein he used to hold her, the more she distanced herself.' Mrs Hall seemed to be enjoying sharing guilty secrets, and Max found it intriguing.

'Do you know, I've never even seen a photo of Diana.

That's odd if she was a model and so stunning,' he said.

'Mr Oliver had them put away after she died. He always found his parents difficult, felt the tension between them, of course. It's no wonder he took off travelling as soon as he could, then had to be bribed to return.'

'Bribed? Whatever do you mean?' Max was lapping it up.

'The old man said he'd stop his allowance and cut him out of the will if he didn't come and pull his weight on the estate. Like a fool Mr Oliver fell for it, and dragged poor Miss Alexis back here with him, as his wife.'

'It's no wonder he's found it hard adapting to the estate work,' Max said.

'Exactly. He should have got a job of his own and left his father to it. Arthur and Diana had enough paid help in those days. But I think they were trying to save money. And then of, course, Diana had her car crash,' Mrs Hall said knowingly.

'I didn't think the crash was serious,' Max said.

'It wasn't really, not physically anyway. She was losing her looks, and that and the crash affected her confidence. I think Oliver felt sorry for her then. You know the police questioned Arthur at the time? She was driving and he was a passenger, and she testified that he distracted her.'

'What, on purpose?' Max had not heard that part of the story before. The complex relationships in Oliver's family were enough to send anyone off round the world travelling, and Carol had once suggested the house was cursed; but it was the people at odds, not the bricks and mortar.

'Of course, Arthur denied any part in it and she took back her statement. We'll never know what really happened.'

'But even though things were pretty tense between Arthur and Diana, your family stuck by them?'

'The Halls have been intertwined with the Trelawneys for generations – man and boy, Reg would say. That's just how it was in these big houses. They needed us and we needed them.' She gave a sad sigh and Max thought it was time to bring the conversation back to the present day.

'Thanks for the water, and the chat. I guess I'd better be getting back to Jenny and Jacob.' He stood to leave.

'I am sorry, I didn't realise they were here and I've been prattling on. I haven't even asked how they are.'

'Not too bad, thanks. Why don't you pop upstairs and say hello?'

'I'd love to. Let me just get this loaf out and I'll come with you.'

<hr />

Jenny and Jacob were being entertained by Celine and the twins in the playroom. On the way there, Max extracted more information from Mrs Hall, who seemed to have an opinion about every other person in the household.

'So, do the lodgers have the run of the house, and what do they do about eating? There are no takeaways around here and the village shop is tiny. Surely you can't feed them all for free?'

'Gus and Oliver have got it all worked out. The third floor has its own entrance up the back stairs, and they only eat as guests on the rare occasion they're invited to the main dining room. Here in the back kitchen I'm allowed to charge them. Sandra helps me write out a little menu each day and she keeps an account of the money. She's a good girl, that Sandra. My Gus needs to hang on to her and put a ring on her finger.'

'Does Tricia help out too?' he asked.

'When it suits her,' Mrs Hall replied. 'I haven't worked that one out yet. One minute she's all pally, asking personal questions and calling me Della; the next she's cold and tetchy, and it's back to Mrs Hall.'

'But everyone calls you Mrs Hall,' Max commented. He hadn't found out for ages that she even had a first name.

'Quite. That girl's after something, you mark my words.'

'How about Mr Hall, doesn't he mind you being so busy?'

'Who, Reg? No. He's always been pretty self-sufficient and, to be honest, he's become a bit withdrawn since his old boss had the second major stroke, and died. Reg does funny things and gets forgetful. I've found him wandering about the house a couple of times now. He never used to come indoors at all. I think he's checking up on me,' she said with a little chortle.

'Poor chap,' Max said.

'He's best if I leave him be, so I just plod on in my kitchen while Gus keeps an eye on him. You see, I'm busier than I expected because that Tricia was going to help us out in the kitchen and the garden centre café, but she and Sandra have fallen out. I wish they'd get it sorted, then we might get Tricia to pull her weight.'

'They are very different types.' Max could guess what they'd fallen out about, and had a feeling it might have been the reason behind Gus and Sandra's weekend away.

'Well, Tricia doesn't seem much of a worker to me. Does a lot of swanning around the place doing nothing since ... you know, since she stopped having Jacob ... I do love that name. Ah, here we are. Hello, lovely boy. How are you?' Mrs Hall went straight to Jacob and ruffled his baby curls. 'My, you look just like your daddy.'

Jenny and Mrs Hall exchanged news on Jacob's progress, while Max helped Celine and the twins pack their toys away in their painted toy boxes.

'Will you all be staying for supper?' Mrs Hall asked. 'There's a hotpot in the Aga.'

'Oooh goody!' yelled Issy. 'We love hotpot.'

Max knew Jenny would decline, saying they had to get Jacob home to bed. She still didn't like to put him to sleep anywhere other than in his own cot, in his own house.

In the car, on the way home, Max put the last few tracks of a CD on, and he and Jenny caught up.

'While you were out running, Jacob got a bit grizzly so Willow and I took him over to see Sandra in the garden shop. Willow pushed Tallulah in her toy buggy and I pushed Jacob. It was so sweet,' Jenny said.

'No Issy?' he asked.

Issy was making a Lego castle with Celine and Tricia and couldn't be torn away. She's a strange one sometimes. I asked her if Lulu would like a walk and she snapped that Lulu couldn't *like* anything because she was only a doll and, anyway, she was dead. That's an odd thing for a little girl to say, don't you think?'

'Yes, very odd indeed. I must say Lulu hasn't been much in evidence recently – perhaps she's lost her?' Max suggested.

'Well, whatever, Lulu has been replaced in Issy's affections by a new, rather alarming doll called Mary.'

'What does alarming mean?' Max asked without too much interest. He was listening to the music and wasn't too interested in dolls, alarming or otherwise. He sensed Jenny had more to say.

'Mary has boobs and curves and made-up eyes, like a Barbie doll. I gather Tricia gave it to her.'

'And Willow too?' Max tapped the steering wheel along with the beat.

'I don't think she got one. I think Tricia and Issy are getting closer and Willow's getting left out,' Jenny said seriously.

'Did you mention it to Celine? I must say Mrs Hall did make some negative comments about Tricia to me in the kitchen,' Max said.

'Sandra did too,' Jenny said, and although not usually much of a gossip she seemed to be enjoying this exchange.

Max wondered if she was suffering from lack of adult stimulation in the world of stay-at-home motherhood. 'Sandra says Tricia flirts appallingly with any man that comes along – and more than just flirts, she thinks. Sandra and Tricia seem to stir each other up, and boil over like one of Mrs Hall's soup pans if they spend too much time together.'

'I'm told Tricia isn't much of a worker, more a hanger-on, quite different from Sandra. Oliver told me Gus and Sandra were having problems at the moment,' Max said.

'I know. Gus is spending more and more time at the big house and less time with Sandra at Oak Lodge. Any excuse and he's over there sorting something out,' Jenny said. 'I think he's also worrying about his dad.'

'Mrs Hall is too. I just hope Gus isn't sorting out one of the lodgers. I hear there's plenty of temptation on the third floor,' Max said.

'Max, what an awful thing to say! I thought they were all his cousins?' Jenny said.

'Cousins aren't illegal,' Max replied.

'Stop it, Max. Poor Sandra. I'll try and have a private word with her next time we go over.'

'With things so unsettled in the house, we need to keep an eye on the twins, do our duty as godparents,' Max said, glancing sideways to see Jenny's reaction. He still had Willow's sketch book in the bedroom. He'd convinced himself they were just childish doodles and had never quite found the time to tell Jenny or Max about it. It was all too easy to distract himself with work and Jacob's needs. He had a major new project on at the office, and Carol coming to stay for another of her visits didn't help. He couldn't possibly discuss it in front of her.

'I think the twins are all right with Celine in charge. We'll have to see about Tricia,' Jenny said. 'Before the spider incident we were happy to have her. I wonder why things have changed so much? She did, after all, save Jacob's life?'

'I know. It's hard to keep things in perspective.'

The CD had ended and the car went quiet for a while.

'Max, my darling, we can keep an eye out, but we can't solve all the problems of the world. I seem to remember we said that when we agreed to be godparents,' Jenny suddenly said as they reached home.

'Yes, we did, but we also said we'd take the job seriously, and that's proving quite hard when we don't understand what's going on half the time. You must admit the Trelawneys are a strange lot.'

'Trelawneys or Trelawney-Smythes?' Jenny asked.

'Quite!' said Max. 'See what I mean? Then there's the Halls too.'

16

***

SOFT SOUNDS

Jenny sensed Max was unsettled in bed that night. 'What's wrong, Max?'

'Just stuff. Sorry, am I keeping you awake?' he replied, turning over and stealing most of the duvet.

'Well, it's not easy to sleep with a fidgety gibbet next to you. It's like sleeping with a scrabbling stag beetle. Give me some duvet back,' she said and tugged at the bedding.

'I think you mean flibbertigibbet,' Max replied.

'Okay, out with it, what's the matter?' Jenny sat up and flicked on the bedside light.

'Can't stop thinking.'

'Yes, and ...?' Jenny was now wide awake and Max even wondered whether to suggest a cup of tea.

'There's something I need to show you now we're both awake.' He got up and dug Willow's sketchbook out from under his socks in the drawer. He flicked through the pages until he came to the two at the back and then laid the book on Jenny's lap.

She looked carefully at the pictures. 'These look very good. Put the top light on,' she said. 'Wow! These are amazing. Five-year-olds have very vivid imaginations.'

'That's what I thought, at first,' Max replied, getting back into bed.

'At first? Why have you got them?'

'Willow gave them to me to show you.'

'How long have you had them, and why are you showing me now?'

Max saw Jenny's face change.

'Willow gave them to me a couple of weeks ago,' he admitted. 'I thought they were just pictures, but I've been thinking ... what if they actually tell the real story and it's not just her imagination? I wish I'd shown you earlier.'

He put his arm round Jenny and she leaned slightly away from him.

'I wish you had too. The detail is astonishing and these could explain things. We can't just ignore them. What does Oliver think?' she said.

'Shall I make a pot of tea, now we're awake?' he said suddenly.

'He hasn't seen them, has he? Oh, Max!'

'I haven't found the right time,' he said.

'We'll never get back to sleep, and tea won't help. You need to speak to Oliver and I'm going to have to speak to Celine and Tricia. I'll invite them over for coffee one day next week when the girls are at school.'

'It might cause trouble ...' Max said.

'In case you haven't noticed, we already have trouble. We have a little boy who's been damaged. We can't just ignore it,' Jenny said. She snapped the book shut and dropped it to the floor.

'Are you mad at me?' Max asked.

'Don't be a fool, Max. I'm a bit cross and upset but I'll get over it. I really need to get some sleep now. Put the lights out.' She turned her back to him and pulled her side of the duvet up to cover her face.

In the dark room Max concentrated on lying still and pretending to sleep while he listened to Jenny's breath drop to a slow and gentle purr. He must have dropped off eventually because when he woke, Jenny was already up and giving Jacob his morning milk. Just for a second he remembered a dream he'd had where Alexis lived in an enormous treehouse, together with Issy and Willow, but the image slipped away as quickly as it came. And then Jenny appeared at the door holding Jacob's hands above his head as he tottered across the room to Max's side of the bed.

'Look, he really is walking. Hurrah for Jacob, well done!' Max pulled Jacob up into bed with him and hugged him until he squirmed. With great relief he saw Jenny's smile was warmer and more full of love than he deserved.

Jenny arranged for Celine and Tricia to come for coffee on one of Jacob's nursery days, thinking it would make the conversation easier. That morning the phone rang just as Max was leaving for work, intending to drop Jacob in at nursery on the way. Jacob was humming, apparently excited about the morning of serious play ahead. Max heard a disappointed note in Jenny's voice when she answered.

'Oh dear, that's awful ... Is Oliver very upset? No of course ... Yes, let's try again Friday ... Bye for now.'

'Now what?' Max asked, struggling to hold his briefcase, a changing bag and a wriggling boy.

'Someone's vandalised Mr Trelawney-Smythe's gravestone in the village churchyard. They've thrown a can of red paint over it. Everyone at the big house is in a real state, and Celine and Tricia have cancelled coffee.' Jenny looked as if someone had burst her balloon.

'That's not good. Red paint again! But how does it affect those two? They're just making excuses if you ask me. I reckon they think you're going to have a go at them and they're scared,' Max said, only half in jest.

'Ha-ha, funny man. No, the police have been called this time and they're now trying to link it with the tree episode. Everyone's being questioned, and when that's done Celine and Tricia have offered to help clean the gravestone.'

'Why them?'

'Oliver and Gus have a meeting with the accountant, and everyone else is busy with some performance Ed is giving tomorrow.' Jenny's matter-of-fact tone made Max feel uncomfortable.

'Oh, I see,' he said, and moved towards the door.

'Did you know about it?'

'What, the gravestone?'

'No, the concert.' Jenny's tone was no longer cool and matter-of-fact. 'You never mentioned it. Why don't you tell me things, Max? What's wrong with you? I bet you haven't spoken to Oliver yet about the pictures either, have you?'

'No, and I was a bit fed up we hadn't been invited to the music evening. I thought you would be too. It's not a concert, anyway, it's some sort of private promotional do and basically, we weren't invited, so that's it. I'll tell you more about it later, but right now I must get off or I'll be late for a meeting. You can have a nice day now, so go shopping or something. Give Mummy a kiss, Jakey.'

'Please don't call him that. His name's Jacob.'

'How about Jake?' Max asked stepping out of the door.

'If you must,' Jenny replied.

Max knew as he drove away that he'd exited a little too quickly, but he really did need to get to work. When he arrived at the office, the first thing he did was check his emails. Top of the list was one from Jenny:

Date 23/09/14
Sender: jenniferbest@physiofit.com
Subject: Secrets

Hi Max, it's easier to write this than keep it bottled up all day. I feel really sad that you've been keeping secrets from me. First Willow's pictures, and now the concert.

What's happening to our relationship if we can't share things? We'll talk tonight, but in the spirit of transparency, I'm just letting you know I'm driving over to Lawn House this morning to find out what's going on (more useful and less expensive than shopping!)

Jenny x

Max knew she must be seriously fed up with him to bother to write an email. He composed an apologetic, some would say crawling, reply and hoped that the fact she'd signed off with a kiss meant she'd get over it soon enough. He glanced through his other emails, then got on with filing the quarterly report ready for his meeting.

———

He got home later than he hoped and Jacob was in the bath. He edged the bathroom door open and pushed a bunch of red roses through the gap. Jacob squealed and made a noise that sounded like "dada", which made Jenny squeal too.

'Did you hear that? He said, dada,' she said, turning to the door. 'For God's sake, Max, you can't just win me over with a bunch of flowers.'

'I can try,' Max said. 'I thought we'd have a takeaway tonight too. It'll save us cooking.'

'Okay, I'll accept that. I've had quite a day. I'll tell you about it when Jacob's gone down.'

Jenny declined wine or beer with their Chinese meal that evening, so they washed it down with sparkling water. Conversation was stilted while Max waited for Jenny to bring up the things that were bothering her, but at last she moved the sticky plates to one side and picked at some grains of rice that had fallen on the table. Max wondered whether now was the right time to discuss Jacob's nickname options … but decided against it.

'Right, where shall we start?' Jenny suddenly said.

'I thought I'd like to start by kissing you passionately on the lips and tasting the flavours of garlic and ginger mixed with essence of Jenny.' Max thought he saw the trace of a smile, but the battle wasn't over.

'You'll be tasting sackcloth and ashes with a hint of washing-up liquid if you're not careful. I know you're stressed with work but we must talk more.'

'I know. I am sorry,' Max said. 'Let's start with the concert, then you can tell me how you got on with Celine and Tricia.'

'Tricia was lying low, but actually that might have been for the best as it happened.'

'Really, why?' Max asked.

'Concert first,' Jenny said.

'There's no need to make a drama of it, there's not really much to tell. On Friday, after you'd gone to bed early, I got an email from Ed telling me about a performance he was giving in the conservatory at Lawn House. It was an announcement rather than an invitation. He was just letting me know about what was happening with his new project.'

'So, tell me what's it all about?'

'Apparently some of his music friends have started up a company called Soft Sounds, which arranges small, intimate – and that probably means expensive – invitation-only music events in people's houses. They'd heard of the success of the studio at Lawn House, approached Oliver, and asked Ed to be one of his guinea-pigs.'

'I don't think Ed will appreciate being likened to a small rodent,' Jenny said.

'Probably not, but Oliver liked the sound of it and the first event is taking place on Thursday. The idea is to create a different kind of musical experience in relaxed and luxurious surroundings.'

'Like a salon in the nineteenth century – nice. Didn't he

think we'd like it? I love it when it's Ed "unplugged", playing the blues,' Jenny said.

'I know, it wasn't that. He didn't ask us because he thought we wouldn't be able to get a babysitter mid-week; besides, the fact is it's mega-expensive and the numbers are tight. His mates have given most of the tickets to sponsors and advertisers, so I wonder how much Ed and Oliver will get. It's going to be recorded and streamed online, so we can catch it later. I was going to show you as a surprise.'

'Were you? Ah! I guess I'm sorry for making a fuss, then,' Jenny said.

Max thought he sensed a touch of sarcasm there, but also thought he was beginning to climb the ladder from the dungeon of punishment and into the light again.

'So, tell me about your day. Hang on a minute – if you went to Lawn House, you know all about the concert already, don't you? You've let me go on about it, you little monkey, and you knew all along.' Max tried to stab her hand with a chopstick, but missed, and Jenny laughed.

'Just testing, slowcoach, making sure you got your story straight.'

'And did I pass the test?' Max asked.

'You certainly did, well done.'

'Phew, what a relief. Your turn now. Tell me about this wretched gravestone. Was it a mess?'

'Dreadful. It was as if someone had hurled a whole tin of Dulux over it and then scratched in some disgusting words before it dried,' Jenny said.

'They'll need a professional cleaning firm, not just Celine and Tricia to clean it,' Max said.

'They thought they'd have a go themselves first. Celine went to ask Reg Hall what cleaning stuff to use. She thought he might have paint remover in his garage.'

'Why Mr Hall, he's hardly likely to have an industrial amount of paint stripper is he?' Max said.

'Apparently Gus still asks his dad for practical advice, and Reg knows what's in the outhouses and sheds around the estate better than anyone, even if sometimes he can't remember his own name.'

'So, what happened?' Max asked.

'Well, Celine found Reg rooting around in his little garden shed at Chestnut Cottage, and in the corner of the shed she spotted a black bin liner, half covered by a blanket. Grubby puppets and dolls were spilling out of it and, on the top, she saw Lulu.'

'What, missing doll Lulu? How did he explain that?' Max said.

'He just mumbled that he didn't know where it had come from. She said he seemed flustered and bundled her out of the shed quickly, but she did manage to hang onto Lulu. She's planning to give her a good wash and spruce her up a bit before returning her to Issy.'

'I wonder if Issy will even care?' Max said.

'Celine didn't seem too worried about her losing Lulu, just said what she always said about the girls being different individuals. I think her mind was more on the job of cleaning the grave, to be honest.'

'But did you talk about the drawings?'

'Sure did, and she, of course, said they were simply the result of Willow's imagination. I managed to get her to talk about that day again, though. She remembered that at one point, when they were cooking the banana bread, Issy had gone upstairs to get a cardigan because she was cold, and Willow went to find her when she took a long time. Celine and Mrs Hall were doing the washing-up, and when the girls came back downstairs, Celine popped out to the shop. She left them eating banana bread with Mrs Hall. The rest, of course, we know,' Jenny said sadly.

'I suppose it all fits, Oh my god! Issy could have taken the spider upstairs and Willow could have seen!' Max said.

'I can't believe Issy would put a spider in Jacob's cot, that's just too bizarre,' Jenny said.

'What on earth do we do now?' Max said.

'Celine thought she might talk to Willow.'

'Do you think it's wise to talk to her on her own? She might lead her on, make her say things she doesn't mean. This sort of thing needs careful handling.'

'That's what I thought. Actually, I was wondering if it might come better from you. You are her godfather, and you have had some training with your charity. What do you think?'

'Maybe, but I'd have to square it with Oliver. He might want to be there too. I'm working from home tomorrow, so I should be able to catch him in the morning.'

'Will you tell him about Reg Hall and the stash of dolls?' Jenny asked.

'I suppose I'll have to. Oh dear, what a mess!' Max said.

'That's enough show and tell for tonight. Let's leave the dishes, I'm exhausted,' Jenny said.

17

FEVER

Max slept like a sloth that night, unaware until morning that it was Jenny's turn to be restless. Jacob had disturbed her in the middle of the night, crying with a slight temperature. She gave him a dose of children's paracetamol and sponged his forehead, and Max heard nothing. Jenny then spent the night listening out for him between spells of superficial dozing on the spare bed in his room. In the morning, Jacob was still hot.

Jenny brought him back into bed with Max. She gave him more medicine, followed by his morning milk, which he promptly threw up, creating a creamy lake in the middle of the duvet. The child grizzled and clung to Max, while Jenny stripped the bed and loaded the washing machine downstairs.

'I think we should take him to the doctors,' Max said, when Jacob vomited a second time. 'Have you checked for a rash?'

'Yes, all clear when I changed him, but have another look while I phone the surgery.'

Max couldn't see a rash but noticed that the scar at the top of Jacob's arm looked a bit red. 'Tell them it's urgent,' he shouted along the hall.

'They say come straight down and they'll see him

immediately. Oh Jesus, he will be alright, won't he?' Jenny appeared at the bedroom door looking frazzled.

'Come on, let's just go. Throw a tracksuit on, there's no time to dress. He'll be fine, but let's get him seen.' Instant Max was back in action.

'He's very flushed. I'll get a facecloth and try to cool him while you drive,' Jenny said with a wobbly voice.

At the surgery they were ushered straight into the treatment room, where the practice nurse took Jacob's temperature while they waited for the doctor. Suddenly Jacob started twitching and shaking.

'What's happening?' Jenny cried. 'Do something!'

The nurse pressed her alarm bell and a doctor came bursting through the door.

'Reduce clothing, recovery position, watch his airway, paracetamol suppository,' said the doctor, 'Have some diazepam on standby. How long has he been fitting?'

'Oh, Jakey-Jake,' Max said quietly. 'It's alright, darling boy, we're here.'

'Ninety seconds,' said the nurse.

Max thought it seemed much longer. He saw Jenny's eyes were wide with terror, watching Jacob's every move. He put an arm round his wife's shoulders and the two of them stood together like statues of petrified wood while the doctor took care of their baby. The twitching stopped as quickly as it started, and Jacob held his left arm up to his mother. Max noticed his right arm hardly moved.

'What's happening?' Max asked. 'Is he going to be alright?'

'He's had a seizure, but he's fine now. Just soothe him and reassure him,' the nurse said, but Jenny was already doing just that.

When the doctor completed his examination, he told them Jacob had a secondary infection in the scar on his upper arm. He hoped the seizure was simply a febrile convulsion as a result of spiking such a high temperature, but because of his past history they wanted to send him to the children's unit in Ipswich for observation.

'We'll take him straight away,' Max said.

'No,' said the doctor. 'We've already called an ambulance, just to be on the safe side in case he fits again. Nurse will stay with you until it arrives.'

'Oh God, will it happen again?' Jenny said, and Max thought she was going to cry.

Pretty soon they were back at Ipswich hospital, and the reception they received made them feel like old friends. Jacob even managed to smile a little. Dr Singh was on the case again, with a new assistant – Dr Webb. Max had rather hoped to see Dr Mercer again, but he'd moved on to pastures new. Max thought it ironic to now have a doctor called Dr Webb dealing with a child who'd had a catastrophic spider bite. He looked at Jenny's distracted face, saw her picking her thumbs, and decided not to share his observation. Max gave his hands another good scrub with hand sanitizer, and tried to feel reassured in this safe environment, while Jenny fussed over Jacob.

Swabs taken during a small operation, done to clean out Jacob's wound, confirmed a nasty bacterial infection – a resistant bug that would need strong, intravenous antibiotics. This nearly freaked Max out and his hand-washing regime escalated. He was terrified that he could have passed a germ over to Jacob, and even more terrified of this apparently virulent bug spreading. His next worry was that by being too clean they hadn't allowed Jacob's natural resistance to infection to build up. Jenny and Dr Webb were both unimpressed by Max's concerns, and assured him none of this was his or Jenny's fault. The important thing was that Jacob was getting better now the infection had been drained.

Before he was allowed home, Jacob had one of Dr Singh's specially requested brain scans, which thankfully showed nothing sinister. His right arm was starting to move a little, and Dr Singh said his patient would be able to go home in a few days. Max and Jenny were given advice as to how to prevent another convulsion if Jacob got too hot, but they were sure this was a tendency he'd grow out of in due course. They tried to be brave, but Jenny shed a few tears and picked her thumbs, and Max washed his hands at every opportunity. They shared an air of resigned déjà vu when Jenny said, 'Looks like it's back to the physio for Jacob, then, and lots more of Ed's drumming exercises.'

Towards the end of their stay in hospital, they had an unexpected visitor: Tricia arrived, with bags under her eyes, looking as if she hadn't slept or washed her hair for days. Her make-up was smudged, and Max was alarmed by the heavy, bitter smell of cigarettes on her breath. Tricia was a non-smoker? He was sure they'd checked that most particularly at her interview?

'I just had to see Jacob and know how he is. I won't stay long, but I heard he's had a setback. Is he all right?' she asked. She seemed apologetic, twitchy, a completely different person to the one they'd trusted with their son's care. Max looked to Jenny for a lead.

'That's fine. He's making good progress,' Jenny said. 'He's having a nap, as you can see, but he's okay. Come and sit with us a while.'

Max found her a chair.

'Actually, I want to tell you something important. I've wanted to say something for a while, but Gus wouldn't let me,' she said in a weird, almost unworldly voice. 'I need to tell you ... it was my fault.'

'What was?' Jenny asked.

'Jacob's illness. I just have to say I'm sorry,' the weird voice continued.

'What are you talking about?' Max said. 'You didn't make the spider bite him. We know how upset you were, but it wasn't your fault. You saved his life.'

'I took my eye off him. I neglected him when he was in my care.' Tricia tugged at her jacket sleeve and Max thought he saw the freshly made line of a cut across her wrist. She shuffled her feet and looked at Jacob, peacefully sleeping in his cot. Max saw something in her gaze, which drank in every element of the child, and made him shiver.

'You were only in the next room and you had the baby alarm on,' Jenny said, gently gathering the sleeping boy into her arms.

'I wasn't concentrating,'

'You said you were reading. What happened? Did you nod off?' Max suggested.

'Not exactly. You see, I wasn't alone. Gus was with me and we were ... oh, I might as well tell you ... we were fucking.'

'You a-and Gus? N-no!' Jenny spluttered. Max stood up and went to Jenny's side, putting a hand on her shoulder as she spoke. 'So, what you're saying is there was a delay? You were otherwise engaged when you heard Jacob choking? Jesus Christ!'

'Why are you telling us now, if Gus stopped you earlier?' Max asked.

'That's hardly the issue,' Jenny snapped. 'How long was the delay?'

'Just long enough to put some clothes on, so not long. I feel really bad. I had to tell you.'

'For goodness sake, Tricia, this is not about you! Jacob was damaged! Are you just telling us this to make yourself feel better? If you're looking for forgiveness, think again,' Max said.

'No, it's not that. Celine said you'd seen Willow's drawings, and I thought you'd put two and two together. It'd all come out, anyway, so I thought it best to confess, do the deed, take the heat.' Tricia's voice wobbled and she made a little snorting sound, laughing at the mismatched phrase. (Max put the strange sound down to anxiety at the time, but much later would wonder if it was something worse and more sinister when the memory of it continued to make him shudder. He'd seen the glint in Tricia's eyes, too, as she'd gazed at Jacob in his cot, and watched Jenny's reflex reaction to scoop Jacob up and hold him close.)

'We could prosecute, sue you for damages,' Jenny said.

'I don't think that's the answer, darling. There are too many other contributory factors, and suing Tricia wouldn't change anything,' Max said. He turned to Tricia. 'Have you told anyone else what you've just told us?' Max tried to sound calm, be the reasonable one and keep his fury about Gus's stupidity under control for the time being.

'I had to tell Celine. You see, I was worried about the stupid pictures,' Tricia said, her voice now sounding flat.

'We were planning to talk to Celine and Oliver about them, but everything went on hold when Jacob got ill again. The girl in the spider picture does look like Issy,' Max said.

'And the couple in the blue room was you and Gus. Jesus Christ,' Jenny added.

'I know, I know, and Issy does like spiders. Now Celine has interrogated Issy, and Issy has gone running off to her father saying Celine and I are ganging up on her,' Tricia said.

'But you and Issy have been so close?' Jenny said.

'I wouldn't say close. I just liked to keep her on side. She's livelier than Willow, can be more of a handful, and I didn't want to make an enemy of her,' Tricia said. 'She's pretty smart, and I thought she'd caught on that I was seeing a lot of Gus and might blab. That girl is perfectly capable of blackmail.'

'Oh, come off it, we're talking about a five-year-old girl. Blackmail? How ridiculous!' Jenny said.

'Are you quite all right, Tricia,' Max asked, trying to get another look at her wrist.

'Don't worry. I'm sorting it. I'm leaving, dumping Gus and going back up north, end of!' Tricia announced, but she still didn't move.

'Not quite end of,' Jenny said. 'What about Sandra and Gus? And *we* still have Jacob's problems to deal with, even if you run off.'

'That's why I'm here. I had to see Jacob one last time and say a proper goodbye. You don't seem to realise how much I love him. I lost my own ...' Tricia gulped and turned her head away.

'Lost who or what, Tricia?' Jenny asked more softly. She waited for the answer.

Tricia simply flicked her wayward red curls from her face and glared back at Jenny. 'Nothing. Forget it.'

'So, maybe just go.' Max was feeling uncomfortable and just wanted this visit to be over and this disturbed woman to be well away from Jacob.

'And Sandra can have Gus back if she wants him. It's Gus I need to get away from. What started as a harmless flirtation has become dangerous and Gus is turning nasty. I daren't stay,' Tricia said.

'What do you mean by nasty? Has he hurt you?' Jenny asked.

'Not r-really,' Tricia stammered, then broke into noisy sobs.

'What does "not really" mean?' Max asked firmly.

Tricia looked shaky. 'He ... raped me. I said no, and he did it anyway.'

Jenny gasped. 'When?'

'A couple of nights ago.' Tricia hung her head.

'Are you hurt? Physically, I mean?' Jenny's expression had changed from one of irritation to genuine concern. Tricia just shook her head.

'Have you told the police or been to the doctor? Who have you told?' Max demanded.

'No one. I've packed my bags and I'm on my way. I've left

a note for Celine but no details.' Tricia hung her head and made that snorting sound again, only this time it was more of a choking sound than a snigger.

'You must report him,' Jenny said.

'No way. It'd be his word against mine. Leaving is the only way,' Tricia said.

She then took one last look at Jacob in Jenny's arms and dashed out of the door.

'Stop her, Max. Go after her,' Jenny yelled, making Jacob jump.

Tricia was surprisingly quick for a woman in distress. Max briefly caught her by the arm but she wrenched it free, and he decided to let her go rather than be accused of assault.

'Let Celine know where you are,' he called after the chaotic figure that ran down the corridor to the exit.

He then sighed and returned to Jacob's room. Jenny was pacing up and down trying to calm her alarmed infant, who'd reacted with loud screams to the toxic atmosphere left in Tricia's wake.

'What on earth do we do now?' she said.

'I don't know. It's all getting beyond me. Let me think,' Max flopped in the only easy chair in the room.

'Rape?' Jenny said. 'Could Gus really have raped her?'

'I don't know,' Max said, 'but did you see the cut on her wrist? Whatever has happened, she's in trouble.'

18

Della's diary, Friday 13th June 1964

We keep having discreet trips to the blue bedroom. I don't seem to be able to stop him (or myself). I don't know if I'm being brave or stupid but it feels very thrilling. The other day Arthur told me I needed new underwear, something more frou-frou, whatever that means. I think he knew that upset me a bit because last evening he gave me a pink rosebud from the garden to take to my room. I've put it in a tooth mug and I can smell its perfume as I write.

Saturday 21st June 1964

Arthur wants me to do different things I'm not sure about. And he wants me to go to the clinic to get a Dutch cap because he doesn't like rubbers. I don't know when I'll manage to go because it's in Ipswich and there are houseguests coming to stay. I might have to go there instead of doing cookery this week. Arthur said I should make people think I am going out with Reg when he drives me to town. Odd thought. I can't imagine ever wanting to go out with Reg.

Thursday 25th June 1964

We've had an accident, one split. He blamed me, said I wasn't careful enough and had been too lazy to go and get a cap fitted. It's not that easy.

I can be irregular, but I've worked it out and I'm due 'the curse' any day, so fingers crossed everything will be okay. I had the hottest bath I could manage tonight just in case. Arthur says guests always want to come in the summer to see the gardens at their best and the busy season is upon us. I've noticed it makes him grumpy having visitors in the house, and I'm grumpy, too, because Diana's not away and he doesn't give me any attention.

19

BROTHERS-IN-LAW

October 2014

Jenny made Max go to the chemists to buy a fancy new electronic thermometer to monitor Jacob's body temperature, and a room thermometer for his bedroom. They'd discussed Tricia's performance – for that's what it felt like to them – but for now the decision they made was to concentrate on Jacob with a wait-and-see approach, giving Tricia the chance to report the rape if she so wished.

Once home, Max avoided checking his emails, hiding as long as he could from any potential communication with Lawn House. Just preparing himself for the arrival of Carol's next stay was enough for him – she'd arranged to come for a few days so Max could get back to work. He didn't know why she still put him so on edge because, on the whole, they were getting on better. Perhaps it was because her first impressions of him had been so poor. She thought him a young man with no focus, no ambition, and simply not good enough for her daughter. Mike had been more welcoming, which helped Carol's eventual acceptance of him as a son-in-law – that and Max actually getting a decent job. He'd since proved over and over how much he loved Jenny and that she could rely on him, but still he felt he had to put his guard up for Carol. Although she now accepted Max, he wasn't sure the compliment was quite as easy the other way around, and he couldn't believe such a tricky woman could produce such a gorgeous and loving daughter as Jenny.

Having Jacob had almost sealed the deal, however, and Carol certainly came into her own as a grandmother who loved to come and help. Sometimes the help became meddling, of course, but he tried to take the rough with the smooth. (He accepted the fact that he'd always been surrounded by strong women: growing up he and his father had definitely been the quieter members of the Brown family.) So yes, he tried to convince himself that Carol was a great help, having more time on her hands than his own mum, but Max and Jenny were agreed that short, sharp visits worked best with her, so she couldn't get too involved or critical about modern child-rearing techniques.

Ed phoned and agreed to wait until after Carol had gone before coming over to see them. Jenny suggested he bring Lucy for Sunday lunch, with the proviso they all helped with the cooking and clearing up.

'Lucy says she'll bring a dessert. She's longing to see Jacob,' Ed said. 'And I can give Jake another music lesson.'

Calling him Jake sounded so natural when it came from Ed, but to Jenny he was still Jacob. Max wondered at what age that would change. His own parents had called him Maxwell until he went to junior school and then, to his great relief, he became Max. Just the occasional teacher and the odd smart-arse student at secondary school clung on to his full name. But then he made the mistake of putting Maxwell Brown on his CV, so the name was reborn in the office. Max always thought names were so important: Jenny hated to be called Jennifer; Ed hated to be called Edward; and he was definitely Max, not Maxwell.

Max spent the week trying to encourage Jacob to say "Mum" and eventually he did a satisfying "mmm" sound. He could say dada quite well, but the name Ed still got the better of him. His speech therapy appointments were few and far between, but the health visitor said not to worry, it was still early days, he was only thirteen months old, after all.

On the Sunday morning Jenny provided him with a drum set consisting of saucepans, a frying pan, and a pair of wooden spoons.

'Someone's looking forward to seeing his godfather,' Max said as he made a cymbal out of a tin foil container he'd found in the kitchen.

'I think we all are,' Jenny said. 'It's so nice to be home and have some normal family activity.'

'I'm with you there. You look tired, are you sure you're up to visitors?' Max said.

'Yes. Tired is normal these days. It'll be great to catch up with Lucy. I wish we could see more of her,' Jenny said.

'I expect we will, now her brother and my sister are about to bring another baby into the family,' Max said.

'I know, exciting, isn't it! I wonder if Lucy and Ed will ever get married?' Jenny mulled over the prospect whilst peeling the potatoes for lunch.

'I think they're content as they are. She's certainly tamed him since they met in Steve Cain's office.'

'Tamed who, Steve Cain or Ed?' Jenny said.

'Both, I guess. That girl has her hands full as Steve's PA in London.'

'And Steve has his hands full being Ed's agent,' Jenny added.

'It works both ways. Steve must be a nightmare to work for. I've always thought him brash and too full of himself,' Max said.

'Alpha male, you mean?' Jenny said. 'He's obviously a good businessman and has been great for Ed. They get on all right. Lucy must be a very clever woman dealing with both of them. She seems to be able give Ed enough freedom to not feel tied down, and enough support to feel loved and wanted.'

'You modern women have to work so very hard,' said Max.

'And you love us all the more because we can,' Jenny said. 'There's the doorbell – you go.'

Lunch was long and lazy and full of laughter. Ed and Lucy played with Jacob between courses, and Jacob demonstrated that he was back on form. After lunch, his music lesson grew into a full-blown jamming session. Lucy was on xylophone, Jenny on plastic whistle, Ed and Jacob on drums, and Max on cymbals, having now made a matching pair. When they'd worn Jacob out, Jenny and Lucy took him up for a nap, while Ed followed Max to the kitchen and helped load the dishwasher while Max made coffee.

'You've no idea how good it is to be in a normal home,' Ed said. 'It reminds me how I used to love Sunday lunch in London with your parents when we were students.'

'I'm glad you thought they were "normal",' Max said.

'Your father was the only decent dad I'd ever met until then. I reckon you're taking after him.'

'Ah, shucks,' Max replied, pretending to be embarrassed.

'Mind you, I had a long chat with Oliver the other night, and his parents – well, his father at least – made mine seem less fucked up than I thought.'

'Steady, we're trying not to use the f-word with Jacob in the house,' Max said.

'Oh, come on, man, I've heard you swear,' Ed replied.

'I said trying, not succeeding. Just be aware and watch your language.'

'Okay, sorry,' he agreed. 'You know, I love all of your family – your mum and dad, and of course your lovely sister, Jo. Hey, Lucy told me Jo and Freddie, that brother of hers, are having a sprog soon. Who'd have thought it when they met at your wedding? Cool, isn't it? We'll be related!' Ed said cheerily.

'Incestuous, you mean! I don't think being godparents to each other's children is quite the same thing as related, but if you get on with it and marry Lucy, you and I will end up as brothers-in-law twice removed or something.'

'I think what you mean is, your brother-in-law will be my brother-in-law and the whole world will revolve around Freddie, as if being a big-shot lawyer isn't enough for him. Lucy says he has a big head as it is.'

'That'll make him and Jo a fine pair of self-obsessed high achievers, then, and I do say that from a position of brotherly love. It's no wonder my confidence used to sag at times, having Jo as a big sister. You've got to feel sorry for their kid,' Max said.

'I feel a bit sorry for all the kids we know at the moment. They all seem to have problems. It makes me think I could never cope with offspring of my own. My parents screwed me up when they separated and I had to bounce between them. I wouldn't want to repeat the scenario,' Ed said.

'Jenny would say the idea is not to separate, especially once you have children. Mind you, she sometimes sees life through rose-tinted spectacles,' Max said, and as he did so had the awful realization he still hadn't paid Dr Grey for his blessed specs. As Ed closed the dishwasher and switched it on, Max got his phone out and tapped himself a quick reminder. 'Does Lucy know you might not want kids?' he asked.

'I suppose I haven't spelt it out. She knows the music business isn't exactly compatible with a well-balanced family life.' Ed had a mildly troubled look on his face.

'Don't you think it should be discussed if you're in it for the long haul? Surely you've been together long enough for the subject to have cropped up?' Max tucked his phone back in his pocket.

Jenny and Lucy came downstairs giggling. 'What subject has cropped up?' Lucy asked.

'Nothing,' Ed said quickly. 'What have you two been up to?'

'Nothing,' Lucy said.

'Ha-ha,' said Ed. 'Touché.'

'Just sharing a private joke,' Jenny said. Come on, then, tell us about your secret performance. What did we miss? We can't seem to find it online yet.'

'Ah, the trouble is, it didn't get recorded.' Ed looked across the room at Lucy.

'But on the whole it went very well,' Lucy added quickly. 'We had a lovely champagne reception, with the most marvellous canapés to start with.'

'I'm amazed Mrs Hall does canapés,' Max said.

'Don't be daft. Soft Sounds brought in their own caterers,' Lucy said. 'The plan was for welcome drinks and nibbles in the drawing room first, with a short set from a new pianist Steve's discovered, after which we'd go to the conservatory for a light, but totally super, two-course supper. Ed's virtuoso acoustic session was to be the finale.'

'It sounds wonderful,' Jenny said.

'Is there a but coming?' Max asked.

'How did you guess? Lucy said. 'The caterer's refrigerated van got plugged into the wrong socket at the wrong time, just as they turned on the electric ovens and the lighting for the stage, and the whole system blew, fusing the first two floors of the house – apparently the electrics are shocking and long overdue for a rewire.'

'It was a bloody disaster. My career teetered on the brink of ruin. We had important guests there – future clients, investors, and Steve Cain himself,' Ed groaned.

'Come on, not a total disaster. We resuscitated most of the food in Mrs Hall's enormous Aga. It was only just getting dark, so the music continued by candlelight, until Gus hitched up the emergency generator,' Lucy said, impressively upbeat considering the desperate look of failure on Ed's face.

'Oh yes, good old Gus, hero of the day, wearing his underpants over his trousers,' Ed said, sounding like a spoilt child whose birthday cake had sunk in the middle.

'Got a problem with Gus, have we?' Jenny asked, wondering if Ed had had too much wine with lunch. But then her own attitude to Gus had shifted a bit in recent days, and she wanted to hear Ed and Lucy's opinions.

'Ed's just feeling sorry for himself, for a change,' Lucy said. 'Gus did what had to be done.'

'The man showed no musical sensitivity. He put Oliver down in public and made him feel worse than necessary about the state of the wiring. Then his noisy generator ruined the atmosphere, and the sound levels were dreadful. Of course, the idiot guests ignored that, because all they really wanted was chilled champagne and hot food. No one cared about the music.'

'That's not entirely true. Don't be a spoilsport. Your set went really well.' Lucy said, apparently earning Jenny's respect for her calmness at dealing with a grumpy Ed.

Max meanwhile thought Lucy was reacting more like a carer or a mother, than a girlfriend.

'It was okay once we'd turned off the generator and returned to candlelight, I suppose. I bet Gus knew the wiring was crap. Why else did he have the generator available? And why was his father there, making things worse and changing all the plugs around? I told you – bloody chaos!' It seemed Ed wasn't ready to drop the subject.

'I'm sure Reg was just trying to help, and the generator was part of some routine back-up plan. Gus would have done a risk assessment for an event like that,' Lucy said.

'Corporate gobbledygook ... risk assessment, my hat! Why didn't he say something before the inevitable disaster and warn Oliver about the condition of the electrics? He just wanted Oliver to look bad and get some credit for himself. He was showing off that evening in front of that Tricia woman who was hanging around too. Poor Oliver, lumbered with that place by an accident of birth. He should be doing something more creative than patching up a crumbling old house, a privilege thrust upon him by his controlling father.'

'It does sound a mess,' Jenny said. 'I wonder how the rest of the house managed if there was a major power cut?'

'Celine had already taken the girls into her room on the far side of the house for the night. They'd set up folding beds and a little tent, pretending to be on a camping trip. They had torches and lamps at the ready and thought it was all a great game.'

'Ah, that's so sweet. You see, Celine does give those girls a lot of thought,' Jenny said to no one in particular.

'Most of the lodgers were in the stables, waiting for the crew to get back for a backstage party. The stables and the top floor kept their power supply – I suppose their wiring had been upgraded when they were refurbished,' Lucy explained, while Ed grunted in agreement. 'Anyway,' she added, 'Oliver got some emergency electricians in the next morning to restore power and now they're doing the rewiring.'

Ed stopped groaning and thinking about himself at last. 'Oliver's really fed up with the mess. He's had to move some of the more valuable paintings and bits of furniture out, to protect them from the dust caused by the drilling out of old wires. I heard him say he might even have to sell some of the art to help pay for everything if the insurance doesn't cover it.'

'That sounds bad,' Max said.

'Meanwhile, Celine and the girls are staying at Oak Lodge with Gus and Sandra until it's finished. There's no room there for Oliver, so he's staying in the big house, and, as for Tricia, she's probably sleeping in the stable block – with anyone who'll have her. It's odd I haven't seen her around since the concert,' Ed commented.

Jenny was picking at her thumbs. Max wondered if, like him, she was thinking about the timing of all this: the concert had taken place while Jacob was in hospital after his seizure, and the alleged rape must have been a day or two after. He wondered how Gus had managed such a thing with electricians all over the place and everyone sleeping in different beds. He gave Jenny a quizzical look.

'What do you mean, "anyone who'll have her"?' Jenny asked.

'I've just heard Tricia gets around a bit. She's getting quite a reputation for herself,' Ed replied. 'You must have seen her in action, Max, seen the way she sidles up to Oliver at every opportunity, asking personal questions? She even tried it on with me once.'

Max realised he and Lucy couldn't have known Tricia had, by now, left for good.

'What?' Lucy shrieked. 'You never told me that.'

'There was no point. Nothing happened,' Ed said.

'Max?' Jenny said.

Max simply shook his head, whilst Ed's wine-lubricated story-telling continued. 'Oliver really didn't need advances from Tricia,' Ed said. 'I spent the evening with him yesterday and he has more worries on his plate than the prime minister. He's finding redecorating the house without Alexis to advise him is too much, and he's still really shaken up about her tree being messed with.'

'You and he seem pretty tight at the moment,' Max commented.

'Yeah, we get on well. He's still furious with Gus, of course, for losing his keys and then not taking it seriously enough. He seems to need to unload, and I've been around a lot lately.'

'Has he told you Celine found Issy's doll in amongst the stuff they took down from the tree?' Jenny said.

Max had to take hold of her hand as the thumb-picking was getting serious. He gave it a warning squeeze: he thought they weren't going to discuss this with anyone until they knew more.

'What, you mean Lulu?'

Blimey, thought Max, *Ed even knows the name of Issy's doll.*

'That's weird,' Lucy said. 'Sandra didn't mention it last time I ran into her. She did say the girls were all over the place, and she looked exhausted.'

'Issy wouldn't have put her doll there,' Jenny said.

'No, I didn't mean that,' Lucy said. I just meant the girls are unsettled, like Oliver.'

'There's something else,' Ed said. 'You know I used to stay in the house when I was recording? Well, one day, a while ago now, I was out early, stretching my legs, and I saw Reg Hall near the stable block moving the wheelie bins about. I heard him drop something heavy into one of them. He didn't see me, and I thought he looked a bit shifty, so I took a peek. It was a can of red paint.'

'No!' Jenny and Max said in unison.

'He could have just been doing his job and clearing up, but Ed thinks he was trying to hide it,' Lucy said. 'Do you think he could have done the paint jobs?'

'No, why would he?' Jenny said. 'He's such a nice, gentle chap.'

'Mrs Hall did tell me he was losing it and doing strange things. He likes to scavenge around the bins and look for things to recycle. She said his shed is always full of his rubbish,' Max said.

'Someone needs to talk to Gus, but I'm afraid we have to get back to London tonight,' Lucy said.

'That'll be me, then. I'll have a word with Gus. I need to speak to him about a couple of things,' Max said.

Lucy started to rummage in her handbag.

'Tea or another coffee before you go?' Jenny asked.

'No, thanks, I couldn't manage another thing,' Lucy said. She took her phone from her bag and read a memo she'd made for herself. 'Sorry to change the subject, but I need to ask a small favour. Steve has suggested we get some old photos of Ed for the promotion of his next album and I said I'd ask you two when I saw you.'

'I've got some good ones from when we were all at uni,' Jenny said.

'And I've got some from our American travels. I think you've even got one of him meeting Steve in California, Jenny? It would be great to show the moment he was discovered,' Max said.

'Excuse me, I am here,' Ed said. 'Don't talk about me as if I'm not in the room.'

'He just likes reminiscing about California,' Jenny said, with a smirk.

'You weren't interested when I asked you for photos, Ed,' said Lucy. 'You said all your pictures were at your dad's and you didn't want to have to go to see him.'

'Correct,' Ed said and yawned. 'Come on, we need to hit the road soon. There's no rush for the pictures.'

'I can go through my computer files and forward you a couple when I've found them,' Max said.

'I'll find my photo album, it won't take a minute,' Jenny said. 'Oh, sounds like the boy's awake, too, just in time to say goodbye.' She rushed upstairs and came down with Jacob on one hip and a dusty old photo album in the other hand.

'Such a sweet, old-fashioned girl. Jenny loves a good album and remains unconvinced about the digital world, don't you, love?' Max joked.

'I have photos on my phone, too, thank you very much. There's just something rather comforting about flicking through an album. A printed photograph holds more emotion than a screen.'

Jenny passed the album to Lucy while she got Jacob a drink. Within minutes Lucy found the print she wanted of a youthful Ed, bathed in California sunshine, shaking Steve's hand. 'Can I borrow it to make a copy? He looks like an innocent child getting the school prize.'

Ed looked over Lucy's shoulder. 'That was the best summer ever,' he said, exchanging a twinkly smile with Jenny.

'Yes, take it, but don't forget I want it back,' Jenny said.

It was clear both women adored Ed, one in a brotherly way and the other as a lover; but his innocent face had changed to an all-knowing weary one, lined with experience. Max thought Ed's life was a story of its own: after an unhappy childhood, he'd survived university, then a dangerous dabble with drugs and excess alcohol, and as a successful musician he'd handled the groupies and neatly negotiated some financial challenges. He remained Max's most entertaining friend, who was proving to be a perfect choice of godfather for Jacob, but Max did wonder what sort of a father his friend would make.

On the way out of the front door Ed produced an enormous belch.

'Oh, that's better,' he said.

20

Della's diary, Wednesday 8th July 1964

I've felt sick all day today with a tummy bug. Had to cancel evening class and have gone to bed early. I don't want to get behind, as we're doing choux pastry next week. I love chocolate eclairs but I couldn't even manage one of those today. I must be ill. We used to buy them from Simmons' shop in Welwyn Garden City. Oh, Mum, I wish you were here.

Saturday 11th July 1964

Still feel queasy, it comes and goes. The curse still hasn't arrived and now I'm worried.

Sunday 12th July 1964

All the visitors have gone back to London, taking Diana with them. I went to Arthur's study this afternoon. He was furious I hadn't been to the doctor. I thought he might hit me when I said my monthly hadn't come, but instead he just slumped in his chair. When I told him, I felt sick and my breasts hurt when he touched them. He called me a stupid girl and I sat and cried while he came up with a plan: I am to flirt and make out with Reg next Wednesday in the car. Then I must try and seduce him, as that is the only way to avoid a scandal. I told him I couldn't do it. Reg is just a friend. But he says I have no choice. Now I can't sleep for worrying. Mum, you'd say write a list, so here goes. What are my choices?

1. Run away to London and seek an abortion (where? who? no money)

2. Throw myself on cousin Rosie's mercy (too ashamed)

3. Take an overdose (too scared)

4. Do nothing and hope to miscarry (gin and hot baths?)

5. Do what Arthur says (God help me!)

Wednesday 15th July 1964

Arthur must have given him ideas and a nudge. Reg was wearing aftershave and had a smart shirt on today. On the way to Ipswich he blushed when he said how nice I looked in my summer dress, and if it hadn't been so contrived I might have thought it sweet. As it was it was just embarrassing and I felt sicker than ever.

On the way home Reg pulled the car over in a remote lane and said he'd admired me ever since we first met. He asked if he could kiss me. I must be a better actress than I thought, because soon Reg was getting carried away and we climbed onto the back seat. I was pretending to join in, and I won't say I enjoyed what I did, but it wasn't unpleasant and was over quickly enough.

21

GUS

October 2014

Max took on the task of talking to Gus, wanting to be a good influence in Issy and Willow's lives and iron out doubts about their other godfather. "Good old Gus" they used to call him, but was he? Max had never been terribly close to Gus, but until now had trusted him well enough, and Jenny got on well with Sandra – but then, so did everyone. The evidence against Gus was mixed. The timing of the alleged rape seemed wrong, and even if he'd been stupid enough to sleep with Tricia, Max really couldn't imagine him as a rapist. As far as he knew there'd been no word from Tricia since she stormed out of the hospital.

It made sense to Max, however, that Gus might want to protect his failing father. He recalled often seeing Reg Hall lurking in the shadows around the estate, looking a bit lost in recent times, and Reg would avoid eye contact and never wanted to chat. Max could never think of him and Della Hall as a couple, as she always seemed a much more positive and an altogether brighter individual. Perhaps it was Reg, in a confused state, who'd desecrated the tree and vandalised the gravestone, after all? How much did Gus know? Gus needed to be honest about his father, and then there was this rape allegation to deal with.

It took Max the usual twenty minutes to drive to Oak House, on the edge of the estate. Gus opened the door with a wide, open smile on his face and a firm handshake – and the cheerful greeting quite put Max off his stride. He wasn't planning to be aggressively confrontational, as Jenny's advice had been to stay calm, but he was aiming to ask some delving questions and put together some of the jigsaw pieces he'd been gathering.

'I've just put the kettle on, want a cuppa?' Gus asked, all pally.

Clever strategy if you have something to hide, thought Max, who decided a similar warm response might lull Gus into a false sense of security.

'Thanks. Having a quick break?'

'Yes, I've been on the go since six. This place doesn't run itself.'

'I guess not, and it must be tough having Celine and the kids staying too. I bet Sandra's knackered.'

'Oh, she's fine. She didn't have to open the garden centre until ten, and Celine's helping there while the girls are at school.'

'How much longer will they be staying?'

'They go back to the big house tomorrow. It'll be quiet without them. I must say Sandra's been great. She can cope with most things, even on top of my demands,' Gus said, and stuffed almost an entire doughnut into his mouth in one go.

Max was taken aback by this degree of openness. What did he mean by "demands"? Sexual demands, dietary requirements, the irregular hours of work on the estate, or the keeping of Gus's secrets? Max looked at Gus's broad, muscular frame, and the thought of him overpowering Tricia made him feel sick. He breathed deeply and pushed the image away. He then tried to channel all the TV detectives he loved to watch, from Sherlock Holmes to Morse and Lewis, convincing himself he could be just as effective as an investigator.

'Tomorrow? So soon. Are the electrics fixed?' Max was pleased with his calm and easy control.

'Yes, almost done. I called in a favour from an old mate of mine who has his own company.'

Hmm, I see, thought Max, *that's how he works, is it? Perhaps Ed was right about who's in charge around here.* But he quickly got his mind back on the job in hand. 'It'll be good to have your home back, though. They must have made a mess with all their toys, especially Issy?'

'Why do you say that?' Gus asked.

'She's renowned for being the wild one, breaking toys and swinging too high. I heard she pushed Willow out of the treehouse recently.'

'She can be a bit lively, but she's been no trouble. Celine has the measure of her. I know she can be a minx, and I think Tricia used to egg her on a bit, but as for the treehouse incident, that was just a sisterly spat. Issy didn't like the decorations Willow put up. Typical women when it comes to interior design. Celine sorted it out.'

'How do you mean, Tricia used to egg her on?'

'It's a bit of a tale ... how long have you got?'

'As long as it takes, I'm intrigued. Hey, that tea should be brewed by now.' Max watched Gus pour two cups of tea and thought how perfectly at ease the man looked with himself. He wondered if he would make it as a sleuth, after all? Or maybe he was much too gullible.

'So, you know Celine and Tricia are only half-sisters, right?' Gus started his story.

'Er, not really. At least I don't know the details. Tell me more,' Max said.

'Yes, same mother but different fathers, or maybe it's the other way around, I'm not sure. Anyway, they grew up apart and hardly knew each other, until a few years ago, and even then, they weren't close. Celine told Sandra and me ages ago about her half-sister, who'd been an awkward teenager, but

I'd forgotten all about it until she turned up here. She'd come good by then, done well at college and got her qualifications. The sisters had resumed contact through Facebook and wanted to try to get closer again.'

'God, that didn't come out when we interviewed her,' Max said, whilst thinking, *troubled teenager come good ... now they tell me*!

'No, she's far too canny to give much away, and she and Celine genuinely wanted to build bridges. There are so many things you don't know about Tricia. We all took her at face value, even Celine. We knew she'd lost her job and we felt sorry for her, and we trusted Celine not to bring anyone unsuitable into the household.'

'Unsuitable?' Max was now getting worried.

'Don't get me wrong, she's well-qualified on paper. It's her personality that's in doubt. It's a blessing she left,' he said.

'What do you mean?' Max tried to put some steel back into his interrogation. 'Are you suggesting we put our baby in danger and nobody warned us?'

'No, course not. Nobody knew in the beginning, Max. This only came out recently, long after the spider bite.'

'She did save Jacob's life, and we will always be grateful for that,' Max said. At the thought of Jacob, his steely centre was already becoming more malleable.

'She did all the right things that day ... eventually.' Gus leaned back in his chair and put his hands in his pockets. From one he pulled out a handkerchief, which he put to his mouth to catch a funny, strangled cough as he cleared his throat.

'Eventually?'

'You'll find out soon enough, so I might as well tell you and get it off my chest.'

'What is it?' Max said, wondering if he was about to get a full confession or an excuse. Maybe there was something else Gus needed to tell him. He felt his own heart rate bump up when he saw Gus take a deep breath in preparation.

'The thing is, Tricia and I were in her room that day, having a quick shag.' Gus lowered his head and blew his nose noisily.

Max stood up with as much authority as he could muster. 'At least you have the guts to admit it! Tricia told us everything, you stupid bastard. She said you raped her, and that's why she left.'

'What the ...? You must be joking! That woman is a piece of work. She actually said that? The goddamn liar.' He thumped his fist on the table. The empty tea mugs jumped and the spoon fell out of the shallow sugar bowl.

'She said you raped her,' Max said slowly and deliberately. 'Jenny wanted Tricia to report it to the police straight away but she said no. This is why I've come to see you.'

'You surely don't believe I could do that?' Gus pleaded.

'You've just said you were shagging her while Jacob was being bitten ... maybe another time you forced her, against her will? What am I supposed to believe?' Max said. He found himself clenching his fists at the thought of Jacob struggling to breathe while those two were at it. 'And what about Sandra? You must be some kind of monster —'

'Hey, stop, hear me out.' Gus tried to interrupt Max but failed.

'Listen? You want me to listen to the man who was fucking my child's nanny while he was nearly dying? I'm phoning the police, even if Tricia won't.'

As Max reached into his pocket for his mobile phone he heard a sound at the door. He turned to see Sandra, her face distorted, tears coursing down her cheeks, dragging black specks of mascara with them through the heavy foundation she was famous for over-applying.

'Sandra!' Gus gasped.

'Get out!' she screamed at Gus. 'I heard it all. How could you? I knew there was something going on and you denied it. We're over! GET OUT!'

Max saw her sway with the explosion of emotion, and

went to take her arm to steady her. Gus stood up as if to go to her, too, then stopped and stood still, feet apart, chest out, broad shoulders pressed down. The buttons on his chequered work-shirt strained as he took a breath. He spoke clearly, with no aggression or fear. His voice was low and almost resigned.

'Will both of you please listen to me. Give me five minutes, and I'll tell you what did happen with Tricia, but I can assure you I did not rape her.'

'You can't talk your way out of this one. If you won't leave this cottage, I will,' Sandra said, turning towards the door.

Gus stretched out his arm, as if to bar the way.

'Get away from me. I don't have to listen to any of this. How dare you?' Sandra snapped.

'Perhaps we should hear him out,' said Max, who by now was feeling calmer than Sandra. She sniffed and wiped her face with shaking hands. She flounced to the sofa and nodded for Max to sit next to her. Gus crossed the room in two strides and settled himself on a tall dining chair facing them – a defendant ready to give evidence.

'Five minutes, Gus,' Max said, taking the role of chief prosecutor, 'then we're calling Oliver. He needs to know what's been going on in his house and he can help us decide whether to involve the police.'

'Sandra, I'm so sorry,' Gus started. 'I've been a fool. I admit I cheated on you but I swear I've done nothing criminal. I certainly didn't rape Tricia. Come on, Sandra, you know me, I just wouldn't do a thing like that.'

'Cut the crap,' she snarled. 'Just tell me why you screwed that tart.'

'Because that's exactly what she is: a tart, and a nymphomaniac to boot. She tried to get cosy with Oliver first, then had a go at Ed, and when they failed to oblige, she worked her way through the guys in the studio before targeting me.'

'Oh please ... so you were a victim? Am I supposed to feel sorry for you?' Sandra said.

'She was all over me, Sandra, touching me at every opportunity, but never when people were around. She was far too clever for that.'

Max listened in amazement. 'She never approached me,' he said quietly.

'Think yourself lucky you were never alone with her. One evening, after a party in the stable block, when you were at your mother's, Sandra, I had too much to drink and that's when she pounced. Like an idiot, I responded.'

'Oh, Gus, how could you?' Sandra's tears started again.

'I told her it was a mistake and it would never happen again, but by then she'd got me where she wanted me. She blackmailed me and said she'd tell you if I didn't give her what she wanted. She was insatiable.'

'Jesus, that's enough, we don't need the gory details,' Max said.

'No, seriously, she was abnormal, like a woman possessed. It was scary. And then she upped the ante and started to involve my dad.'

'What! She tried to have sex with your dad?' Sandra shrieked in horror.

'God, I don't think so. Listen, I think Tricia did those things to Alexis's tree and Arthur's grave. She must have found the toys and broken dolls with all the plastic rubbish in Dad's shed. She tried to frame my dad. She left a trail of clues to implicate him.'

'Why on earth would she do that?' Max asked.

'Because she's crazy. She knew Dad was losing his grip and I'd do anything to protect him. That's where the next level of blackmail came in, and the fact she could punish Oliver for rejecting her must have added to her satisfaction. She had a huge chip on her shoulder, and wanted to punish the ruling class in general, as well as any personal stuff.'

'This all sounds a bit warped, Gus. Are you just putting us off the idea of rape?' Max asked.

'I told you, I did NOT rape her. And my dad would never do anything to hurt Oliver. He loves the whole family.'

'It's looking suspicious, though,' Max said.

'Tricia said she'd drop him in it if I wimped out on our agreement, and Mum and Dad would lose their lifelong home and their comfortable retirement. She ranted on about telling Mum. She said Mum was her friend and had told her fascinating things about Mr Arthur's past. Tricia was getting more bizarre by the day, especially after Jacob's accident. Maybe it was guilt – if she's capable of such a thing.'

'So, you serviced Tricia regularly to keep her quiet. How convenient for you.' Sandra sounded unconvinced, and Max also had his doubts.

'Celine said she saw the stuff brought down from the tree in your dad's shed. She saw Issy's doll in the rubbish bag. Explain that,' Max said.

'Dad could never have got hold of Issy's doll. He hardly ever goes into the house.'

'That's not quite true, is it? People have seen him wandering in the house recently. Celine told me she asked if he was looking for his wife on one occasion when she saw him, and he said no, he was looking for Mr Arthur. Mr Arthur's been dead for over three years.'

'Okay, so he gets muddled. But I still reckon Tricia planted the wretched doll in the pile of rubbish. I found my missing keys in her room one day soon after, so she must have taken them from my pocket to do the tree job.'

'If you'd kept your trousers on she wouldn't have got her hands in your pockets,' Sandra said through gritted teeth.

'It was when I found the keys she started to turn nasty. She said Dad had given her the keys, but there's no way he got them from me. I bet it was the other way round and she lent him the keys. She said he did the damage to the tree and the grave because everyone knew he really hated Oliver's old man.'

'This is all a bit convoluted ...' Max said.

'I think Tricia thrived on a slowly drawn-out revenge. It added to the excitement she craved. Anyway, the morning I found the keys, I happened to ring Dad, and when he told me he'd found a pot of red paint, I told him to put gloves on and dump it in one of the bins before everyone was up and about.'

'So, you knew he had the paint. That must have been when Ed saw him acting strangely,' Max said.

'Yes, but Dad didn't have a clue where it had come from. Did Ed tell anyone what he'd seen?' Gus asked.

'Only Jenny and me, I think, and Lucy of course. We told Ed about the rape allegation too,' Max said.

'Oh God, the rape!' Sandra said, with desperation in her voice again.

'There was no rape, I've told you that. Can't you see the woman was a manipulative liar? I would never rape anyone. Why don't you believe me?' Gus pleaded.

'I don't know what to believe. You may not be a rapist, but you are an adulterer and a fool, full of your ridiculous excuses.'

'I am a fool, but I love you, Sandra. Tricia tricked me, manipulated me and turned me into the idiot you now see. Try to understand I had to protect my dad. He's nearly eighty and he's ill. He could have been prosecuted, lost his good name, lost his home and his wife.'

'So, you put your mum and dad before me. That's about the measure of it. Family first, girlfriend second. You call me your fiancée, with this cheap ring on my finger, but I'm just a girlfriend, not family, and I doubt I ever will be.'

'Now, guys, we're straying off the point. You two can sort out your differences later,' Max interjected.

'Can we? I very much doubt it,' Sandra said sadly, even though her tears had dried.

'Look, you two, it seems that Reg still isn't in the clear yet, and what on earth do we do about Tricia? When did you two last have sex? Did you do it the night before she left?'

'No. That's the night I refused. To be honest, I couldn't have performed even if you'd paid me, besides which there were electricians all over the place. I wanted it to stop,' Gus said.

'Jesus, enough,' Sandra said, with a huff.

'I'd managed to avoid her for quite a while, that's why she was so pent up and angry. That's why she lied about me,' Gus said.

'I think I believe him, Sandra. The idiot is no rapist.' Max gently put a hand on Sandra's arm.

'I know,' she said quietly. 'But it's still over.'

'I think we do need to tell Oliver. He is your employer, and was Tricia's too. This all happened on his patch, and he needs to think about his family and all the other staff. Lots of people could have been affected by what's happened,' Max said.

'I feel rather sorry for Celine,' Sandra said all of a sudden. 'Do you think her job is safe?'

'She's done nothing wrong. She knew nothing about this,' Max said, very much hoping that was true.

Gus was sitting with his head in his hands, clearly opting out of any further discussion.

'Bad judgement in trusting her half-sister, though,' Sandra said.

'We're all guilty of that,' Max admitted. 'Perhaps with Tricia gone, Celine will remain a perfect nanny for Issy and Willow. They love her so much. She must have an odd existence. What is she, into her forties, with no personal life of her own to speak of? That's why getting to know her half-sister was so important to her. She wasn't to know how it would turn out, and probably doesn't know the half of it. She'll be devastated when it all comes out.'

'Oh, Max, you are so kind,' said Sandra.

Max didn't always feel kind, although Jenny often said that

about him too. He hoped she knew he was a soft touch who loved her, despite the teasing, and that she loved him back. Sometimes he just felt gullible and inadequate. He quashed the thought that he hadn't even been attractive enough to be seduced and blackmailed by a crazy nymphomaniac, but also realised he should be grateful for that. He'd come to Oak Lodge to pin down a rapist, and here he was being all understanding and thoughtful, trying to justify other people's errors of judgement. The detective and prosecutor had vanished and he wanted to go home to Jenny and their well-ordered life, away from these complicated people whose issues he hardly understood. He wanted Jenny to reassure him the world wasn't entirely bad.

Sandra jumped to her feet, while Max was wallowing.

'This is it, Gus, don't go. I'm the one who's leaving. I'm going to stay with my parents. I'll be back for my stuff tomorrow.'

22

Della's diary, Friday 31st July 1964

Old Mrs Hall thinks we're dating and is okay with it. Phew! Perhaps I can carry this off.

Reg took me to the cinema to see 'Dr Strangelove'. We sat in the back row and snogged and did it again. I still feel sick!

Arthur and Diana go away tomorrow for two weeks in France and I feel quite relieved. He's been very distant and cold towards me. He called me to his study yesterday to give me instructions – if I contact a doctor before he comes back there'll be trouble.

Cookery course is finished. I miss my college friends. Wonder what Bill's doing?

Sunday 23rd August 1964

Arthur and Diana have been back a week. Arthur took me to one side to go over the plan he's worked out, as if it's a board game and not real life. He's told me he doesn't want to but he could throw me to the wolves if our secret comes out. I think that means he'd sack me without a reference and, in effect, I'd be homeless. I can't believe he is threatening me like this. If I keep quiet and go along with it, I will have a home and a job for life, and he will always look after me. I'm stuck.

I've decided I must make the best of things, but I'm worried about his orders that I must not see a doctor because a doctor would work out my dates and know they are not right. He says healthy young women don't need antenatal care. I wonder if Mrs Hall will agree when she finds out? I guess I soon need to tell Reg.

The only communication I've had from Dad is a note to say he's let our house in Welwyn out to tenants.

Monday 24ᵗʰ August 1964

I told Reg the news last night and he was more thrilled than I thought possible. He wants to stand by me and has asked me to marry him. He says we can live in Chestnut Cottage with his mum. I said I'd think about it.

Perhaps in a week or two I'll have come around to the idea of Old Mrs Hall being my mother-in-law. She'll never replace you, Mum, but I could do worse.

23

HALF-TERM HOLIDAYS

October 2014

Oliver was busy with important business meetings in London that week and Max wondered what he could be up to. Whatever it was, their talk had to wait. Tricia had disappeared, the children were being safely looked after, so what was the rush? When he finally made contact, the reception on his mobile was dreadful.

'Hi, Oliver. You're a hard man to track down. Where the heck are you, you sound as if you're under the sea?' Max said.

'Ha, not just yet. I'm on hands-free in the car and we're on our way to Ebbsfleet, about to pick up the Eurostar.'

'Why?'

'Last minute booking for Disneyland Paris for the girls.'

'Nice. I wasn't expecting that,' Max said.

'Yep, the girls have been on about it since a school friend told them about the Swiss Family Robinson treehouse. You know how obsessed they are with treehouses! Celine's been a bit upset by Tricia's sudden departure, and I think we're all ready for a break before term resumes.'

'Good for Celine,' Max commented. 'I can't remember when she last had a holiday.' Max wondered if Oliver would react to the not-very-subtle dig.

'Thanks, Max, I am here, so watch what you say,' Celine called out in the background.

'Hi, Celine,' Max replied. 'I'm amazed you got a booking at short notice, Oliver.'

'I'm paying over the odds, I can tell you,' he said. 'Half-term and only the most expensive accommodation left, but it'll be worth it. Sorry I haven't replied to all your messages. It's been hectic around here.'

'I know the feeling,' Max replied.

He could hear the girls in the background, chattering with excitement.

'Did you phone for anything in particular?' Oliver asked.

'No, it'll wait. Have a great time and take care. We'll catch up when you get back, cheerio.'

'Shout goodbye to Uncle Max, girls.'

There was a chorus of 'Bye-bye, love you, don't miss us too much!' before connection was lost.

'Won't Issy and Willow just love it at Disneyland? I can't wait to take Jacob when he's old enough,' Jenny said.

'It's about time we took him for his first holiday, not Disneyland just yet, but how about the seaside?' Max suggested.

'Yes, he's too young to remember we went to Aldeburgh as a baby, but we've not had much opportunity since, what with one thing and another.'

'I know, surely we're due for a quieter spell. Let's squeeze in a seaside holiday before his speech therapy appointments get going,' Max said. 'We should do a real bucket-and-spade job with sandcastles and donkey rides.'

'People don't do holidays like that these days, darling. We could take him to my grandparents in Majorca. Mum and Dad could come too,' Jenny said. She hadn't really experienced the joys of a UK summer holiday, exploring the coastline in the wind and the rain like Max and his family had. Jenny Best and family had always taken their holidays in the sun, and usually in Spain.

'I'm not sure about taking him anywhere too hot, yet, so maybe Majorca next year. How about Blakeney this year, to see the seals?' Max said.

'Or Brighton?' Jenny offered. 'I went to Brighton on a hen weekend once and I loved it.'

'I don't remember that,' Max said.

'You weren't there.'

'Well, I'm not sure you can remember much about it, either. You can't have seen the beach! It's mostly pebbles on Brighton beach, not sand.'

'I've heard they've imported some sand recently, and made nice play areas along the front. Then there's the pier and the Sea Life Centre,' Jenny told him.

'I see you've been doing some research,' Max said.

'I have indeed.'

'Okay, get your diary out. What's it to be, Norfolk or Sussex?' Max said.

'We could toss a coin, or we could just do both. I'll make enquiries about Brighton and you look up places to stay near Blakeney.'

'Sounds like a plan,' Max said, trying not to think about the expense.

Before they arranged their own holiday, they called in to see the twins, to hear about their trip.

'Oh, the train was lovely, you'd love it. We had breakfast on the train and it went chug-chug, toot-toot,' said Willow, tickling Jacob in time with the sounds.

Jacob chuckled and said, 'Choo-choo' back.

'It went really fast and we were under the sea.' Willow produced a picture of a green train under a wavy blue sea.

'I met Mickey Mouse and Minnie and we stayed in a

hotel like a castle with pink curtains dripping all over it, just like Mrs Hall's strawberry icing. And I met Sleeping Beauty and Goofy,' Issy said.

'And we stayed up late every night and ate lots of chips,' Willow said.

'That sounds my kind of place,' Max said. He could almost taste the thrill of salt and vinegar in his mouth as he thought about eating fish and chips with Jenny in Blakeney – it would be a rare treat, conscious as they now were of healthy eating.

'Did you do lots of rides?' Jenny asked.

'Did they!' Celine groaned. 'They were unstoppable. Oliver and I had to take turns to go with them. We got so dizzy on the spinning cups that Willow got addicted to.'

Willow broke into song, '*It's a small world, after all. It's a small world, after all,*' and Jacob hummed along with her.

'Very good, Jacob, but can you give it a rest now, Willow,' Oliver said kindly. 'We've just about had enough of that particular tune. You've been singing it all week.'

'Tell us about the treehouse. Was it big enough for you?' Max asked.

'Huge,' Willow said.

'Massive,' said Issy. 'We climbed up ladders and walked on wobbly paths so we could look down on everyone in the park, just like spies. We like spying, don't we, Willow?'

'Yes, Celine says we don't miss a trick.' Willow brought out another drawing showing an enormous treehouse. 'This is the add-on we want Uncle Gus to build for us.'

'Extension,' Issy said, pulling a face at her sister.

Oliver interrupted the chatter. 'Didn't you want to speak to me about something, Max? Why don't you and I have a quiet word in my study?'

Max was relieved to escape from the Disneyland promotion being provided by the girls and suspected Oliver had probably had enough too. As he slipped out he heard

Jenny ask Issy which ride was her favourite, if Willow's was the spinning teacups. Pirates of the Caribbean or Phantom Manor? He didn't hear the answer.

Oliver sat behind his desk in the study and Max settled himself opposite. Old Mr Arthur as usual glared at Max from the portrait hung behind Oliver on the back wall. Max declined the offer of a small whisky, and then Oliver off-loaded first before he could get started on his concerns about Gus.

'Oh, Max, I must tell you about Disneyland,' he said. The tone of his voice made Max realise this wasn't going to be just another advertisement.

Oliver explained that the four of them went on the ride called Phantom Manor. The girls stood with straight backs and were only just tall enough to get in. The attendant, a student of English, warned it could be scary, with spooks and ghosts and things that made you jump. Issy and Willow insisted they'd be fine, and Issy added that they were the bravest girls in England and people had told them that ever since their mummy had died. The student looked horrified and pushed them to the front of the queue. They only had a short wait in a dimly lit entrance hall and Oliver saw Willow take Celine's hand and whisper, 'Oh, it's not at all like our manor.'

'I didn't know whether to laugh or cry,' he said. 'I just hoped Willow wouldn't be too much of a scaredy-cat. We all got into little carts. Issy sat with me and Willow was with Celine, still gripping her hand. We were ferried through shady corridors scattered with skulls and laced with cobwebs. Skeletons popped out of cupboards and made both girls squeal, while ghosts flapped overhead and brushed across our hair like puffs of wind. That even made me jump.'

'Sounds a bit much for a pair of five-year-olds,' Max said.

'Just you wait,' Oliver said. 'I could hear Willow squeaking, but it seemed to be with delight, and her howls of horror sounded put-on. We were laughing, and I guess I started to relax. In the dark, Issy clung on to my arm and I thought she was just joining in. Then halfway round an enormous rubber spider dropped from above and I had to push it away to let us pass. Issy screamed a most awful scream. She completely freaked out. It was awful. And she started crying and I had to undo her safety belt to pull her onto my lap. Well, that caused the security guard to stop the ride, which only made things worse, until he could get Issy and me taken off the ride. It took me ages to calm her down.'

'What a nightmare,' Max said, with only gentle concern. It was a nasty experience, but why was Oliver was making such a big deal about it? The child had survived and presumably no one was injured. 'What happened to Willow and Celine?'

'Oh, they stayed on until the end and emerged to find Issy licking a consoling ice cream.'

'All's well that ends well, then?' Max suggested.

'Not really,' Oliver said. 'She wouldn't go on any other ride after that. Poor Celine had to endure more spinning teacups while I took Issy back to the hotel. When she started crying again I asked her why the rubber spider that had upset her so much, and do you know what she said?'

'Tell me ...' Max was beginning to see where this might be heading.

'She said she hated spiders so much it hurt. That's a weird statement for a child to make, isn't it?'

Thinking it a rhetorical question, Max simply grunted. He wondered briefly whether to say he'd heard Issy liked spiders.

'I think it's something to do with Tricia,' Oliver went on. 'Tricia had found a spider when she moved into the blue bedroom and she kept it there as a little pet. Tricia never ever killed a spider, or tipped one out of the window like most people do.'

Max smiled. If Jenny found one in the bath, he had to trap it in a cup and do just that.

'Issy became obsessed with Tricia, who, in turn, lapped

up the attention of an adoring child. Tricia encouraged Issy's natural mischief and they made quite a team.'

Max was surprised at the emotion he heard in Oliver's statement. He felt the significance of it all the more, knowing what he now knew about Tricia's behaviour. He let Oliver continue, not wanting to interrupt his flow.

'It was then she told me the truth, Max, and ... I'm so sorry. She told me on the day they baked the banana bread, she'd seen a giant spider in the back kitchen, near the bunch of bananas. It was a very unusual spider and she thought Tricia would like to see it, maybe keep it as a pet. Tricia was meant to be reading, while Jacob had his nap, so Issy scooped the hairy beast up with a cup and covered the top with her hand.'

'Jesus!' said Max. 'She wasn't scared that day, was she? She's lucky she wasn't bitten.'

'I know. Anyway, she made an excuse to go upstairs and went to Tricia's door. It opened a bit when she leaned against it and she peeped through the crack. She saw Tricia lying on her blue bed cover next to her Uncle Gus. They were kissing and playing tickling games, she said, and they made funny noises that scared her, so she ran away.' Oliver let out a long gasp, as if he'd been holding his breath for a week.

'Oh my god, that all happened months ago, and she's only just told you. Poor little girl,' Max said.

'It gets worse. She ran into Jacob's room to show Jacob the spider. He was gurgling so she knew he was awake in his cot. As she leaned over the side to show him, the spider slipped out of the cup onto Jacob's blanket. She said she tried really hard to catch it, but it scurried down the side of the mattress and disappeared.'

'Why didn't she tell anyone at the time, or soon after?' Max asked.

'That's what I asked her, but she got upset again and begged me not to be cross with her. Eventually she told me she thought Tricia would find the spider as a nice surprise when she went to get Jacob up. I think she took a fright and went back downstairs.' Oliver looked uncomfortable and embarrassed.

'Why take fright?' Max said. 'She didn't seem frightened by the spider.'

'She didn't understand what was happening in Tricia's room, but I think she sensed it wasn't right.' Oliver looked at Max, as if willing him not to judge.

Max cleared his throat. It was plausible that Issy had acted in innocence, but then Issy wasn't stupid and could just as easily have made half of it up to get attention. 'Have you seen Willow's pictures?' he asked quietly.

'Celine only just mentioned them, in Paris, but I haven't seen them myself,' Oliver admitted. 'Celine thought they were the result of Willow's imagination, drawing her own story around what she'd heard about the spider's bite. They both must have got the gist, even though we tried not to go into too much detail in front of them. Perhaps I should have talked to them more at the time. I think I've messed up, Max.' Suddenly his hangdog expression changed to one of startled realisation. 'Why, have you seen them?'

'Willow showed me a while ago. She wanted me to show them to Jenny next, hence the delay. That's why I've been phoning. I wanted to talk to you about the pictures. They seem to support what Issy told you.'

'What did Jenny say?' he asked, as if he trusted Jenny's opinion over his.

'Like the rest of us, she thought it was Willow's imagination, but now everything's changed. The pictures are in my car. I'll run and get them.'

When Max returned Oliver was gazing out of the study window, surveying his land and twiddling his wedding ring. He turned and snatched the sketchbook from Max's grip, almost tearing the pages in the process.

'I think Willow must have followed Issy upstairs,' he said.

'So, they've both been worrying about this for ages. God, I'm an awful parent,' he said.

'I wanted to tell you that day I phoned and you were on the way to Eurostar. But really, none of this is your fault, Oliver,' Max said.

'Shut up, let me process this. I just thought Issy was being naughty in those weeks after Jacob got ill, attention-seeking, as is her wont. And I thought Willow was just being uncommunicative, like a moody artist with her head in a drawing book all day,' Oliver said.

'Celine can't have been too worried about them or she'd have said something,' Max suggested.

'Celine isn't their parent, I am. They must have felt so confused. What the hell do I do now?'

'I guess you talk to them.'

'Yes, I can't leave everything to Celine, I have already decided that, and together we had a good talk with the girls about the spider after Issy's confession. I must say I glossed over the issue of Tricia and Gus, though, that's how much of a coward I am.'

'I think it's time to stop beating yourself up, Oliver. Celine must feel awful, too, but neither of you can change what happened, you just have to move forward. Jenny and I are learning that.'

'Here am I bleating on about my girls and it was your child who was injured. I don't know how you can still be my friend. Alexis was your real friend, and you only got me by default.'

'Jenny and I promised you we'd stay friends when Alexis died. At the girls' christening we both agreed to care for them, too, and don't forget, so did Gus.'

Oliver groaned, as if he couldn't quite cope with thinking about Gus, and thankfully Jenny tapped on the door and popped her head round.

'Jacob's getting fidgety. I think we need to go home.'

'Okay, love. I'll be with you in a tick,' Max said. He'd had enough for now, but there was still so much more to say.

'Sorry, I've kept you too long,' Oliver said.

'No, it's alright, really it is,' Max said stretching his legs and turning to the door. 'Hey, how about I come back later and meet you at the pub? We can continue where we left off. Gus might be able to join us. He has a few things to get off his chest too.'

Oliver pulled a face. 'I suppose we'd better hear him out, but the pub's too public. Are you okay to come here? We'd be better off being somewhere private if we're going to clear the air.'

'Fine, I'll be driving, so won't be drinking anyway. Shall I leave you to call Gus and I'll see you about eight?'

In the car on the way home Jenny seemed subdued, and Max thought she looked pale. 'Everything all right?' he asked once Jacob was safely strapped in.

'I'm shattered,' she said. 'I had a fairly intense time with Celine while you and Oliver were chatting.'

Max didn't let on that his chat had not exactly been warm and cosy, either, and he was pretty knackered too. He concentrated on driving and let her continue.

'The girls put jumpers on and went out to the swing, and Jacob was playing happily on the rug with his bricks, mostly using his left hand,' she said, pointedly, and Max felt sorry that Jenny still had to say things like that. He knew Jacob's right hand was sluggish, so why did she have to keep going on about it? It was going to be all right.

'Anyway, Jacob was quite content, so Celine and I had time to talk properly. We had a chat about Tricia and then she told me some worrying things about the holiday. God, you should have heard what happened with Issy. Poor little thing. It's no wonder she's been such a troublemaker when you hear what's been going on.'

Max and Jenny were almost relieved the stories told by Celine and Oliver matched, however awful that sounded, because at least there were no more curveballs to distract them. The worst thing was that at the end of it all, Celine told Jenny she was handing in her notice. She believed she'd let the girls down.

'I tried to tell her she wasn't the one at fault,' Jenny said, 'but she thought she'd been so keen to reunite her own family, she'd put another family at risk. I think she feels really hurt that Tricia abused her trust, and she was so cross about her targeting Gus.'

'Not surprised,' Max said. 'I'd feel bad if it was my sister.'

'Half-sister,' Jenny said. 'I think Celine feels she dropped her high standards and, if not for her poor judgement, Jacob's accident wouldn't have happened. Then she went on about how much she was going to miss the girls. It was awful.'

'Did she cry?' Max asked. Jenny shook her head. 'Presumably you told her the girls needed her and she doesn't have to go? She didn't know her sister was deranged.'

'Not sure that's a good word, Max,' Jenny said.

'I can tell you Oliver is feeling responsible too. They're a right pair. There was still so much for me and Oliver to talk about, and I've agreed to go back after we've had something to eat and got Jacob down. We're going to fathom it out once and for all – the tree, the grave, Mr Hall's role if any, and of course, Gus's position. Gus is joining us too.'

'Poor you, it'll be a late night, and you've got to work in London tomorrow.'

'I know, but the time is right. It'll be a grand inquisition, and all the jigsaw pieces will be put in place.'

'You are good, Max, helping Oliver like this. Let's hope that's how it works out. It'll suit me to have an early night. I'm going to meet the team at the physio practice tomorrow and I want to look chirpy.'

When Max was ready to return to Lawn House, he kissed

Jacob, who was snoring quietly in his cot, and then hugged Jenny, who was already settled on the sofa under a throw. Max would have loved to snuggle there with her, watching TV. He could not have regretted his decision to return to Lawn House more.

24

THE AGENDA

The car almost knew its own way back to Lawn House so Max could give most of his concentration to the evening ahead. He found himself feeling strangely nervous, until he spotted Gus who must have been feeling even worse as he trudged up the lane towards the wrought iron gates. He parked and waited for him. With his broad shoulders slouching down, Gus had lost the bold stance he'd demonstrated when the men last met in Oak Lodge. His face looked drawn, and there were grey bags beneath his eyes. His checked shirt was crumpled and Max thought he'd lost weight. Life without Sandra was obviously taking its toll and, by the looks of it, the threat of a prosecution for rape had been disturbing his sleep and his appetite. Max smiled at him weakly and banged the brass knocker.

Oliver was in formal mode when he greeted them and he led them straight up to his study, where they were met by the welcoming smell of strong coffee and biscuits fresh from Mrs Hall's oven – the smell estate agents recommend when you are selling a house.

'I thought we might need something to keep us going, unless you want anything stronger?' he said.

'Coffee's fine for me, thanks, and I can never resist a

biscuit,' Max said. He knew the caffeine might disturb his sleep later, but for now he felt in need of the energy. The warm cookie crumbled in his hand and a shower of sugar dropped onto his jeans. Max brushed them off discreetly and licked his sticky fingers. Delicious.

'Same for me, thanks,' Gus said. He leaned over and took two of his mother's cookies. He'd obviously done it before and deftly caught his crumbs with his other hand.

'Good,' said Oliver. 'Thanks for coming. There are a few things going on that concern us all. I haven't exactly compiled an agenda, but here is my list for starters. Add anything you want.'

Oliver pushed a piece of paper across the desk and Max heard Gus sigh. He felt sorry for the man who was about to be interrogated by his childhood friend. The list just about matched the one Max had thought up in the car:

Tricia and Celine
Mr Hall
Alexis's tree
Dad's grave
The children – Issy, Willow and Jacob
The house/buildings etc

'How's that for starters?' Oliver asked.

Gus grunted.

'Fine,' Max said, 'but I'm conscious some of these things don't really affect me. Kick me out if you have private stuff to discuss.'

'You're here as our friend, Max, almost a family member, besides which I think the presence of a third party might help keep things calm. You okay with that, Gus?'

'Sure,' he replied.

God Almighty, Max thought. This was sounding more like an official tribunal than the friendly chat amongst friends he'd hoped for. He began to realise why he felt nervous, and looking at Arthur's portrait behind the desk wasn't helping ... he wondered if the painting might have open ears as well as piercing eyes.

'Let's start with Tricia, then, and that'll probably lead us on to everything else,' Oliver announced.

Gus grunted again.

'I have to admit she was very pleasant to have around at first and, of course, I allowed her to stay in the house for Celine's benefit. The girls seemed to like her company, especially Issy. But once Tricia settled in, I found her somewhat ... how shall I put it – intrusive?'

'You never told me that,' Max said.

'Well, you know what I'm like with women, have a tendency to hold back. But she was really quite pushy, kept asking me personal questions. And she was always hanging around, popping up when I least expected her.'

'You know she made a move on Ed? Happily, he declined her offer of some "special attention". Did she actually try to seduce you, Oliver?' Max asked.

He heard Gus groan.

'No, nothing like that. She just followed me about and made me feel ... uncomfortable,' Oliver said. 'I thought she was after money, to be honest. I didn't realise until much later what a liability she was, or how she'd been trying it on with every man on the estate.'

Listening to him speak, Max thought how old and staid Oliver sounded, like a man twenty years his senior, rather than just nine or ten. (Oliver and Gus must have been about the same age, but Gus seemed much younger.)

Looking embarrassed, Gus confessed he'd been one of the men taken in by her charms, made susceptible on the night of the party by an excess of beer and whisky. One stupid mistake and Tricia had got him where she wanted him Max realised.

'She started to blackmail me, saying she'd tell Sandra we were having an affair, and Oliver would be told that Dad had vandalised the tree and the grave. It was just after I tried to end it with her she told Max I'd ... I'd ... raped her.' Gus looked as if he might collapse with the effort of even saying the word.

'For God's sake, no one's mentioned rape before?' Oliver leapt to his feet and turned to the window. It was dark outside and his anguished face could be seen reflected in the glass. He turned back after a long pause. 'Why, Gus, why?'

'I didn't rape her, you must believe me. I knew nothing about the stupid allegation until she told Max and Jenny the day she left. I just hoped once she'd gone the accusation would go away too,' Gus said.

'You bloody idiot. Things like that don't just go away,' Oliver said with a raised voice. 'And you knew about this, Max?'

'Hey, I only heard just before you went to Disneyland,' Max responded. 'You know I tried to get hold of you to talk, and it wasn't just about Willow's pictures. But you can now see how it's all interlinked.'

'I did not rape her,' Gus said firmly. 'I admit I was wrong to have sex with her, but it was entirely consensual, and my god do I regret it. The consequences have been dreadful for Sandra and me, and poor little Jacob ... to think I contributed to his troubles just destroys me.'

Max saw Gus shake trying to hold back tears. Seeing this big man on the brink of tears stirred up his own emotions about Jacob and brought a sharp pain to Max's throat. He felt strangled, hardly able to swallow his own saliva.

'I believe you, Gus,' Oliver said, his tone softening. 'I've known you since we were kids and you are no rapist. The trouble is, it'll be your word against hers. Has she reported it?'

'She told us she wouldn't,' Max said.

'Well, that's weird for a start,' Oliver said. 'Why hasn't she told the police if it's true?'

'Her word against Gus's,' Max pointed out. 'But she can't

be trusted not to change her mind.'

Gus pulled himself together. 'I've spoken to some of the other lads about her – not mentioning the supposed ... rape, of course – and they were all very outspoken about her behaviour. The consensus is that she's a predatory slag. I think if ever I got taken to court I'd have plenty of character witnesses on my side.' He was obviously trying to make light of the prospect.

'For goodness sake, Gus, let's hope it doesn't come to that; but she might carry on with a bit of blackmail, even if she daren't risk your word against hers in court,' Max said.

'I haven't got much money, so she'll not get much out of me,' he said. 'I like to think she's used up her blackmailing options, anyway.'

'So, how did she arrange what she did? You'd better tell us all about it,' Oliver said.

Gus then unloaded the baggage he'd been carrying on his shoulders for a long time. He admitted he'd lost his keys to the gate of the arboretum, but swore he was always fastidious about keeping them safe. He kept them on a separate key ring, away from his other keys, he said, and only Sandra knew where he put them when they weren't in his pocket. The sad thing was that Tricia got access to his pockets.

'I think she damaged the tree, partly to get back at you, Oliver, after you gave her the cold shoulder, and partly to keep me in my place,' Gus said. 'She framed my dad and knew I'd do anything to protect him.'

'Odd reasoning, but the woman is a bit crazy,' Max commented. 'There could be another explanation, though. She could have taken the keys and given them to your dad. He might have actually been involved.'

'She did know his memory was going and that I was worried about him. She could have persuaded him to hang some of the rubbish he liked collecting in the tree. The devil in her would have got pleasure from simply organising it. Sticking Issy's doll there confirmed it as an in-house job, as no outsider would be blamed, and the finger would be pointed firmly at Dad or me.'

'I wondered if she was that clever at first, but the more I hear, the more I think Gus might be right,' Max said.

'I don't remember Lulu being there when I took the rubbish down,' Gus said. 'I bagged it up and left it by the bins for Dad to clear when he did his tidying and recycling. Now he says he can't even remember what he had in his shed before I got it all down from the tree. We don't know why he started scavenging in the first place. Mum and I used to tease him about it ... so maybe Tricia did put the idea into his head.'

'Or maybe seeing his collection put the idea into her head,' Max said.

'Poor Dad thought he must have got into one of his muddles. He's beginning not to trust himself as it is. The last thing he needs is someone messing with his head ... Oh God!' Gus suddenly gasped.

'What?' Oliver said.

'I remember before I took the stuff down, Dad said the tree looked very pretty with its decorations. What an awful thought he might have actually done it!'

'He couldn't have done it on his own. I reckon it took two of them, as they'd have needed ladders. I reckon Tricia planned it and roped Reg in,' Max said.

'She must have been disappointed not to get more of a reaction from her little escapade,' Oliver said.

'Mainly thanks to the walking group, I suspect,' Max commented, and the three of them briefly shared smiles of wry amusement at the thought of her plan being thwarted by a group of walkers.

'I think that's why she moved on to her next attack. She must have made Dad paint Mr Arthur's grave,' Gus said. 'I'd told her we had to stop what we were doing in bed, and her response was to get Dad to trash the gravestone. That day he told me the paint pot was in his shed and he didn't know why, I really believed him. I told him to quickly chuck it away and not to tell anyone. I just wanted to keep him out of the frame and I'd figure out how to tackle Tricia later.'

'How did you propose to do that?' Oliver asked.

'By looking round her room for evidence, for anything to get me out of this mess, and that's when she caught me. She saw me picking up a shoe that had a smear of red paint on the sole. She said that was from the clear-up operation, then went ballistic and screamed she'd done nothing and I should look closer to home.'

'Oh dear, this is worse than I thought,' Oliver said.

'But listen, there's more – she tried to hit me. Why do that if she was innocent? God knows I was tempted to thump her back, but I kept my cool and put her into an armlock. I told her all this had to stop and she should pack up and leave; leave us alone or else I'd tell everyone what she'd been up to. Needless to say, she still swore she'd done nothing wrong.'

'That was risky, Gus, and you didn't mention the armlock before. She could have got you for assault even if you didn't rape her,' Max said.

'Not helpful, Max,' Oliver chipped in.

'I didn't bloody rape her,' Gus declared. 'And I didn't have much choice but to restrain her! I had to stop her in her tracks, but I wasn't vicious. I held her 'til she calmed down then told her to make an excuse to Celine, and get out of here.'

Max saw Oliver try to delve into Gus's mind with a penetrating glare. He opened and closed his mouth without saying a word, and shook his head. Gus paled visibly and Max imagined some sort of silent communication passing between the two of them. Gus and Oliver then exchanged another look, more a minor curl of the lips than an actual smile. That's when Max realised that the closeness these two had shared since they were kids was deeply entrenched. He was very much the new boy in town, and the only one who felt awkward in the silence.

After a while Max spoke. 'Does anyone know what she told Celine?'

Oliver shrugged his shoulders. 'Just some sort of guff about not having found what she was looking for; that it was a mistake to come here and try and make a relationship with her sister who was more devoted to her employer's family than her own. Said she was bored and we were all a bunch of country yokels; that there were no decent men around and she missed the bright lights and buzz of the city. She thought she might go to London for a while before she returned to Manchester and would be in touch. That was it,' he said.

'No decent men – bloody cheek,' Gus said.

'Steady, Gus! I wonder if that's the last of her?' Max said.

'Perhaps that's hoping too much,' Gus said seriously.

'Now, before we relax, can I assume you've talked properly with your dad about the tree and the paint. Are you absolutely convinced he is innocent? It's by no means cut and dried who the vandal is yet, is it?' Oliver asked.

'To be fair, I didn't get much sense out of him. I was all too happy to think he was innocent, but looking back he did keep changing his story,' Gus said.

'What about his mental state?' Max asked. 'Is it so bad that he could be made to do things he didn't understand?'

'Probably. He did start saying Tricia was a nasty woman and he didn't like her after the tree thing. I thought it was because he thought she'd done it, but it could have been more than that, couldn't it?'

'It makes little difference now. Even if Reg did the dirty work, Tricia was probably prodding him from behind. It's hard to blame a man in his condition,' Oliver said sadly. 'What does your mum say, she usually has an opinion on things?'

'I've spoken to her, but I didn't say too much about Tricia, just said we had a minor flirtation and that's why Sandra was upset. Mum's not impressed.'

'I can well imagine,' Oliver said.

'She's much more worried about Dad than she is about me, though. We've booked a GP appointment for next week to get Dad checked. Mum'll take him, and she doesn't want me to go with them.'

'She'll be alright on her own with him, won't she?' Max said.

'She'll be fine,' Oliver said. 'She's always been pretty grounded and sensible – often against the odds, I might add. She had to be capable, dealing with my parents like she did. If Reg did these awful things, there's not much we can do about it now, other than look after him better.'

It was only much later that Max learned the significance of this statement about Della Hall. For now, he was pleased to see Gus nodding in agreement that his mum was a good, capable woman.

'Let's move on,' Oliver said.

'I guess next on the list we have the children,' Max said. 'Do you want Celine to stay on as the twins' nanny?'

'Course I do, and so will the girls,' Oliver replied. 'She's been the most constant figure in their first five years, and I can't imagine replacing her with anyone else. She seemed happy with us before Tricia came and upset things. If I can convince her to stay I'm sure she can be happy again.'

'Maybe even happier, if you look at her work-life balance. That's what Jenny thinks, anyway,' Max said. 'She thinks Celine needs more free time and opportunities for some friends of her own. She needs a life outside work.'

'Jenny usually knows the score?' Oliver said, throwing him a knowing look.

'You've spotted that have you? Celine needs to join in a bit more with the real world. She needs to have holidays. I bet she doesn't even have a proper contract with terms and conditions of employment,' Max said.

'Afraid not,' Oliver said sheepishly. 'We did draw up a basic list of responsibilities in the early days, but we never got around to updating it. The job seemed to grow organically as the children grew. I'm afraid the pay rises have been a bit random too.'

'Why don't you get Celine to write her own job description? That would be a good place to start, and might come in very useful if ever she does leave and you have to replace her,' Max said.

'Good plan. I'm sure I could get her to stay if I make it right. And I can throw in a long-overdue bonus now the accounts are looking healthier.' Oliver smiled properly for the first time that evening, and Max thought maybe the fog was clearing. 'As for Issy and Willow, I've already decided to spend more time with them and not leave it all to Celine. I need to listen to them more and share things. I especially need to talk to them about their mum, so they feel they know her. I feel so bad we've not had family holidays until now. I've been pretty selfish, so busy thinking about my own survival and busy running this place that I forgot my own children's needs.'

'Don't be too hard on yourself. It's been a tough few years,' Max said. He looked at Gus and wondered how he was coping with all this honesty.

To his surprise Gus, joined in the support. 'Yes, you lost Alexis and then both your parents – that's grief in triplicate.'

'The three losses each had a different impact,' Oliver said, 'but you're right, of course. I just thought keeping this house going and putting food on the table was enough. I forgot about being a real dad. Look at you Max.' He nodded in Max's direction now. 'You're a real dad. When I think of what you and Jenny have had to deal with, I could just give up. I'll always feel guilty about Jacob ... I think others will too.'

Gus grunted in agreement.

'Look, what happened to Jacob was crap, but he's doing all right now, and I sense things are looking up for all of us. All three of our families share a close connection with Lawn House. Perhaps it took a challenge from the likes of Tricia to show us what's important.' Max knew he hadn't worded his thoughts well, but it was getting late and he was tired. Surely they'd nearly finished Oliver's list? He was ready to creep away and let them discuss the house without him.

'You say things are looking up ... maybe for you two, but I'm not there yet.' Gus sounded as if he'd suddenly woken up. 'I've been a fool and I'm left with worries about Dad, terrified Tricia will return to catch me out, and holding the biggest share of guilt. All I have is my work. I loved it here with Sandra beside me, but now it's sheer torture, seeing her about the place and not being together.'

'Would you like me to speak to her?' Oliver offered.

'I doubt it would make any difference but you can try.' Hopelessness dampened his voice like a heavy sponge.

'Have you considered relationship counselling?' Max suggested.

'Not really my thing, all that talking and baring of souls,' Gus said, the sponge still clinging to his vocal cords.

'I don't know, you've done quite well this evening. I'm presuming you want to save the relationship, but does Sandra?' Max asked.

'That's the trouble, I don't know,' Gus said.

'So, you've got to try everything,' Max said.

'Could Jenny talk to Sandra? We need to make Sandra feel wanted and make sure she stays. I'd hate to lose her too,' Oliver said. 'You know, now Tricia isn't around to help in the café, Celine might like to do a bit, when the girls are at school. That would keep Celine in touch with the outside world and she'd meet people. I only mean the odd morning. She and Sandra get on quite well, don't they?'

Max coughed indiscreetly.

'What's your problem, Max?' Oliver asked.

'Erm, Jenny thinks Celine might fancy Sandra and says Sandra can sense it and feels a bit uncomfortable.'

Gus and Oliver both spluttered at the same time.

'What?' Gus said. 'As in *fancy?*'

'You are kidding?' Oliver added. 'Are you saying she's gay? Never!'

'That's what Jenny says. She thought I was stupid not realising. I'm glad you two didn't know either – makes me feel much better.' Max suppressed an embarrassed laugh, while the other two let the idea sink in.

'I thought she was nothing. That sounds bad. What I mean is celibate. You know, just a nanny-type person with no sexuality. How thick am I? I just didn't think, I suppose,' Oliver groaned.

'That won't have gone down too well with Tricia, then,' Gus said. 'I heard her make some really homophobic comments about a couple of the guys at the studio.'

'Heavens, a psychologist would have a field day with that woman. If she tries to take you to court, Gus, you'll have to ask for a full psychological report.'

'Shut up, Max,' Oliver said. 'She won't take him to court. Too much other stuff would come out. It makes you wonder why she really left her last job, though.'

Max tried to recall the references he'd seen on Tricia's job application but couldn't remember anything weird. They were rather bland, as if written to a formula, but lots of references are these days. He really was ready for home now, but Oliver had started to talk about the house, in what was beginning to sound like a presidential address. He read from notes on his desk, and Max's mind started wandering between Oliver's words and phrases. 'Long evening ... house my concern ... value your hard work Gus ... business interest Max ... Ed's investment ... accountant ... Inland Revenue.' He poured a glass of water from the bottle on the desk and tried one last attempt at concentration.

'I'm even managing to plough some of the profits back into the business and planning more improvements,' Oliver went on. 'The fabric of the house needs upgrading and much of the routine maintenance work is long overdue. The gardens could be made even more spectacular. I'll need a landscape gardener to look at the grounds, but first my idea is to bring in a contractor to sort out the utilities and infrastructure of the house, once and for all. That power failure did rather pre-empt things and, now it's been made safe, we need to future-proof. The electricians messed up the décor so that needs some attention now too.'

This must have been all news to Gus, who was listening with a frown.

'The power failure was a blow. I didn't know the electricity was so fragile. You know Tricia was helping the caterers set up? You don't think she could have overloaded the system on purpose, do you?'

'Let's not even go there, Gus. If she did, she might have even done us a favour, making us get on with the rewire.'

So much for Ed's theories about Gus, thought Max

'I was hoping to make you the estate manager, Gus, with a salary increase. You never know, but that might help you win Sandra back, too, when she knows I still value you.' Oliver grinned.

'I can't believe it. Even after my recent stupid behaviour, you still believe in me?'

'I do. You're a good worker and you've never let me down before. I'll have to regard your dalliance with Tricia as an aberration. I was going to tell you sooner, but had to hold fast until things settled a bit.'

'I don't know what to say,' Gus said, his voice suddenly sounding clear.

'Just one thing – you alone will be in charge of the arboretum. Agreed?'

'Agreed,' said Gus and the two of them shook hands. Max thought he was witnessing congratulations on a winning result at an election.

'It might mean some changes on the residential side of

things. I'll be asking the lodgers to leave when the building work starts. In the redesigned house we might create some bespoke apartments at the top that I can rent out to people who can actually pay their own way, with proper tenancy agreements. Things have got to change around here.'

'Will Chestnut Cottage and Oak Lodge still be safe?' Gus asked.

'Yes, of course,' Oliver replied.

It was almost as if Oliver had experienced a visitation, or a premonition, giving him a clear view of the future. Max couldn't hold back from adding a note of reality, however. 'Sounds great, but these changes sound mighty expensive, especially if you have to install a lift to the top floor.'

'It's all about security and sustainability, Max. You know, putting those paintings into storage while the rewiring was done made me realise I didn't need half the stuff I have hanging around. I'm getting some up-to-date valuations from an old university friend. We'll see what we might get at auction.'

'I'd forgotten your degree was in Art History. You can't sell the family portraits, though, they're part of the girls' heritage,' Max said, with a keen desire to protect his god-daughters. 'Perhaps you could just put your dad somewhere less prominent, though, I always feel he's looking down on me.'

'He is,' Gus said with a smirk.

'We'll keep the portraits, but there are a couple of old Cornish landscapes that won't be missed and a small Munnings' horse I could live without, lovely though it is. I haven't much idea what some of the older pictures are worth, but my friend is coming up to view them soon and give me some advice.'

'And what about the recording studios?' Gus asked.

'We'll keep them as they are, unless Ed wants a change. We might just try to make them more self-contained.'

'When did you plan all this?' Max asked.

'The power cut gave me a kick-start – as I said, it did me a favour. Since then, the thoughts have trickled through on a drip feed. I know it's a challenge but I feel ready for it.' Oliver stood up, yawned and stretched. 'Time you two went off home. I need my bed. We'll keep in touch. Oh, and Gus, all the best with your dad's doctor's appointment. Hope your mum can get some help for him.'

25

Della's diary, Saturday 26th September 1964

Arthur has got the photographs back from last weekend. Here I am wearing the white shift dress Reg's mum made for me, with her pale blue shawl round my shoulders. The pink roses, picked from the garden by Reg, made a nice bouquet that hid my bump perfectly. Mum, we look quite a good couple, me and Reg on the veranda at the back of the big house. No one will know how sick I was feeling. There's another one of us with Old Mrs Hall, holding my hand, and looking with a smile at the gold band on my fourth finger. I'm looking at my wedding ring now, as I write, and can't quite believe I went through with it.

It was ironic to be 'given away' by Arthur at the registry office. Reg's mum made a cake and Arthur took photos at the little party we had afterwards, for which he provided champagne. I allowed myself one little sip. Diana looked bored and drank lots. No sign of a baby for her yet. Shame I had no family here. Dad's somewhere in the Pacific and cousin Rosie's got glandular fever.

No honeymoon for us. We just stayed on our own in Chestnut Cottage for a few days while Old Mrs Hall had some time away. She said she needed a rest after all the excitement. She's gone back to the coast for a few days with Reg's older sister, Maureen, who was my matron of honour – weird as I'd never met her before!

So, I'm now 'Young Mrs Hall' and I live in Chestnut Cottage and I'm not as unhappy as I thought I would be. I've accepted the situation and I plan to make the best of it. I won't let Arthur think he holds all the cards, so don't be too disappointed in me, Mum.

Saturday 17th October 1964

I still feel sick. Old Mrs H is back and says I need to try to eat more but I just can't. My back aches, too, so I'm on light duties at work. At least Arthur is still paying my wages. Mrs H thinks I'm due about Easter-time next year, but I know it'll come before that. At least eating so little means I'm not getting too big and I can fudge the dates.

I've secretly been to see a midwife at a clinic in Ipswich, rather than a local one, so Arthur won't know. I lied about dates, said I was uncertain, but she thinks I'm about 22 weeks and the baby will come in February. She's booking a scan, but I won't keep the appointment. I've told her I'm moving out of the area and I'll make my own arrangements with a new doctor. I'm pleased she said I'd always be welcome at Ipswich Hospital. At least I know I can go there if I need to. Arthur's keen on a home birth and, when necessary, he'll get me a private midwife. I suppose that's okay. I'll think about it after Christmas.

Thursday 29nd October 1964

Mrs H is tired by the time she gets back to our cottage after working at the big house all day. She does some knitting then goes to bed early. I wonder if it's to give us some privacy. She had a fall today and was quite wobbly after. I do all I can, but wish I could help out more. I've noticed her hands are shaky when she knits. Reg wants her to go to the doctor but she's too stubborn to go.

Arthur keeps asking me how I am. I'm fine and the baby's kicking well. I wish he'd just let me get on with it. He still lends me books from the library, but I don't have much time to read now I'm married.

Diana seems to hardly acknowledge that I am pregnant. I wash her smalls and help her pack her weekend case and that's about the extent of our relationship. She seems less and less part of this household, just as I am feeling more a part of it.

Friday 13th November 1964

Mrs H has got Parkinson's disease and the doctor's given her tablets. He's advised her to retire. Poor thing suddenly looks old. She told Arthur and Diana her diagnosis and Diana was more concerned about finding a new cook in time for Christmas than anything else. Mrs H says she'll try to battle on until the New Year and give them time to find a replacement. I always thought I might have that job when the time came, but it's not to be. I feel sad for us all at Chestnut Cottage this evening.

26

UNSETTLED TIMES

October 2014

Jenny was asleep when Max got home from the meeting but in the morning, she needed information so was up early. The offer of scrambled eggs for Max's breakfast made the later train suddenly seem possible, and they talked while she scrambled.

'Extraordinary, three men talking constructively with emotional intelligence! You should write it up in an academic paper – a social breakthrough, no less,' she said when Max finished giving his report. 'Mind you, I need to know more about this uni friend of Oliver's. Male or female?'

'Female, I think.'

'And?'

'What?' Max said. 'Let me eat my eggs.'

'Did you get any details?'

'No, why should I?'

'You are hopeless. It's the first time we've ever heard of Oliver having a close personal friend and you didn't ask any questions!'

The teasing that followed while Max cleared his plate suggested that Jenny had enjoyed an excellent night of restorative sleep. Jacob presumably had, too, and was sitting in his high chair guzzling milk from a feeder cup. Max wished he'd slept well and felt as refreshed as they did. He wasn't particularly interested in Oliver's friend at this stage. He really needed to get the next train, where he was hoping he might get his head together, ready for his first meeting. His sleep had been disturbed by the evening's discussions and the coffee he'd drunk. He needed to get up to use the bathroom and then couldn't get back to sleep, thinking, worrying about Jacob and how his little boy's life would pan out if he still had a weak right arm and mild learning difficulties once he started school. Jenny hoped that with the right support he'd achieve his full potential, and Max had to admit she was usually right about such things, but it didn't stop him beginning to accept that Jacob could have longer term problems.

Jacob started bashing at a small piece of toast with a red plastic spoon held in his left hand. Looking at the handsome little chap in his high chair that morning, Max thought a stranger would never know what had gone on. The scar at the top of Jacob's right arm was covered by a Mickey Mouse print pyjama top from Disneyland, and when Jenny put a matching red plastic fork in his right hand he hardly needed any help in stabbing at some slices of banana. Yes, bananas were allowed in the house again, but Max secretly checked every bunch if he unpacked the shopping, and he suspected Jenny did the same, just as they both checked down the sides of Jacob's cot mattress each time they tucked him in. Max even turned his shoes over and tapped them before he put them on in the mornings.

Jacob smiled sweetly when Max got up to go. He nearly got a poke in the eye when he leaned to give him a goodbye kiss.

'See, he's moving his right arm better,' Jenny said. 'We'll do some drum practice before I call in to see my new physio friends. They said Jacob could come too. Say goodbye to Daddy.' She helped him wave with his right arm.

When Max returned from his day at the London office and the joys of public transport he felt tired and grubby. He went into the downstairs cloakroom and scrubbed his hands before greeting the family. Jacob was bathed and ready for a bedtime story from Max while Jenny cooked supper, and once he was settled they flopped in front of the TV for the evening. It was only on the way upstairs for an early night that Max spotted an official-looking brown envelope on the console table in the hall.

'What's this?' Max said.

'Sorry, I forgot to give it to you. It'll only be a bill, it'll wait until the morning,' Jenny said, stifling a yawn.

'I'd better open it now. You go up and I'll join you in a tick.'

Half an hour later Jenny trudged back down, wearing her white towelling robe and silver slippers. Her hair was brushed out ready for bed and her face free from make-up. Max thought she looked like an angel.

'Aren't you coming? Don't fall asleep on the settee, you'll only regret it,' she said, then a look of doubt spread across her face. 'Are you all right, you don't look well? What is it?' She sat by him and felt his brow.

'I'd better show you this,' Max said.

'What is it now? Has something happened?' She took the letter Max held out to her.

'It's nothing serious, just a bit of a nuisance,' he said.

Max still hadn't told Jenny about the little accident with Dr Grey and his glasses. It was not exactly his finest hour, and because she had been recovering from the accident he didn't want to worry her. He had to tell her now, though, as she was holding a letter from Dr Grey's solicitor with a look of amazement on her face.

'It says you assaulted a doctor, Max. For goodness sake,

why didn't you tell me?' she asked.

'Because I didn't assault anyone. There was a minor incident, an accident, and the daft man had a nosebleed and broke his glasses. I was more worried about Jacob and you, than the stupid doctor, you were both so poorly,' Max tried to explain, but can't have sounded very convincing.

'Why, then, does he need compensation? You'd better tell me the whole story,' she said, as if talking to a child.

At the end of it, Max finally persuaded Jenny he wasn't a thug. He reassured her that the whole episode had been witnessed, by a nurse, who confirmed his innocence. The hospital had investigated, completed an accident report, and concluded there was no case to answer.

'Then what's with the compensation claim? Why didn't you just say sorry and offer to pay for his wretched glasses?' Jenny was losing her patience and was starting to sound irritated.

'I did. I wrote him a note saying sorry that we'd had a clash and offered to pay for his specs. I just ... didn't get around to writing the cheque.'

'Oh, Max, for goodness sake. You never paid, and now he wants to sue you in the private courts for the effects of post-traumatic stress disorder, as well as a pair of designer specs. Great, as if we have money to give away!'

'He's trying it on, Jenny, don't worry about it. PTSD is a hard diagnosis to prove, anyway,' Max said.

'Even harder to disprove! It's the fact you didn't tell me that's most upsetting. We've talked about sharing things before and said we wouldn't keep secrets, not even to protect each other. Looks like you've done it again.'

'It was a very stressful time, Jenny, give me a bit of understanding,' Max said.

'Oh, if what you say is true, it'll never get to court. He must have inveigled a tame solicitor who's after some easy fees,' she said.

'They didn't look like designer glasses, Jenny, honestly,

they looked like those NHS ones little kids used to have.'

'Whatever,' Jenny said. 'Just write a cheque now and we'll deliver it first thing. We'd better speak to a solicitor ourselves in the morning too. There's not much we can do about it tonight. Let's try and get some sleep.'

'Some hope,' Max said as he followed Jenny up the stairs.

At first, they took it in turns to go to Jacob in the night and deal with his intermittent grizzling. He had a mild fever and red cheeks could be seen by the glow of his nightlight.

'Teething,' said Jenny eventually. 'Those big teeth at the back.'

She gave him paracetamol and decided to sleep on the single bed in the nursery. Max knew it was so she could watch over him, for fear of a fit, but part of him thought she didn't want to sleep with a man who kept secrets from her. Of course Jacob's needs came first, but as he struggled to get back to sleep, alone in their double bed, Max felt a little sorry for himself.

<hr />

In the morning Jacob was as fine as a sunny day. Jenny's not-quite-so angelic face was shadowed by a light peppering of cloud, whereas Max felt he was in the midst of a low-pressure zone of depression. There were no eggs for breakfast, just porridge, and they both focussed on Jacob's spoon skills.

'I'll be working in Colchester today, then Ipswich,' Max said. 'I'll ask if anyone knows a good local solicitor and arrange an appointment.'

'Okay, good luck with that,' Jenny said.

Her goodbye kiss was a staccato peck rather than the warm hug of reassurance Max would have liked. Bloody Dr Grey. Max was sorry he'd broken his specs, albeit accidentally, but he just couldn't see that getting a bit of compensation would benefit the man much. This could be money they could use to help Jacob. He really had to stop himself thinking like this. It was an accident, he wouldn't be liable, he'd write a cheque for £480, and that should be the end of it. More importantly, he had to get back on side with Jenny. It would be much more positive to be planning a treat for her than to worry about Dr Grey. A holiday for them as a couple might be worth thinking about rather than a family holiday just at the moment.

He didn't get around to ringing for a solicitor's appointment until the end of the day, by which time he'd already got a nice weekend in Blakeney planned, and his depression began to lift. It was just what Jenny needed before her ankle op, and his parents were thrilled to be asked to look after Jacob for two nights. This was a win-win opportunity.

But when he told Jenny it was all organised she told him off for not running it by her.

'I wanted you to have a surprise,' Max said.

'You are a twit, Max. It'll be lovely.' She smiled and looked excited for a second, then added, 'But it'll be hard leaving Jacob behind.'

'That's why I thought I'd get the experts in. He'll be fine with two GPs looking after him.'

The solicitor had suggested he make an appointment, and the only one available was on Friday morning, the day of their departure. He'd considered postponing the weekend break – the one he'd only just managed to organise – but to cancel would have disappointed everyone. He'd done enough letting people down of late, so that morning Max made an excuse to slip away, while Jenny finished packing and running through Jacob's needs with her mother-in-law. Grandpa, however, was apparently too busy playing with Jacob to listen to any instructions or, for that matter, to notice Max had disappeared. Happily, he was back within the hour.

Saying goodbye to Jacob was tougher than they both thought. They were both thoughtful and unusually quiet for the first few miles of the journey to the east coast, giving Jenny in particular, time to compose herself.

'I know Jacob will be fine with your parents, and I'm getting over this ridiculous hospital nonsense already. I just hope that solicitor was sensible. What did he have to say?'

'Well, to start with he was a she – Frances Freeman, junior partner at Smith & Sons,' Max said.

'Ha, great name for a lawyer. I see, Frances with an "e".' Jenny laughed a nice normal laugh and already the front of low pressure again hovering over Max lifted by a few millibars.

'Yes, Frances with an e says she should be able to settle him with a firm but fair letter. She thinks he'd be a fool to pursue it in the civil courts with no evidence, and all I have to do is pay generously for the glasses.'

'What, so we can stop worrying and ignore the PTSD?'

'Yes, I suppose so. I did ask her how "generously" she meant, and did she actually mean an out-of-court settlement, because that sounds expensive. I mean, we'll have to pay her fees too,' Max said.

'Hey, stop, you are such a worry-guts. There's nothing to settle, so let it rest. Presumably you told her you'd done the cheque for four hundred and eighty quid?' she said.

'Yes.'

'Sure?'

'Yes!'

'In that case, let's forget about it and leave it with dear Frances.'

Max breathed out, letting go of some of his worries. He smiled, and then Jenny almost ruined it all by teasing, 'We'd better have one last weekend of luxury before we have to live on bread and jam. I'm starving. It's a good job I'll be bringing in some money soon, once I've recovered from the surgery.'

They arrived at their seaside inn in time for a late lunch and then a slow stroll. Max noticed Jenny was walking slowly, with a limp. He realised she could no longer pretend, and disguising her painful ankle was getting harder.

'We'll not overdo the walking,' Max said. 'Let's just potter about and enjoy the scenery.'

'Suits me. Sorry if I'm holding you back,' Jenny said. 'You can go off for a run or a power-walk if you need the exercise. I'll be happy just watching the world go by.'

'I don't think you'll ever hold me back, Jenny. You do know how much I love you?' Max kissed her and put his arm around her as they stood looking out to sea across the sand dunes. The squawking of seagulls over the rolling of the waves was like the score of a modern opera.

'Shall we book a boat trip tomorrow and go seal hunting?' Max asked.

'I hope you mean seal spotting? Yes, let's. When's dinner? Have we time for a phone call home, then a little rest?' Jenny said, and Max had a feeling everything was going to be all right.

They enjoyed two lazy mornings with breakfast delivered to their room – freshly squeezed orange juice, fluffy scrambled eggs on wholemeal toast, and a pot of Columbian coffee to get the day started. They marvelled at the light over wide Norfolk seas, breathed in the salty air and found a renewed inner calm. The East Anglian landscape refreshed their souls and balanced their worries. Max didn't need a run, and the damaged skin round Jenny's thumbnails healed and grew strong.

They walked a little and talked a lot. They meandered slowly round Blakeney Point, along the coastal marshes, then took the car to nearby lovely towns like Holt and Wells-next-the-Sea. Jenny found a homemade pottery studio and bought an azure-glazed bowl for Eleanor and Richard to say thank you for looking after Jacob, then persuaded Max to buy a pair of matching mugs for themselves, to remind them of their stay. They ate pub lunches and scoffed Cromer crabs and local cheeses with weird names. The fresh, wholesome food filled their stomachs, and for two nights they slept like sloths.

Seal spotting didn't happen, they simply ran out of time, but it didn't matter because they vowed they'd come back when Jacob was old enough to appreciate it with them. By Sunday they were missing him, and the longing to see him again, nudged them back to reality.

Carol was due to arrive the next week, in preparation for Jenny's surgery. She would be minus Mike again, so Max would have no buffer, and he had to keep reminding himself they were getting on better these days. She was to look after Jacob while Jenny got back on her feet, and so Max could still go to work. He had a follow-up meeting with Frances with an e planned for that week, and really didn't want to have to discuss the issue with his mother-in-law. Tension in the house built up as Jenny's admission date grew closer, and Jacob became clingy, which made Max irritable too.

'Stop fussing, Max, it's only routine. I'll be in for just one night after they've removed the pin and recovery will be quick,' Jenny said.

'I know, and you'll feel more comfortable immediately, according to the surgeon. I just want it over and done with for your sake.'

'Look, when I'm home and Mum's here, why don't you take the opportunity to see Ed one evening?' she suggested.

'I'd feel as if I were deserting you,' Max said. "And she'll only criticise me for leaving you.'

'No, she won't. It'll be fine. Sometimes it's easier to keep her happy when I'm on my own. She's great with Jacob, and I know how to just go along with her. I mean it.'

Once he knew the op had gone well and Jenny was home, Max arranged to meet Ed after a day at work in the London office, and he got Jenny's permission to stay overnight to avoid the drunks on the late-night train home. Ed met him in East London, and they went for a Vietnamese meal in a scruffy place that could just as easily have been in Hanoi as Hackney. They were the only Europeans in the place, and Max's taste buds started to dance with the smell of garlic, tamarind and lemongrass as they sat on the plastic chairs at a Formica-topped table. He gazed at the unintelligible menu, then looked to see if he could see the men's room, where he could wash his hands.

'Don't look so worried. This place is the best. They don't serve wine, will beer do you?' Ed said.

'Fine, thanks. I'm just off to the Gents, back soon,' Max said.

He made his way between crowded tables to the back of the restaurant and had a look at the open kitchen on his way. Chefs, red bandanas round their heads to keep the sweat off their faces, tossed stir-fry delights in clattering woks over fierce gas burners. Steam hissed into the air and the atmosphere was equal parts exciting and scary. Max was able to push the door to the Gents open with his foot. He tried not to analyse the grubby grouting around the urinal and the edges of the sinks as he did a three-minute hand-scrub. He dried his hands on two paper towels and used a third to grab the handle of the exit door.

'Better?' Ed said when he returned. He watched Max pull his chair out with his hand covered by the sleeve of his jumper. 'Having trouble, mate?'

'No, I'm okay. Minor relapse.' Max smiled and shrugged his shoulders. If anyone understood, it was Ed. 'I'll get it under control when my world settles down a bit.'

The waiter introduced himself to Max as Loc. He shook Ed's hand like an old friend. 'Are you ready to order?'

'Two beers please, Loc, and a selection of starters, two beef pho, then enough of the special for two hungry men please,' Ed ordered confidently.

'That was easier than I expected,' Max said. 'I was wondering what to have. How do you know this place? I must say it's not quite what I was expecting.'

'I found it by sheer luck, literally fell into it one day, years ago when more than a little drunk. They looked after me so well I've been back too many times to count. I try to place a large order and then tip generously to pay them back. They seem to think I'm part of the family now.'

The beers arrived with some small plates of spring rolls and prawn pancakes.

'I can't believe I've not brought you here before. Good, isn't it?' Ed said, but Max was too busy eating to reply.

When the pho arrived, Max started to sweat. 'Blimey, they've been a bit heavy with the chilli,' he said and mopped his brow with a paper napkin.

'I'll get another beer.' Ed's solution to the heat was perfect.

Dumplings arrived next, followed by sticky rice with a wonderful selection of pork and chicken and shrimp in unrecognisable sauces. The overall smell was strange and exotic, the flavours quite delicious. The two men attacked each dish with enthusiasm, only stopping when every bowl was empty and their stomachs full to bursting. They laughed and talked their way through the evening, just as they had when they were students, laying their troubles and their joys on the table. There'd been little time for such indulgences since adult life took over, so there was a lot to say and to share over more beer at the end of the meal.

Ed was still haunted by insecurity, and the worry that he wasn't good enough to sustain the career he'd made as a recording artist. He still hadn't had the courage to propose to Lucy, and still leaned on the excuse of his dysfunctional parents and their dodgy marriage. Max found it odd that he was the only person who knew how difficult Ed sometimes found life. The rest of the world only saw the laidback musician with the world at his feet.

Similarly, Ed knew Max better than almost anyone, apart from Jenny. He knew that even though Max looked controlled, organised and sensible on the outside, he often shook on the inside. He knew that Max was kind and thoughtful, but was sometimes a ditherer and that could make him seem reticent. He knew why Max was addicted to running, and how he reacted to stress – other people's as well as his own – with hand-washing and other classic OCD symptoms. And Ed knew how exhausting Max must find it to remain strong for Jenny in view of Jacob's difficulties.

When Max told Ed about the "Dr Grey Debacle", as it had become known, Ed simply laughed at him.

'You worry far too much,' he said. 'You can't be taken to court for accidentally knocking someone with a door.'

'He won't stop it. His solicitors want him to go through with a court case,' Max said. The joy of the evening suddenly disappeared.

'For God's sake, just leave it to the solicitors to sort out. It'll never get to court.'

'But if it does, we haven't got much spare cash these days. I've paid for the specs but I can't manage much more. Our weekend away won't have helped our finances either and we can only just pay the mortgage anyway some months,' Max said.

'You're talking rubbish. All you might need is a little bit to cover solicitor's fees, and I can help with that,' Ed said.

Max shook his head.

'Consider it a gift to my godson. I can afford it. If you want to think of it as an interest-free loan then that's okay, but I'll never call it in.' Ed held his hand out as if to seal the deal.

Max hesitated ... he had a feeling Jenny would agree to anything to help Jacob, but some sort of stupid pride was threatening to hold him back.

"I seriously don't know what to say,' he mumbled.

'A gentle thank you will do,' Ed said. 'I seem to remember

you helped me out when I got my girlfriend into trouble in California. I was skint and traumatised and you got me through it.'

'Yes, that was a bad time,' Max said.

'Bad! It was a bloody disaster: an unplanned pregnancy and a traumatic miscarriage. The poor girl didn't deserve that,' Ed said.

'At least she survived, and so did you, even though you split up,' Max said.

'Guess so. You and Jenny helped me out then and now I want to help you.'

'Fair enough. I'll just say thank you, then, and I'll find out what we owe the solicitor.'

Then they shook hands.

Back at Ed's apartment Lucy joined them for a nightcap.

'We need a brandy to help us digest that feast,' Ed said.

'And a bottle of antacid to take to bed,' Max added.

Sipping brandy, the conversation turned to Lawn House.

'How are those poor girls? Has all this rubbish with Tricia upset them?' Lucy asked. 'Hey, I must tell you I thought I saw her today.'

'No, surely not, you mean Tricia? Where?' Ed said in amazement.

Max nearly choked on his brandy.

'I was waiting for a taxi outside the office and a bus crept past, in the queuing traffic. This woman looked out of a side window straight into my eyes,' Lucy said. 'We had one of those do I or do I not recognise you moments. We didn't smile or acknowledge each other, she just stared, and the bus moved off. It was a bit disconcerting.'

'She did say she might go to London. Are you sure it was her? How did she look?' Max asked. He couldn't understand why he felt so unsettled at the thought of Tricia being so near. London was a huge city ... what were the chances of it actually being Tricia?

'Her hair was all over the place, and it was the big, messy red curls I first noticed,' Lucy said. 'She didn't look great, a bit spaced out. I watched to see if she got off at the next stop but she didn't.'

'Why has it rattled you so much? There's nothing for you to worry about,' Ed said.

'I don't really know. The thought of her trying to steal you from me perhaps,' Lucy said, with an unconvincing smile.

'Tricia has caused a lot of trouble, but Ed's right, Lucy, there's no reason to think we'll ever see her again,' Max said. 'It might not even have been her, just a woman on a bus who looked like her.' He did a good job reassuring Lucy, but didn't know if he believed his own words.

'Yes, it was probably just a double, they say we've all got one,' Ed said. 'I hear Oliver has persuaded Celine to stay on – that's good for the girls, isn't it?'

'Yes,' Max agreed, 'And Oliver's going to spend more time with them too. Mind you, he'll have his hands full with his big new plans for the house and gardens.'

'I'm coming up next week to see him. He wants to discuss some studio business with me,' Ed said.

'Surely not another Soft Sounds evening?' Max asked

'Not at Lawn House, thank you, not after that last attempt. At least not until the upgrade is completed.'

'It's going to take ages,' Max said. 'He's got to raise some money first. He's still going on about selling off more art.'

'That's just an excuse to meet that bird he knew at uni – Charlotte, the mystery blonde who works for an auction house. I thought I might buy something from her and start my art collection,' Ed said.

'How come you know more about Charlotte than I do?' Max said.

Ed just chuckled enigmatically.

'You know nothing about art,' Lucy said.

'I can learn,' Ed replied. 'Since you ask, Soft Sounds have asked me to do a couple of sessions elsewhere, haven't they, Lucy? Lucy is helping with the negotiations.' He gave her his most charming of smiles and slid up the leather sofa to hold her hand.

'He's doing a country pile in Derbyshire first, just before the next German tour,' she said.

'Then after that we've got one pencilled in for a castle in Scotland, the one where that film star got married last year, what's 'er name?'

'What's 'er name? Honestly, Ed, you are hopeless,' Lucy said, once again smiling.

'At least I knew Charlotte's name.' He smirked at Max. 'As long as the Scottish castle has electricity, and they'll pay me enough, I really don't need to know anything else. I trust this wonderful executive organiser sitting here next to me to make it all perfect. I can peruse the art on the castle walls and the money I make can kick-start my collection.'

27

NOVEMBER STORM

A pint of water before bed and an undisturbed night in Ed's spare room allowed Max to wake up feeling remarkably fresh. He rang Jenny to say he missed her and would be home by teatime, as he only had a few jobs to attend to at the office. On the train he debated whether or not to tell her about the possible sighting of Tricia. At the risk of unsettling her the answer, of course, was yes – he didn't dare be accused of keeping another secret.

When he walked into the cottage Jenny was up and about, her ankle already feeling less painful. Jacob greeted him with a toothy grin and a quick burst of 'Dada.'

'Look, Daddy, five teeth,' Jenny said proudly.

'All he's said for the last two days is Dada,' Carol growled from the kitchen. 'I've been trying to get him to say Granny and all I get is Grrrr.' Max smirked as she continued. 'I do hope his speech therapy makes a difference before too long. He really should have more words by now. Jenny could say at least a dozen by the time she was eighteen months and little sentences when she was two.'

'He's not eighteen months yet, Mum. Anyway, we've explained Jacob's development has been slightly interrupted. Give him time and we're sure he'll catch up,' Jenny said, looking to Max for encouragement.

'Look how scrumptious he is,' Max said, sweeping Jacob up into his arms for a giggly, tickly cuddle. Jacob did a major burp and everyone laughed, then the wind came out the other end and Jenny said enough was enough, it was time for some quiet before bathtime.

'Mum, would you like to read Jacob a story while Max and I go and run the bath? It'll be your last chance before you go home tomorrow.'

Max gave Jenny a hug at the top of the stairs. 'Has everything been all right? Has she driven you mad?'

'It's been fine, but I am ready for her to go. She doesn't mean to be so tactless but it is wearing. It'll be good to be just the three of us again. How was London?'

'Great, but I missed you both.'

Carol puffed her way up the stairs, carrying Jacob. 'You are getting a big, heavy chap, Jacob. You need to start climbing the stairs for your mummy or she'll be doing her back in next.'

Jenny scowled.

Max took Jacob and announced, 'Let bathtime begin! Drum roll, please.'

Jenny did a pretend drum roll on the bannister and, much to Max's relief, Carol went downstairs and poured herself a glass of wine. While Jacob was splashing and playing with his plastic boats, Max told Jenny about Ed and Lucy and gently slipped in Lucy's improbable sighting of Tricia.

'It can't have been her. Celine seems to think she's gone up to Manchester,' Jenny said, seeming surprisingly unperturbed.

Max saved the news about Ed's offer to until they were in bed.

'That's so kind of him; mind you, it won't even make a dent in his bank account. Surely solicitor's fees aren't so expensive, though, and we're not so tight for money, are we?' Jenny said.

'I was a bit worried we might have to pay Dr Grey some compensation. But Ed says I'm stupid to even think it. Trouble is, the nursery fees are adding up,' Max told her.

'Good job I'll be working again soon, then,' she said and fell asleep almost immediately.

———◆———

By the weekend Jenny was walking almost normally again, so on the Sunday a visit to Lawn House was called for. Issy and Willow were well wrapped up in winter coats, playing outside on the see-saw, and Issy's newly cut, short bobbed hair bounced as she shrieked on the up and grunted on the down. Celine had brushed out the plaits from Willow's hair and tied it into bunches, which whipped her face with every bump. Celine was acting as referee between the two ends.

'Hey, who are you? I don't recognise you,' Max said, pointing at Issy.

'You silly thing, it's me,' Issy said.

'I'm here, too, I'm Willow,' Willow added, and the three adults laughed.

'I love the makeovers,' Jenny said. 'I think I need one. What do you recommend?'

'I think you'd look nice with streaks like Sandra's,' Willow suggested. 'Shall we go and ask her?'

'Good idea. I expect she's at the garden centre. Who's coming with me to find her?'

The twins led Jenny to find Sandra, with Willow pushing Jacob's buggy. Max was left alone with Celine.

'I'm so glad you're staying,' he said as they walked to the house.

'I'll stay for now, but I can't say it'll be forever. Nothing stays the same, and the girls are already growing up. They're less dependent now they're at school.'

'They still need you,' Max said.

'I know, for now. Oliver has helped me write a new contract and he's going to let me rent a cottage on the estate. If I'm always in the house I feel I'm never off duty. I got a pay rise, too, so how can I refuse?'

Max knew it wasn't about the money, but smiled in agreement.

'All good, then,' he said. 'Do you mind me asking if you've heard from Tricia since she left? Is she in London?'

'Haven't heard a thing. I doubt she'd stay in London, she doesn't really know anyone there. No, she'll be back in Manchester, visiting her old haunts and trying to cadge off Mum while she lies low for a bit.'

'Let me know if you hear anything, would you?' Max said.

'Don't hold your breath.'

The girls came rushing back ahead of Jenny and Jacob. 'Jenny's coming back to have her hair done tomorrow!' yelled Issy at the top of her voice.

'With foxy highlights!' squeaked Willow.

'That's the colour ... blonde fox,' Issy explained.

'How very exciting, I can't wait,' Max said, and Jenny did a pretend punch to his arm. 'Ouch! The girls are in good form,' he added as they made for the kitchen.

'Shoes off,' ordered Celine.

Mrs Hall had heard the arrival. 'Kettle's on. Who wants cake?' she asked, getting up slowly and picking up pair of gold-rimmed glasses. Max had never seen her wear glasses before and thought she suddenly looked older.

'Yes, please, but we can't stay too long,' Jenny said.

'The old girl needed an outing and wanted to see the twins, but she needs to get off her feet again soon,' Max said.

'Less of the old girl, just wait until you see my highlights,' Jenny said. 'Actually, let's skip tea. We need to get home. Just look at those clouds.'

The sky in Max's rear view mirror was bathed in a strange light as they made their way down the long driveway. The silhouette of the house was like a gothic castle, wrapped in dark mauve clouds, which tried to chase the car once they were out on the road, and now a fine, grey mist covered the windscreen as well as the back window. Max switched on his wipers but the mist just kept coming back. A vague hint of the sun, which was sinking fast in the west, gave a menacing glow between more banks of cloud. The coal-smoke greyness deepened and, even though it was early, headlights were needed.

'This wasn't forecast to come until later,' Max said. 'Never mind, we'll soon be home.'

Heavy plops of rain hit the windscreen, and Jacob let out a blood-curdling cry from his car seat, as if he thought the world was coming to an end. Jenny patted and stroked him between the tight straps of his seat, trying to give comfort as Max drove. They arrived in their drive as a bolt of lightning flashed across the sky and Max counted ... and fifteen seconds later kettle drums of thunder boomed. The temperature had plummeted and they rushed inside to get warm. Jenny held Jacob to her chest and rocked him. Max took one last view of the sky before drawing the curtains, just as a sudden strobe of lightning shot across the front lawn. One, two, three, four, five ... crash! It was just a mile away. Electric energy shook the clouds as the storm came overhead, and there it stayed, banging and crashing, unlike any percussion band they'd ever heard. Jacob clung to Jenny and whimpered like a trapped animal. Max heard her hum a tune to try to calm him.

The wind roared around the outside of the house now, and forced itself through gaps under doors. It threw sheets of rain at the sash windows of the cottage, which rattled in furious objection. Even Jenny looked terrified as she cradled

Jacob, and when there were two more crashes outside, Max peeped between the curtains and saw a pair of roof tiles skid across the bonnet of his car, just missing the windscreen. The next interval between lightning and thunder was seven seconds, then eight.

The centre of the storm finally grumbled off into the distance, but the wind and rain would not give in. Whenever they thought it was stopping it would rise up again and batter the windows once more. The electric lights in the living room flickered and the cottage seemed to creak with the effort of staying upright, and Jacob's moans again turned to screams, despite all efforts to comfort him.

'God, I hope the electrics don't go off. Can you fetch a torch in case, and flick the kettle on, Max?' Jenny said.

'Have we got candles?'

'In the kitchen drawer next to the sink.'

Max looked out of the kitchen window onto the back garden and heard yet another crash, then another: the fence panels were coming down one by one, and the dustbin somersaulted across the patio. Next-door's trampoline then hurtled across the lawn like a creature from Star Wars. Only the garden shed stopped it, and Max almost expected an alien to emerge from the wrecked framework.

'Everything alright?' Jenny called.

'Can't find the matches.'

'Cupboard to the right of the oven.'

The kettle boiled and the lights blinked again.

'I think it's settling.' Max set a line of candles in a hotchpotch of candlesticks on the mantelpiece.

'It looks like an altar,' Jenny said.

'I hope you're not expecting me to pray,' Max replied. He flopped onto the sofa next to Jenny and Jacob, and they listened to the infant's grizzles, waiting in case the storm turned around and hit them again.

'He's bound to be terrified,' Jenny said quietly. 'I've never experienced anything quite like it before. I think it's moving on. We're safe now, little man,' Jenny comforted Jacob. 'I'll get him some milk.'

Jenny passed Jacob to Max, whereupon he buried his head in his father's armpit. Max felt the little body shake and wrapped his arms around the bundle he'd been given, holding him until Jenny returned.

'Wow, that was vicious. I'll go and check for damage in a minute. Are you alright here?' Handing Jacob back was like passing the parcel.

Max threw on his waterproof and nervously stepped outside, wondering what on earth he'd find. There was still a cold edge to the wind, which caught the door and slammed it shut. He went straight to check the car and saw that the fallen tiles had gouged tracks across the red bonnet, making deep scars, reminding him of the scar on Alexis's tree. The car would undoubtedly need surgery, or maybe even a bonnet transplant. He loved that old car – they'd bought it together before they were even married, and it had become part of the family. They'd never had enough ready cash to replace it, but never really wanted to. He hoped now the repairs wouldn't be too expensive or, even worse, be the end of her.

A potted bay tree lay on its side across the front path, wounded and spilling soil like a flow of blood towards a brown puddle on the drive. A large branch from the neighbour's oak tree lay like an amputated limb across the front garden, and brown leaves were scattered on the grass. Max lifted the bay tree back onto the porch and decided to leave the rest until morning.

He came in, rubbed his hands to warm them, and tried the television, hoping for the local news. It just buzzed and displayed a screen of white speckles.

'Aerial must be down,' Jenny said. 'And my phone's out of charge. How about the computer?'

It worked.

'Clever things these computers! They can keep going through anything!' But as Max spoke they lost all power, and were plunged into a half-hearted gloom, too dim to see, but too light to call dark.

Max found the torch and lit the candles and they set up camp ready for a disturbed evening in the living room.

'I'm ravenous,' Max said.

'Don't panic, I can make a sandwich by torchlight, and you can play "guess the filling",' Jenny said. 'It's mighty chilly. You light the gas fire and I'll fetch blankets.'

She fetched Jacob's pyjamas, extra jumpers as well as some blankets, and announced that bathtime was cancelled. They entertained Jacob by singing songs and making shadows in the candlelight until he drifted off to sleep on the sofa. When they went up to bed they carried him to his cot and rigged up a torch in the hallway outside his open door.

The torch had run out of juice by the time Jacob woke them up with a squawk in the morning light. The atmosphere was still strange, but the clouds had gone and a watery sun was pushing up into a pink and blue sky. Max tried the light switch in their bedroom and it worked. The television worked too. Further evidence that the electrical world had come back to life came from downstairs with the buzzing of the clock on the oven timer, which always made a nuisance of itself after a power cut. Jenny picked up the phone and heard a dialling tone.

'We're back in action, Jenny,' Max said. 'Cup of tea?'

'Yes, please. I'll bring Jacob into our bed. What a weird night! I'm amazed I managed to sleep.'

'It's a bit early, but I'll go and check the neighbours are okay when I'm dressed,' Max said. 'I think the garden might need some attention too.'

'Oh, you are a good chap, in fact a double good chap,' Jenny said when the morning tea arrived.

They watched BBC Breakfast in bed, waiting for it to

switch to the local news. Disruption on the roads in the south and east was reported, with fallen trees but no major casualties reported. The trains, of course, were severely affected by debris on the line and damaged overhead wires.

'What a surprise! I knew I wouldn't be getting into work today. I'll try and work from home,' Max said.

The weather lady was saying the storm had caught them unawares and showed a chart explaining why it hadn't been forecast.

'I'm glad someone can explain it, otherwise we'd be talking about angry gods,' Max said. Jenny suddenly grabbed his hand and he nearly spilt his tea.

'Sshh! Look. Oh my goodness!' She pointed to the television.

On the screen they saw a picture of Lawn House with a rolling headline: "Georgian Manor battered by freak storm".

Max gasped. Oliver's house looked like a warzone. One of the tall, brick chimneys was down, lying on the ground. Part of the tiled roof was hanging like a fringe, leaving rafters and purlins bare, and the woodwork within the belly of the house was exposed to the outside world like an anatomical dissection.

'Look at the trees,' Jenny said. 'Poor Oliver, what will he do?'

Twisted wisteria branches, as well as ivy and and other climbing shrubs, torn from the red bricks that supported them, now lay sprawled across the surrounding lawns. A second, lesser chimney hung precariously over the side of the roof, and a bent chestnut tree leaned against the kitchen extension as if kneeling in prayer, its bare branches poking through a broken window.

'There must be glass everywhere,' Max said. He dared not even think what had happened to the beautiful conservatory Oliver was so proud of. It was like a scene from a movie, not a live view of their friend's home.

The television reporter on site told of how an unprecedented tornado had torn the roof off the historic house, causing tens of thousands of pounds-worth of damage. A small fire, possibly caused by the use of candles when power was lost, had also contributed to the chaos.

'Jesus, we used candles,' Jenny said.

'Sshh, he's telling us about the people,' Max said.

The reporter looked earnestly into the camera. 'The family members are safe, but two people who had lodgings on the top floor are still unaccounted for. Engineers are on site trying to ensure structural safety and are assisting the fire service and police. Now over to the rest of our news ...'

'I can't believe this is happening. I wonder who's missing,' Jenny said, giving Jacob a hug. 'What about Oliver and the girls?'

'They said the family are safe.'

'Should we go over and try to help, or invite them to come here?' Jenny said.

'We haven't got much space.'

'We can't just sit and do nothing. We need to drive over and see if we can help.'

'We'll only get in the way. We won't be able to do much and, anyway, the roads aren't good after the storm. Let's see if we can speak to someone first,' Max suggested. He tried Oliver then Gus but got no answer. Eventually Jenny got through to Sandra. Max listened in as well as he could.

'Sandra, are you alright?'

He couldn't hear the answers, just Jenny's ongoing questions.

'And Oliver and the girls? ... Celine? ... You're with Gus's parents ... Where's Gus? ... Helping with the search, that's good.' Jenny then listened while Sandra told her the details, then asked more questions.

'Should we come? Is there anything we can do?' Max hissed in Jenny's ear.

Jenny shook her head at Max. 'No, I understand. Keep us informed. Let us know if we can help at all. Promise? ... Okay, speak later. Bye.'

She put the phone down and shrugged her shoulders.

'Not much we can do, then,' Max said and put his arm round Jenny.

'She says not. It makes you feel so helpless.'

Jacob banged his fist on Max's arm demanding breakfast.

'Let's go down. I'll switch the TV on downstairs.' Max thought about the clear-up task which lay ahead for Oliver and Gus. It made tidying his own little "estate" seem a minor problem.

'We still don't know if anyone's been injured,' Jenny said as they stared at the television screen. 'And we need to listen out for news on the missing people too.'

The coverage continued as various experts on historic houses and their architecture were wheeled in from universities and local history groups, and were commenting on the significance of the Lawn House and the tragedy of the damage. As Max suspected, the beautiful conservatory, which a reporter said had been added in the nineteenth century by ancestors of the current owner, had been badly damaged, and specialists in historic glass would need to come in to repair it. It was apparently one of the finest Victorian conservatories still in use.

'If only we'd known that we might have taken more notice of it,' Jenny said as she fed Jacob with banana and yoghurt. He held his own rusk and chewed on it between mouthfuls.

'I guess we always gave more attention to the people of the house than its history and structure,' Max said, pinching a corner of rusk and a piece of banana from Jacob's bowl.

'Hey, get your own,' Jenny said. 'Tell you what, it's a blessing so much of the artwork is still in storage after the rewire – the bits he hasn't already sold off, that is. I wonder how much is left?

28

STORM-CHASER

Max realised there was no way Jenny's hair appointment would happen, and the chances of him doing any office work from home were slim. He made the garden look a little better and checked on the neighbours as promised. He helped return the trampoline to next-door's children, and borrowed a saw to cut the fallen branches into more portable pieces. He was rather proud of the neat little stack of wood he built near to where the side fence should have been.

Inside, Jenny was writing a list: fence panels, bay plant pot, car bonnet repair, candles, matches, batteries, milk, bread. It probably made her feel she was doing something useful, but Max knew she still had Lawn House on her mind – they both did.

He interrupted her list-making. 'I'm going to go over and see it for myself.'

'We offered and they said no. Leave it, Max. I love it that you care, but don't go. You do realise you've become obsessed with the place, don't you?'

'You can talk! I won't stay long and I promise I won't get in the way.'

Driving was a precarious business. Max had to avoid fallen branches and steer his way through lanes made narrow by leaning hedgerows. Two police cars were parked at the front gate of Lawn House, and just inside he saw a white van blocking the drive. A female police officer was guarding the entrance, while a group of journalists milled about outside. Max drove on, beyond the scene, and parked a little way up the road. Walking back, he kicked twigs and leaves as he went, all the time peering over the perimeter wall at the injured house.

A photographer took his picture as he approached the gate. Max scowled at him and strode on. He explained to the WPC that he was a family friend, here to help. Jenny would either think it hilarious that her husband had been papped by the paparazzi, or furious at the intrusion of privacy. Max just felt irritated. The officer made a call on her mobile and he was allowed in. The gardeners had already cleared much of the drive, and stacks of sawn-up tree trunks and gnarly bits of wood lined the way to the front door. (Each pile dwarfed Max's little collection at home in Stowmarket.) He decided to turn right and aim for Oak Lodge rather than make a nuisance of himself in the big house. On the doorstep of the lodge, Sandra and Gus were standing awkwardly together, looking across the tattered lawn at what remained of the manor.

'Sandra's come down to check we're all right,' Gus explained.

'Hi! How are things in the village? Any news of the missing pair?' Max asked.

'No, they're still searching,' Gus said, and shrugged his shoulders.

Sandra looked exhausted as she leaned on Gus's side, and she accepted his arm being placed round her shoulder.

'It's mostly tree damage in the village,' she said.

'I'm afraid Lawn House received the worst of it,' Gus added.

'Yes,' agreed Sandra. 'Bob, from the pub, saw the storm arrive up the road. He said it was like a liquidiser chopping and stirring everything in its way, and apparently a funnel of cloud and water whipped along the lane, aiming straight for the main house. He followed it like a storm-chaser and watched the roof lift and then half of it literally flipped over.'

'He caught some of it on video, wants to put it on YouTube, but his wife won't let him,' Gus said. Sandra gently pushed his arm off her shoulder and straightened herself.

'Yes sounds like a tornado to me. We don't get many of them in East Anglia, do we? I expect the weather people will want to see the film and analyse it,' Max said.

'That might be more helpful than posting it on YouTube,' Sandra said with a slight sneer. 'We're just wondering what the police are up to. They're having a very long conversation with Oliver. How about tea?'

Sandra went into the kitchen as if it were her own. It was really, supposed Max.

'Things getting better with you two?' he asked Gus.

'A bit. Lulling me into a false sense of security probably, but at least we're talking. That's better than nothing.'

Max patted him on the back, knowing that in truth, Gus was still standing on fragile ground where Sandra was concerned.

'The girls haven't gone to school today, what with the disturbed night and the roads in such a mess. They're inside drawing pictures with Celine. Come in and join us until Oliver's free,' Gus said.

Issy and Willow still had their pyjamas on beneath grey tracksuits, Issy's edged in purple and Willow's edged in pink. They looked as if they hadn't had a wash or seen a hairbrush yet that morning. They were bouncing on their chairs, leaning over the dining table creating a muddled mess, with paper and crayons all over the place.

'Not much drawing going on,' Max said. The girls responded with squeals of 'Uncle Max! Uncle Max!'

'Caged animals,' Celine said. She looked more tired than Sandra. 'Just look at us. We could only grab the bare essentials before we were evacuated. Sandra's lent me these, she's ever so kind.' She stood up to show off a long, baggy sweatshirt worn over a pair of ill-fitting jeans, and Max realised how short she was compared with Sandra.

'There's something happening up at the house. Look!' Gus interrupted the fashion show.

Sandra, Gus and Max gently jostled for position at the front window of Oak Lodge, trying to get a good view of the big house. In a sudden burst of activity, officers dressed in white overalls were led from the front door, carrying two large white boxes and a small brown suitcase. A couple of colleagues in uniform were protecting them, scanning the surrounding area like the security men seen in American films. (The fact the house had been used on odd occasions as a film set did not make this scene appear any more normal to the onlookers, however.) They saw the overalled men being helped into the back of the white van, and saw it driven away, before spotting Oliver walking over to the garden centre.

'There's Oliver. Come on Max, we can catch him over there at the office. They don't want too many people in the house while they complete the search, and investigate. I heard someone say arson has to be excluded,' Gus said.

Oliver had bags under his eyes the size and colour of used tea-bags. Max considered this par for the course if your house has fallen apart and caught fire; in fact, having not checked a mirror yet that morning, he wondered if he looked much better himself.

'What were the police taking away?' Max asked.

'Some sort of evidence, and now they've sealed off the attic with blue and white tape. It's like a crime scene.' Oliver went to the filing cabinet in the corner, unlocked it with an unsteady hand and pulled out a large bottle of whisky. He held it up to Gus and Max, who both shook their heads. It was only eleven thirty in the morning, but Oliver poured himself a large one.

'How're you doing, Oliver, you look worse than you did first thing?' Gus said.

'Knackered. It's all a bit much.' There was an awkward silence before he continued. 'Something's not right. I don't know why they're talking about evidence and arson. It was certainly a bad storm, but there's something else going on and they won't say much. They seem to have found something.'

'Like what? The missing people?' Max said.

'No. There's no sign of them anywhere in the house.'

'What did they find then?' Max asked.

'Old boxes. The insurance assessors went into the loft with the structural engineers and they found them,' Oliver said.

'All attics have old boxes, what's the problem?' Max said.

'I don't really know. I don't store anything up there; the access is too difficult. I haven't even looked around it for years. I thought it was fairly empty, apart from a few bits of old rubbish belonging to Dad.'

'Must be something interesting for them to take it away,' Gus said.

'Apparently, they were tucked under the eaves and when they moved them to check the rafters, the fastenings came undone. They thought the embossed seals must have melted in the fire.'

'Don't tell me they were full of gold doubloons and your dad was a pirate in a former life?' Max said.

'This isn't Disneyland, Max. All they'd tell me was there were documents of interest, written on House of Commons stationary, dating back to the '60s and '70s and marked "Private". Heaven knows what that's all about and why such security was needed.'

'And the suitcase?'

'More of the same, I guess,' Oliver said.

'Was your dad a political man?' Max asked.

'Not really, that's what I can't understand. He tried to throw his weight around a bit on the parish council and in the local Conservative party, but was never involved at a government level. Anyway, the police want to look into it, but I still can't see what it has to do with the fire.'

Gus suddenly caught up with the conundrum. 'Unless the fire was started on purpose to get rid of them?' he said.

'That's a bit far-fetched, but maybe that's why arson crossed their minds,' Max said, suddenly sounding like an expert. He saw Oliver's face drop and realised he and Gus might be getting carried away with fanciful theories, while Oliver was being overwhelmed by the practicalities of the disaster.

Just then someone tapped on the door. The handle was stiff so Gus opened it, letting the fire officer in. He had an old rusty tin under his arm.

'I have news for you, Mr Trelawney. Our investigations have ruled out arson.' He stroked his moustache with a confident air.

'That was quick, how do you know?' Oliver asked.

'The missing persons turned up and gave us statements. They'd been having a "romantic session", shall we say, in what they called "The Blue Room". Thought it wasn't in use so chose it for a night of passion, playing lords and ladies, I imagine.' He gave a gruff laugh, but no one laughed with him. 'Yes, ahem,' the officer continued, 'anyway, they decked it out with candles and the like. A flame caught the curtain while they were at it.'

Gus groaned and turned away. Max felt the need to interject, 'So they weren't "missing" at all?'

'Yes, they were, but only briefly. They took fright and ran when they heard the crashing outside; thought they'd snuffed out the candle before they escaped, but it must have caught the curtain. Those heavy satin curtains can certainly smoulder. All it took was a broken window and a gust of wind to feed the fire again. It's lucky only one side of the house got caught. I expect the heavy rain helped.'

'For God's sake,' muttered Gus. 'I'll skin 'em alive. Who was it?'

'No need to trouble yourself, sir. We're dealing with them.'

The fireman turned back to Oliver and offered him the tin. 'This old tin was found below the floorboards in the blue bedroom, sir. Looks like personal stuff and not needed for our reports.'

Oliver prised open the stubborn lid, tearing a fingernail in the process. 'Shit,' he said and sucked his finger. 'Oh, just some cards and letters, and an old piece of cotton. I'll have a closer look later. Thanks.'

Della Hall appeared at the door as the fireman was leaving. She seemed to have visibly shrunk since Max had last seen her, and her eyes were puffy and red behind her gold-rimmed spectacles. She clutched a white handkerchief.

'I saw them bring you the tin ... and I recognised it. I heard you say cards and letters. They're mine you see, just personal stuff. I sometimes stayed in the blue room before I was married. I think I know about those boxes in the attic too.'

'Leave it to the police, Mum. Don't get involved,' Gus said.

'Gus, I want to explain. It's time to clear the air around here.'

'Sit down, Mrs Hall, would you like a medicinal tot?' – Mrs Hall shook her head – 'No? Well, tell us what you know,' Oliver said kindly. 'These boxes, do I need to be worried?'

'I don't think so, not now your parents are gone.'

Oliver sniffed. 'This doesn't sound good.'

Della straightened herself in the chair. 'Perhaps I will have a little tot.'

Oliver obliged and she took a sip before she began. 'You must remember I was a young girl when I started as a maid in the house and we're talking about the '60s. The Swinging Sixties had bypassed Trelawney Manor – that's what it was called then – and Mr Arthur had not long been married to your mother.' She turned to Max and added, 'Mr Arthur used to be Arthur Trelawney. You know he added the Smythe with a fancy hyphen to impress Miss Diana when they got engaged?'

'What, so he wasn't always Arthur Trelawney-Smythe?' Max said. 'How odd ...'

'Oh no, dear, Smythe was his mother's maiden name, and she died just before the engagement. He was unusually close to his mother,' she said. 'So he also did it as a mark of respect.'

'I regarded it as a mark of pomposity,' Oliver said with another sniff. 'Anyway, back to the point, Mrs Hall.'

'I'll just say the marriage seemed strained from the start. Mr Arthur liked to be at home in the country, and Diana preferred the city. She was always dashing off to London to see her society friends – of course, they kept an apartment in Kensington at the time.' She looked at Oliver for confirmation, and he nodded. 'You know your mother was much younger than Mr Arthur, and having been a catwalk model she had so many contacts there. You get your looks from her, Mr Oliver.'

'Thank you, but do carry on. I know very well what they were like and I have no illusions, so don't feel you have to hold back.'

Colour had come to Oliver's cheeks and he began to shuffle his feet. Max sensed how uncomfortable this was for the poor man, but he had to admit to being intrigued by the story.

'I think these days we'd call her a "trophy wife", if there is such a thing, and he was quite a catch with a double-barrelled name and a country estate. She liked his status and the impression of wealth, but he really didn't give her enough attention – and she liked to be the centre of attention so it was no surprise to me when the rumours started.'

'Do we need to go over all this, Mum? Is it relevant?' Gus asked.

He wasn't sure if Gus was bored, or as uncomfortable as Oliver about the story, but Max wanted to know how it ended. He never had liked unanswered questions or loose ends.

'Yes, shush, Gus, Mr Oliver wants to know about the boxes,' she told him.

'Go on then, what rumours?' Gus agreed grudgingly.

'It was said Diana struck up a friendship with a Westminster MP, a rich old Etonian called William Du Bois. Married with two children he was, too, and it went on for a while before Mrs Du Bois caught them in a compromising position and created merry hell.'

'How come I didn't know about that?' Oliver said.

'You weren't even born, dear.'

'Jesus, when exactly was this? I'm not that man's child, am I?' Oliver's face twitched horribly.

'Most certainly not, you are a Trelawney-Smythe through and through,' she said with a bizarre sense of pride.

'It's Trelawney now, Mrs Hall. You know I never liked the Trelawney-Smythe tag, and just at the moment, I'm not sure how pleased to be with your assertion,' Oliver said sharply.

Max realised long ago that Oliver and his father had a major clash of personalities, but was surprised at how vehement his views remained. He still couldn't let it go, even though the man had been dead for years. Whatever had harmed their relationship must have been pretty serious; psychological abuse or emotional neglect, who knew? He wondered if Mrs Hall did. She seemed to know most things around here.

'So how come you know all this, Mum?' Gus asked.

'It was all over the papers at the time, and Mr Arthur used to talk to me a lot when he was home alone. We became quite close back then,' she said, and Max noticed her take a deep breath before she continued. 'Anyway, the papers accused the MP of a conflict of interests and some sort of fraud – I believe they'd call it "insider trading" these days. He was forced to resign from the government and it ended his political career. Your mother came straight back home with a show of remorse and made peace with your father. I think they made some kind of deal.'

'Sounds true to form,' Oliver said.

'You see, Mr Arthur couldn't face the fuss of a divorce and he desperately wanted an heir. If she would promise to leave the MP and produce a child with Arthur, he would publicly stand by her and even help sort things out with the authorities and the press. Part of the deal involved him storing some of William Du Bois' documents, things he hadn't shown to the government at the time.'

'I think you mean hiding, then, not storing?' Gus said.

'Perhaps,' his mother replied, 'but I think Mr Arthur held those papers as an insurance. If William and Diana got back together, which they could have done because it was a real love affair, Arthur would go public with the documents and William would be prosecuted. Arthur held the trump card.'

'I wonder what happened to William?' Max said. He was surprised this scandal had faded away quite so easily; they wouldn't have got away with it these days, with social media chasing every misdemeanour. This was only just after the Profumo affair, and Max knew about that, but had heard nothing about the Du Bois affair. Arthur Trelawney-Smythe must have had more power than he'd realised. Max looked at Oliver with a new understanding.

'Du Bois had a heart attack a few years later,' Mrs Hall said. 'I remember Diana was grief-stricken when she heard, but she was pregnant with you at the time, Oliver, and I think after that the boxes in the attic were simply forgotten.'

'Well, that's a sorry tale,' Oliver said, rather stoically. 'I expect it'll crop up in the papers again now. Let's hope it's forgotten just as quickly. MPs having affairs and accusations of insider trading are more prevalent these days, or certainly more publicised. Surely no one will be interested in a historical scandal about some dead chap no one remembers.'

Max hoped Oliver wasn't being naïve. He actually seemed relieved the truth wasn't any worse. He picked up the metal tin and gave it to Mrs Hall, as if to show he'd heard enough. Max wondered if he was the only one thinking about the suitcase.

'I'm off to have lunch with my girls,' Oliver announced. 'You'll lock up the office for me, won't you, Gus?'

Mrs Hall looked unsettled. All this sharing of secrets had taken it out of her. Gus and Max offered to walk her back to Chestnut Cottage.

'I need to be getting Reg his lunch too,' she said.

'Is Dad okay?' Gus asked.

'A bit rattled by the damage to his precious gardens, but he'll settle down. Actually, Gus, I was going to ask if you'd keep an eye on him for a few days. I want to go and visit cousin Rosie. I haven't seen her for a while, and I could do with a break and a bit of a chat.'

'About Dad?'

'Amongst other things. Yes, now's a good time to go. There's not much I can get on with in the house at the moment, and Celine says she'll make sure everyone gets fed. She's a good one that one, not like her sister.'

'Okay, I'll move in with Dad. How long will you be away?'

29

THE SUITCASE

Mrs Hall stayed away for longer than expected. Max phoned Gus to see if the park was fit for him to resume his running there. Gus was still staying with his dad and Sandra had moved in to help him.

'You're back in favour, then?' Max said.

'Separate rooms,' Gus replied, 'but at least we're talking again, and she's great with Dad.'

'How's your mum?'

'We chat on the phone a couple of times a week. She says she's okay, but not ready to come back yet.'

'Fair enough. She has been looking tired lately, probably due a good rest. How's Oliver bearing up?'

'Hard to tell with him. It's all change around here: he's moved into Oak Lodge with Celine and the girls.'

'Separate rooms!' Max said.

'Ha-ha, very funny, but yes. The girls are back at school, and we're all carrying on with the big clear up, but you're welcome to come over for a run anytime.'

'Great, thanks, I'm getting out of condition,' Max said.

'It'll be a while before the general public are allowed back. All the trees in the park need safety checks and the fences and walls need mending before we open for business. Until then, we're just keeping the garden centre going, and guess what? Celine is helping Sandra out there and it's all going well. Your theory about them was rubbish, Max. Anyway, how are Jacob and Jenny?'

'Jacob's good and Jenny's starting two days a week at that physio practice in town soon, while he's at nursery. My office is hectic as usual and, of course, I could do with a pay rise,' he said jokingly.

A casual phone call was not the time to admit that money really was tight and he was looking forward to Jenny's contribution starting. The charity sector was naturally cautious with pay rises, so Max just pretended to Gus that all was well in his world, because his niggling worries were nothing compared with Oliver and Gus's.

'Has Oliver spoken to you at all this week?' Gus asked.

'No. I expect he's busy. Why do you ask?' Max said.

'It's just that he's been going to the police station almost every day since Mum went away and I can't get anything out of him. I've been asked to go to the station tomorrow, too, and so have the other gardeners. It must be bloody Tricia.'

'Surely they'd have told you if it was to do with her?'

'You would hope so, but perhaps they're trying to catch me out. I'm shitting myself, Max. When you come for your run, can you try to catch up with Oliver?'

'Sure,' Max said. 'Keep me informed, and all the best.'

As he hung up Max sensed more dramas were about to unfold. Whatever next? He hoped the police were still just talking to people about the damage to the house and those wretched white boxes.

Before Max made it over to Lawn House, however, Oliver invited himself to Stowmarket for supper. Max was relieved to have heard nothing more from Gus and decided Oliver must simply be missing Mrs Hall's cooking and probably just needed to get out of Oak Lodge for a while: he wasn't used to living in a normal-sized house. They got Jacob to bed early and Jenny had just prepared a chilli when Oliver turned up, and she left the pot to simmer gently on the hob. Oliver was carrying a holdall from which he produced a bunch of flowers, and a nice bottle of Shiraz.

Once the pleasantries were out of the way, the real purpose of his visit became clear.

'I want to tell you about the suitcase,' he said. 'I warn you, it's pretty bad. There's no nice way to say this.'

At last! Max thought the suitcase had been forgotten.

'What is it?' he said impatiently.

'Inside the suitcase the police found the mummified body of a baby,' Oliver announced.

'What?' exclaimed Jenny. 'How old?'

'Depends what you're asking? The baby was probably a newborn and might have been there about fifty years.'

'Jesus! Do you know where it came from? Whose is it?' Jenny had her hands on her chest, as if steadying her heart.

'They can't tell if it was a natural death or foul play at the moment. They've been doing carbon dating and forensic tests on the body. Now they've moved on to taking DNA samples from anyone whose family had close connections with the house in the '60s and '70s,' Oliver said.

'That includes Gus and you, then?' Max asked.

'Exactly. It must be something to do with my bloody father,' Oliver said.

'Or Diana and William De Bois?' Max suggested.

'How old are you, Oliver?' Jenny asked.

'Why?'

'Just thinking. And what year were your parents married?'

'1963 ... or 4, I think.'

'Hmm, I wonder,' Jenny said.

Suddenly the smoke alarm went off. Jenny leapt to her

feet and opened the kitchen door. The smell of burning chilli wafted in to the sitting room.

'Max, stop the alarm, quick, before Jacob wakes up,' Jenny called and then shut the kitchen door behind her. Max heard her open the back door to let the smoke out and the alarm stopped as quickly as it started. Max listened for Jacob at the bottom of the stairs but all was quiet.

'I'm so sorry, Oliver, I think it might just be cheese and salad for supper. I've got some nice bread and some pickles too,' Jenny said when she returned from the kitchen. 'Come and sit at the table and we can at least pick at what we've got.'

'I think we've all lost our appetites, darling,' Max said, and Oliver nodded.

They sat at the table. Oliver put some cheese on his plate but didn't touch it. He fiddled with his napkin and took a gulp of water.

'I wanted to let you know before it hit the local papers, maybe even the nationals. It won't be long before it leaks out, as now they're testing some of the villagers who worked for us.'

'Oh dear, how awful,' Jenny said. 'Will the DNA results take long?'

'I'm not sure, but the police now want Mrs Hall to come back from the coast. They've already questioned Reg. Gus went with him and said he was about as much use as a friendly scarecrow. I think they're sending a car for Mrs Hall in a day or two. They might have some DNA results back by then.'

30

Della's diary, Friday 25th December 1964

Happy Christmas! At least I got a card from Dad with a cheque in it to buy something for the baby. Cousin Rosie has sent a Mothercare voucher. Reg has bought me a woollen cardigan with a matching scarf – nice but not very romantic. Still, I only bought him a wallet. I'm only nineteen and I feel middle-aged.

The new cook has already started at the big house so Reg, his mum and I will have a small turkey at Chestnut Cottage. It's in the oven now and smells good. I was allowed to put the tree up and it feels quite homely. Old Mrs H is going to stay with her daughter Maureen for a while in the New Year. Reg says we can have a second honeymoon. He'll be lucky with this bulging great tummy and nagging backache.

There was a staff party last week when Arthur gave out our Christmas bonus envelopes and served sherry. (It was orange juice for me!) The extra cash will be useful for next year. Arthur is talking to me more warmly again. He's told Reg about getting us a private midwife when the time's right and Reg thinks he's being kind to us. I suppose he is.

Thursday 22nd January 1965

I felt sad waving Reg off in his green Hillman. I wish I'd gone now. I know I'm a dreadful wife but I just couldn't cope with a long drive to the coast just to see a dying woman. It would have brought it all back, Mum. Being with you those final days was the hardest thing. It's less than two years since you went and I can still hear the rasp of your final breath. When Maureen phoned to say their mum had pneumonia and might not make it, I packed his overnight bag and let him go to her. Now I feel guilty and alone. Told you I was a rotten wife.

The baby is kicking less now. Not so much room for it to move and it's leaning on something tender in my back so I just can't get comfortable. I wish you were here to rub my back, like I rubbed yours when the cancer got into your bones and you could no longer walk.

From my window I can see the glow of lights from Arthur's study in the big house across the lawn. There aren't many other lights on. I think Diana went to London for a Burns Night dinner this weekend. He's alone over there, and I'm alone here, but I know I mustn't think like that.

Reg phoned to say he's arrived safely but it's snowing like mad on the coast. His mum's really poorly. I've been reading the pregnancy book Arthur and Diana gave me for Christmas. I don't even know which way up this baby is. I'm scared and I'm cold. Hot water bottle and bed for me. Night-night.

Friday 23rd January 1965

Would you believe it, I'm writing this back in the blue bedroom, resting, propped up on top of 'our' bed? Arthur sent Bridget, the new young maid, across to fetch me this lunchtime. It snowed so heavily overnight he thought I shouldn't be home alone in my condition. The radio says there's more to come, so perhaps it's a good thing as I do feel safer now I'm here.

The path from the cottage to the house was really icy so Bridget had to carry my bag and hold my arm. She's only seventeen, not been here long, and just a bit younger than me when I started. She treats me as if I'm a woman twice her age. All the other staff were sent home while they could get through the snow so it's just me, Bridget and Arthur here. Bridget comes from Ireland so can't go home. Poor girl, I know how she feels.

I phoned Reg and he's completely snowed in at Maureen's and his mum is dying. Sounds bleak. He's just glad Arthur's looking after me. My back's paining me something shocking and I've got terrible wind. Indigestion, I expect – although I haven't eaten much today.

The snow's still falling and Bridget's brought me a heater and a sandwich. Oh God, I think I've just wet myself!

31

DELLA HALL'S RETURN

November 2014

Oliver phoned Max a few days after the night of the burnt chilli.

'Mrs Hall's back and I think we could do with a meeting, Max, with everyone present. Sandra's coming, too, so can you and Jenny make it on Friday afternoon?'

'We'll have to make some arrangements. Is it important?' Max asked.

'It is really,' Oliver replied.

Okay, leave it with me,' Max said. He could easily work from home on Friday morning, then get away after lunch. Jenny had nothing on the calendar and maybe Jacob could go to nursery.

Max knew Oliver liked the image of Lawn House functioning like a small community, with its own council of representatives. The council consisted of Oliver as chairperson, Gus and Sandra, Della and Reg Hall, and new co-opted members Max and Jenny. Oliver explained that the three families most affected by recent events at Lawn House were to be gathered together, round the long table in the breakfast room now that Mrs Hall had returned. *Clever*, thought Max, *more space and more formal than the study, and less formal than the main dining room.*

'How does she seem?' Max asked.

'Withdrawn but okay,' he replied.

'Does this mean the DNA results are back?' Max said.

'Well, yes, but they've not really helped. Mrs Hall's told me a few things, though, and she's given me her diary to read. She presented me with a large brown envelope as soon as she got back. She's written a diary ever since she came here, and I think she now wants to share some relevant bits with the rest of us. She'd like to tell her own story, however, so I won't say anything else for now.'

'We'll do our best to be there, then,' Max said.

'Hope to see you Friday, about 2 o'clock. I think Mrs Hall might let you and Jenny read her written account for yourselves after Gus has finished with it. It makes interesting reading, Max, be prepared ...'

32

Della's diary, Wednesday 12th November 2014

I'm sitting at a small writing desk, by a window, looking out at the sea. I'm trying to add to the diaries I wrote between 1964 and 1965 but I feel very out of practise. After the trauma of 1965, I know my entries became brief and I got lazy (or scared). Cousin Rosie has read those early pages and seems to think it'll help me to finish the story I started to tell you, Mother dear. (I now feel too old to call you Mum.) I've stayed here in her cottage on the coast for nearly two weeks now but my head is not much clearer. Maybe Rosie's right: if I make myself remember the things I've tried to forget, it will all fall into place. Here goes:

That night of 23rd January 1965 I went into labour in the blue bedroom at Trelawney Manor, or Lawn House as we call it now. Bridget asked Arthur to call for help and, at first, he wouldn't, as he said it was too soon. He insisted the baby wasn't due yet, but Bridget had grown up in a large, Irish farming family and had seen it all before. I remember crying out for Reg, and Arthur saying he couldn't get through to him on the phone – maybe the lines were down at Lowestoft where Maureen lived? He said later he'd tried the local doctor and the private midwife he had on standby, but both were snowed in, unable to get to us. Looking back, I wonder if he really did make those calls or how hard he had tried.

I remember a long night of pain and torture with blood and vomit all over the bed. I heard Bridget scream at Arthur to do something. I must have passed out, I've no idea how long for, but I came to with a new surge of agony, only to hear Bridget shouting at me to push. I don't know where I found the strength but I did what she asked. Ages later I felt the baby come out, followed by a warm flood of what must have been blood, or placenta, or probably both. I'm sure I heard Bridget say, 'It's a boy ... very small.' She told Arthur to cut the cord, rub the baby's chest until he cried, then wrap him up to keep him warm. I suppose that's what he did. He picked the baby up, anyway, and turned away as he wrapped him in a sheet. I believe I heard a little tiny baby sound, more of a whimper than a cry, then everything went muffled and the world went black.

The next thing I remember is waking up. It was the 25th January 1965, I think. I woke up with Reg snoring, slouched in an armchair by the side of my bed. The blue satin curtains were half drawn and the outside light seemed too bright. The room looked clean and tidy, as if nothing had happened, but the searing pain in my undercarriage said otherwise. I must have gasped as I briefly lifted my arm to attract Reg. His eyes were red when he opened them and I knew he'd been crying. 'He's gone, Dell,' he said. 'He's not here.'

I thought Bridget must have taken the baby to the nursery. My eyes were heavy and I drifted off again, holding Reg's hand. Looking back now I realise I didn't even ask about Reg's mother – what sort of wife was I? Reg told me later that I was in and out of consciousness and hallucinating for days. The snow had eased enough for him to travel home, but it then turned heavy once more, so the house was still quiet and they left me to rest.

Next time I woke there was a private nurse in the room. She said it was Wednesday 27th January and she was here to look after me. She was an older woman, of few words. She washed me, bathed me gently where I was torn, and put pads in my bra to catch the weeping milk. She tried to make me eat and drink. When I was awake enough I asked to see my baby. I can still recall the look of horror on her face. She rushed out saying she would find my husband. I wished I'd never woken up that day.

Reg told me the baby was stillborn – that's what Arthur had told him. I think I was almost too tired to weep. I asked to speak to Bridget and was told she'd gone back to Ireland. He passed me an envelope she'd left for me, and I tucked it under my pillow for later.

I asked Reg if he'd named the baby and he said no, he was waiting for me. (Fifty years later he still waits for me to make all the decisions. I might have realised it would always be this way). So, I called him John Jacob, after both our fathers, and said we must arrange a funeral. It was then I learned what the men had done.

In a break in the weather, with the snow beginning to melt, Arthur persuaded Reg, (and the obliging local undertaker) not to wait but to bury the baby in a little coffin in the corner of the cemetery. Beyond belief, this was like a second bereavement for me; a blow to my very soul. I gave my husband no understanding for the double loss he had also endured. I was incapable of expressing any sympathy for him, even though he'd buried his mother in the very same week as the child that could have been his. I simply sent Reg away, refused to speak to him or Arthur for days, and they left me alone with the close-mouthed nurse. She found Bridget's envelope when she changed my sheets. It had no address and was not dated.

"Dear Della,

I don't think I can speak to you before I have to leave. I hope you are all right. I am very sorry you lost your baby. I did all I could but he came too soon and was so small and poorly. I have to tell you he did taste life for a few precious minutes. Just as you fainted away, Sir took the little mite, wrapped him tight and took him away so you would not hear his feeble cry. He knows I wonder if he might have smothered him. He's given me money to go away, back to my family in Ireland, as soon as the snow allows. I wanted to stay and help you but I can't. I'm so sorry.

My thoughts will be with you. God bless you and your son.

From Bridget (the little maid who held your hand)."

Then I knew that my son had lived, but I couldn't believe Arthur would have smothered his own child. I had a lot of time to think and consider my position, and then another envelope containing a picture-postcard of *a lily was pushed under my door that evening and, in a way, that helped me decide.*

"My dear D,

You know how much I care for you, especially at this time of great loss. What passed between us must never be spoken of and nothing like this will ever happen again. Just know that I will always be there, watching you, looking after you.

ATS"

I had to believe John Jacob's death was inevitable and that he was too weak to survive. This was God's will and I had to accept my mistake and make the best of it. Arthur meant it and he would always look after me. In that time of grief and hormonal chaos I believed I loved Arthur like no other man.

I tucked the letter and the card, along with a tear-stained hanky and some personal bits and pieces, into the bottom of an empty biscuit tin Reg had left lying around – I think he must have lived on biscuits during my lost days. I seem to remember I covered the contents with a folded sheet of newspaper from the local rag which Reg had brought in, and closed the lid. I then locked it all away, deciding to leave everything in the blue room. Lifting a corner of carpet, I used the handle of my hairbrush to push the flat oblong tin to a secret place, under a floorboard I knew was loose.

Then I was ready to move back to Chestnut Cottage. Nurse was sent away and I allowed Reg to look after me at home. When I was fit he walked with me to the far corner of the village cemetery and we said a prayer for John Jacob. The snow had melted by then and the ground was flat and barely disturbed. I couldn't believe a little body was buried there. I let Reg hold my hand, and we stood for ages, and I was grateful for the quietness of the man. It was only on the walk back to our cottage that we spoke at length of his mother's death and at last I was able to briefly comfort him.

I stayed at home, making nourishing soups from the garden's winter vegetables. Reg helped me kneed homemade bread and gradually I got my strength back. Arthur did visit once. He gave me strange and shadowy looks. Whether they were sorrow or guilt or love or loss, who knows? When Reg slipped out Arthur repeated that he would always look after me, and Reg and I had jobs and a home for life. I sensed an unspoken message in his words and knew my half of the bargain was to keep quiet.

Later that year, when the cook left, I got the job I wanted. Running my own kitchen brought purpose back to my life. I became part of Arthur and, I suppose, Diana's world again. My spirit returned and life got more comfortable.

After nearly a year of grieving Reg asked if we might try for another baby, but it was still too soon. I remember saying, 'Give me time, maybe next year.' Next year became another year, and another year after that. And so it continued ...

Diana gave birth to Arthur's son, Oliver, in 1972 and Gus was born in the same hospital by Caesarean section, shortly after.

Rosie is calling me for supper, Mother dear. I'll pause for now, but I'm not finished yet. There's still another piece of history to be told.

33

Della's diary, Thursday 13th November 2014

I've visited John Joseph's unmarked grave every week for nearly fifty years. Reg used to come with me from time to time, but not since his mind started to go. He sometimes seemed angry when he was at the graveside and it became easier to go on my own. I think I know why now. And we never said much to Gus about what had happened, just suggested I'd once had a miscarriage ... perhaps we should have said more.

So what else shall I tell you? I won't bore you with the minutiae of family life on the ever-changing estate, but we plodded along in reasonable comfort, trying to keep up with the modern world. There is, however, something else I need to explain. Once again, here goes:

In 2012 Arthur had his second stroke. He was in hospital for weeks, having treatments and therapies which made little or no difference. Eventually he came home as a different man, totally dependent on paid carers and his unfortunate wife. She'd been reclusive and non-too robust herself since a car accident eighteen months earlier. Arthur lived for months as this disabled, cranky old man. Diana arranged for a hospital bed to be put in his study and, unable to walk or talk, he became isolated there. I was a regular visitor, encouraged by Diana, who thought he seemed calmer when I was around. He'd lean back on his pillow support and gaze up at the ceiling.

One day he tried to tell me something but the words wouldn't come. He grunted with frustration, pointing and almost choking on his spittle with the effort. In the end his gesticulations led me to a key to open his desk drawer and there I found two envelopes. One contained a contract he'd made with William Du Bois, Diana's ex-lover, agreeing to store politically sensitive documents for him, so long as he ended relations with Diana. Well, I wasn't interested in unlawful documents, so I didn't take too much notice. In the other envelope was a letter to me, and a beautiful gold chain, wrapped in tissue paper. I tended not to wear jewellery, Mother, but I could tell from the weight of it that this was no cheap gift. I never wore it, but I might start wearing it now, if life settles down a bit. I destroyed the letter, but only after memorising every word. It was dated 2010, so written just two years before his stroke and when, as I recall, he was still in good health.

"Dearest Della.

You have been my faithful friend for many years and most have little idea how much we have shared. If you are reading this, I will be dead, and Oliver will be in charge of the family estate – good luck to him.

Please accept a small and inadequate gift as a mark of the esteem in which you are held. This chain belonged to my mother, and her mother before that, and each of them wore it daily. I hope you will be able do the same in my memory.

Our child was not destined to live in this world. He was born in a state of distress, hardly breathing at all and from the moment he emerged, I was sure he would not live long. You were on the brink of life and death yourself, Della, so forgive me if I did wrong and let him go without a struggle. I was in despair at the thought I might also lose you.

I found I could not let him be placed in the cold and lonely graveyard, so even though all my family were there, I arranged for a coffin containing only a small bag of sand to be buried. Then I put our baby somewhere close to me, where he would be safe. Dear Della, I couldn't tell you where, because in those early days you were so fragile, I thought in your grief you would disclose our secret. When I believe my time to leave this world is near, I will privately give you details of our baby's place of rest. By then it will be safe for me to do so. Meanwhile, forgive me once again.

Now I am gone, please know how much your presence has enhanced my world. I hope you have found yourself some happiness along the way.

Forever, Arthur."

Arthur died at home just two days after I read this and that's when I burnt the letter. Bizarrely, Diana died just three weeks later of a sudden heart attack (perhaps her smoking caught up with her, despite the long cigarette holder she used so ostentatiously, swearing it made it safe). They both were buried on the family plot, near to what I now know was John Jacob's sand-filled coffin.

For weeks I scoured the house at every opportunity, looking for possible places where a second coffin could be hidden. I looked in wardrobes and cupboards, ottomans and chests. I checked for hidden panels in the corridors and library. I cleared out spaces under the stairs and in the hallways. All ten bedrooms were given a special spring clean, so no space was left undisturbed. I regret I didn't try to get up to the attic, but the ceilings on the top landing were so tall and the entrance so inaccessible, it just wasn't an option. I was also sure Arthur could never have got up there without assistance. Eventually I gave up my search, accepting that I might never know John Jacob's whereabouts, but trusting he was somewhere close by.

After the storm, when they found a tiny body up in the attic, right above Arthur's study, I knew he must somehow have struggled up there, to put John Jacob in just the right place. That's why I've run away to Rosie's house to get my thoughts straight before I return to face Oliver and Gus. I feel blessed to finally know where John Jacob is, and knowing has given me some peace. Perhaps we can soon bury him properly.

So, thank you for having me to stay, Rosie. I shall always be grateful for your patience, the loving environment you provided, and the wise counsel you gave me. I'm sure Mother would thank you too.

Della Hall.

34

THE MEETING

November 2014

On Friday afternoon Issy and Willow went to a friend's house for a play date after school and Jenny booked Jacob in for an extra afternoon at nursery. Sandra had offered to mind him, but Gus wanted her there with him. Max could see how badly Gus needed her moral support, even though it meant paying for the nursery. Max wasn't surprised when Mrs Hall turned up alone – Reg had a headache and was resting. Celine made tea for them all then discreetly slipped away.

Oliver sat next to Mrs Hall at the head of the table and Max saw him quietly touch her arm at intervals, so she knew he was at her side. She looked nervous and fiddled with a heavy, gold chain necklace round her neck, which seemed unusual as it was known she never wore jewellery other than her wedding ring, her gold-rimmed glasses and a practical-looking watch. Oliver looked quite calm next to her, and Max thought he must already know most of what she was going to say. Oliver had intimated to him that he'd offered to speak on her behalf but she'd declined, insisting if the story had to be told, it was to be her story, delivered from her own mouth.

Max inspected the gathering, almost expecting to see a secretary taking notes. Across the table Gus looked wretched, and Sandra was holding his hand to try to stop him fidgeting.

Sitting next to him Jenny was picking her thumbs, but on this occasion Max decided to leave her to it.

'Thanks for coming everyone,' Oliver said, as chairperson starting the official proceedings. 'I know you've all been worried about Mrs Hall, and the first thing to say is that the police are happy for her to talk to us. As you know, various things have come to light since the suitcase and the boxes were retrieved from the attic.' He looked to Max and said, 'Gus and I have both had a chance to read Mrs Hall's diary now, Max, but Mrs Hall hasn't wanted to talk about it openly until today. We all know about the white boxes, but we've only just discovered the facts behind the tragic discovery of the baby in the attic. With Mrs Hall's help the police have confirmed the identity of the baby in the suitcase. The gossips in the village are warming up and Mrs Hall wants to tell you her story before it gets distorted.'

Max saw Mrs Hall sway as she stood up. Her gaze did not lift from the table.

'You don't have to stand, Mrs Hall,' Oliver said.

'I think I should,' she replied, and she took a deep intake of breath. 'About fifty years ago I ... had an affair with Arthur Trelawney-Smythe and I carried his baby. But it wasn't as simple as that sounds ... and I'd like to tell you what happened, if you'd care to listen.'

Gus couldn't contain himself. 'Mum, must you? We don't want all the gory details, just tell them the baby in the attic was yours and admit who the father was. We know if it was Dad's the poor soul wouldn't be in the attic.'

Sandra gasped at the harshness of his tone, while the others waited in stunned silence for more revelations. Max was catching on to what might have come to pass, but glancing at Jenny, he saw she was totally confused.

'Listen, Gus, she wants to tell you in her own words,' Oliver said.

Mrs Hall spoke up now, eyes lifted but looking straight

ahead, avoiding any eye contact. Max thought the rehearsals she must have had, first with her cousin and then the police, had paid dividends. She succinctly told them about Arthur and their relationship, the pregnancy and the wedding. She told them about the snow of 1965 and the disastrous delivery in the blue bedroom, and the help she had from the Irish maid called Bridget.

Max whispered to Jenny, 'God, that bloody blue room again ...' and she shushed him.

Mrs Hall then spoke about the baby. 'I called him John Jacob,' she said.

Jenny put her hands up to her eyes. 'I never knew,' she gasped. 'Another Jacob!'

Max was just as surprised. He had a vague memory, no more than a flicker, of a conversation he'd had in the kitchen with Mrs Hall when she'd said how fond she was of the name. He took Jenny's hand and gave it a squeeze.

Mrs Hall continued, unaware of the jolt she'd given Jenny and Max. She talked about her own little boy being buried and how, without knowing, she'd visited an empty grave for years. Only now, since the storm, did she realise her baby had been in the attic, above Arthur's study all that time, although she did wonder if Arthur had tried to tell her on his death bed.

She went on to say what a fine husband Reg had become, dependable and constant, unlike Arthur who was exciting but dangerous and, above all else, used to getting his own way.

'I'm sorry you have to hear me say that about your father, Mr Oliver,' she said.

He patted her hand gently, like a son comforting his mother, and Max considered she probably had been like a mother to him in the unhappy household of the past. The close relationship between master and servant harped back to days long gone, and was so very different to that of today's world of employer and employee. At least contracts with terms and conditions had built-in safety, however much Max moaned about their complexity in his own workplace.

'And Arthur definitely was my father? You're sure it wasn't that MP?' Oliver asked.

'Yes, it was Arthur, I've already told you that. Check the timing if you don't believe me,' Mrs Hall said.

'Okay, sorry,' Oliver muttered like a chastised child.

'Can I ask what happened to the Irish maid?' Max asked.

'Bridget was paid off and sent home. She left no address and Arthur wouldn't say where to,' she said. 'The police traced her last whereabouts but found she died of breast cancer some years ago.'

A wave of sympathetic sighs rippled round the table and Max saw Gus's angry face soften a little.

'This is all worse than I'd realised. I knew Mum had lost a baby before she had me, but I just presumed it was Dad's and she'd had a miscarriage. Poor Dad. I still don't understand why didn't he speak out when all this was happening, Mum? I just don't get the relationship between him and Arthur.'

'I think they call it co-dependency, my love,' Mrs Hall said simply.

'No wonder Dad went peculiar when the old man died,' Gus said. 'How about Diana – can you explain her part in all this?'

'I believe Arthur told her everything in the end. He must have bought her silence by standing by her after her affair with the MP went sour. The press got hold of it, and there was an election coming up, so she came home and played the dutiful wife. Trouble is, she brought those blessed boxes with her. That just meant more secrets and lies entered the house. Oliver, your mother's main aim in life was to keep up appearances. She had no moral compass ... I'm sorry, but I expect you knew that already.'

'Well, that's put both of them in their place,' Oliver said.

'Not quite, there's a bit more to come. One day, when I

was with Arthur in his room, when he could hardly speak following his stroke, he pointed to the drawer in his bedside cabinet. I knew it had been locked for years. He pointed to his bookcase and only stopped pointing when I pulled out a bible. It had a false compartment cut into its pages.'

'Ironic,' said Gus.

Mrs Hall shot him a dagger-like look. 'Inside the cut-out space there was a small brass key.'

'And guess what, the key fitted the lock. Is this a fairy tale now?' Gus snarled.

'Oh, Gus, just shut up and listen,' Sandra said – her first contribution to the meeting.

'I opened the drawer and inside I found two letters. One was a sort of contract between him and William Du Bois concerning the documents Arthur was storing, and the other was addressed to me labelled, *Della, to be opened in the event of my death.*'

'Did you open it there and then, or wait for him to die?' Max asked, and Jenny tutted with disapproval at his bluntness. 'Sorry,' Max added.

'He nodded so I opened it and I almost wished I hadn't. He wrote that our child was born too young and hardly breathing. I believe he allowed the baby to die, without struggling to resuscitate him. He then bribed the undertaker to bury a coffin containing a small bag of sand in the corner of the cemetery because he wanted to keep the baby close to him, but honestly, he never said where. I searched the house for weeks after Arthur died and never found a thing. I didn't really consider the attic.'

'It had to be somewhere it wouldn't be easily found,' Gus said.

'Oh dear,' Sandra said and took out a tissue to blow her nose.

'So, you never knew the body was in the attic? How awful,' Max said.

'I'm furious I only found out when the storm came. I should have guessed. On his death-bed Arthur kept raising his eyes to the ceiling, and I thought it was because he was going to meet his maker. Only when the roof came off did I realise that the brown suitcase was placed directly above the bed, in his study.'

'Can I see that last letter?' Oliver said.

'I burned it. I had no need of any more painful memories, and the man was dying.'

Only then did Mrs Hall start to weep. Nobody moved and no one spoke for a while, then in a strangled voice Oliver stood up and turned his back to the table.

'So, we don't think my father actually killed his own son, but he did let him die without trying to save him, as an act of kindness. Is that manslaughter – I'm not sure? Anyway, when he hid the body, surely that concealment was illegal? I need a break ... will you excuse me for one moment?' He slipped out of the door, leaving the others in an awkward void of silence, which Max eventually filled. He always was the person who couldn't bear the silence when a lecturer asked, 'Any questions?' at the end of a talk.

'I'm puzzled about the undertaker and the burial. Don't you need a death certificate to bury a body?' he asked, just as Oliver came back.

'Never mind that,' Gus snapped. 'I didn't even know I had a brother.' Gus was working himself up again, and Max was relieved that Oliver had chosen that moment to return.

'Okay, I know a bit about the false burial,' he said. 'The police found some paperwork at the Co-op undertakers who'd bought out the old undertaker. They indicate the old guy had made false declarations about the baby, saying it was a stillbirth. They think my father must have bribed him to do a sham burial and that fits in with Mrs Hall's understanding of things. There was no birth certificate, and no death certificate.'

Gus seemed unhappy to leave it. 'Dad must have been

involved, too, don't you think? He was there when baby ... John Jacob was meant to be buried. Don't tell me Dad was in on the dodgy bribe too?' He lifted his hands to his face and rubbed his eyes.

'This isn't time for any more allegations, Gus, and Reg isn't here to speak for himself, and bear in mind he'd just lost his mother too. Just leave it for now,' Oliver said.

Mrs Hall spoke up. 'All I can say is I think Reg must have believed Arthur when he said the baby was stillborn. He just went along with the early burial because that was the easiest thing for both of them. There's no evidence Reg thought the baby could be Arthur's though and no evidence he knew the little coffin just contained sand. You'll have to ask him if you want to know more.'

'As if he can give me a straight answer now his brain's falling apart,' Gus barked.

'Leave it, Gus,' Sandra whispered.

'I think you could both have colluded with Arthur in a cover up – yes, you too, Mum. There I was, always looking out for Dad and feeling he needed protection. I thought you shut him out, acting all superior, thinking the status of cook and housekeeper was far above that of a gardener. I felt sorry for him, but he was as bad as the rest of you – a weak man and a coward for not standing up to Arthur.'

'Standing up to the boss, risk losing his job, his home and probably me in the process? I don't think so. Your Dad wasn't weak; he was the strong one. I won't have you speaking of him like that,' Mrs Hall replied. Max was astonished and impressed at her return of strength.

'My dad was the weak one, Gus, not yours,' Oliver said.

Max was tired and ready to go. He wanted to get away from events in the blue bedroom, the house and its secrets. He wanted to get to the safety of home. Jenny's expression suggested she'd had enough too. He checked his watch.

'We're going to have to go and pick up Jacob soon,' Max

said. 'Just one last thing – do the police know about the MP's papers? And what about Tricia? Did she trash the tree and the gravestone or was it Reg all the time?'

'The police know all about Du Bois, so that's now in their hands. Tricia is next on my agenda. Celine's putting out feelers to try to find out where she is.'

'Okay, good, but we really must be off,' Max said.

'Sure. Thanks for coming. We'll speak soon,' Oliver said, standing up to shake Max's hand and kiss Jenny's cheek.

'I need to go and see Dad,' Gus said and left with them, without even looking at Oliver. Sandra stayed back with Mrs Hall.

Max took Jenny's hand as they walked to the car and, as Gus caught up with them, he wondered if Gus and Sandra would ever truly get back together.

'I'm really sorry you had to hear all that,' Gus said.

'I know you are. Let's try and move on. No news from Tricia, then?' Max said.

'No, thank goodness, but I still live in dread. Sandra and I are getting on a bit better and she's accepted the rape thing was a false allegation, what with the mismatched timing, but – oh, you know ...'

'It's Tricia who has the problem, Gus, not you,' Max said. 'It's as if she sensed bad things had happened in this house. She spotted a scar and decided to pick at it like a child picks a scab. I wonder if she and Reg could have acted together?'

'But they really didn't like each other very much,' Gus said.

'No, but through Reg she could get at both you and Oliver,' Max replied.

'I just don't know,' Gus sighed.

Max and Jenny were glad to drive away. They passed a taxi in the drive, which was returning Issy and Willow to the house, and Max pretended to be concentrating on driving. He didn't even look at their faces, but was aware that Jenny give them a sad little wave.

'Were you there when your mother claimed Lawn House was cursed?' he asked once they were out on the road.

'When was that? I don't remember,' Jenny said.

'When you were in hospital, that first time. I didn't think much about it at the time, but maybe she was onto something, after all,' he said.

'Oh, Max, you know what Mum's like, you can't take her comments seriously,' Jenny said with a cynical laugh.

'Perhaps not,' Max said, unconvincingly.

They went quiet for the rest of the ride home. They collected Jacob from nursery and he nodded off almost immediately, leaving Max and Jenny with their own thoughts. Max tried to run through the details of the immoral and illegal activities that winter, fifty years ago, and how a bizarre ripple effect had gone on to involve his own family. It was an easy cop-out to say that at the centre of the house's curse was the wretched blue bedroom. That's what Carol would have said. He knew a room couldn't be blamed; it was the men and women who used it and slept in it – people like Della and Arthur, Tricia and Gus, making bad decisions and, of course, the lodgers who set fire to it. Why, oh why did Oliver have to give Tricia the blue bedroom?

'You all right?' he asked Jenny after a while.

'Yes, just a bit tired and frankly bemused,' she replied.

'Nearly home,' he said.

'Do you know, I think we should let the Halls and the Trelawneys sort out their own mess for a while, maybe maintain a little distance?' she said.

'I've been thinking much the same,' Max said. 'But we needed to find out the identity of the baby first.'

'Okay, but now that's done, and without getting too involved, we can still see Celine and the girls for play dates with Jacob. Perhaps they can come over here, rather than us go to them?' she said. 'We can still be good godparents.'

'And I can easily find somewhere else to run,' Max said. As always, Jenny tended to be right.

35

THE PAPERS

December 2014

Celine brought Issy and Willow to the cottage in Stowmarket at least once a week during the Christmas holidays. It was helpful to get them out of Gus's way at Oak Lodge now he'd been relieved of his live-in duties at Chestnut Cottage. Max sometimes went running in the park if it was a weekend, but more often stayed to hear what was going on and play with the kids. He knew Jenny found herself appreciating Celine's company more and more as time went by.

'Jacob's saying real words now, getting so much clearer. You must be pleased with his progress,' Celine said.

'Yes, I'm sure the nursery's really helping. Seeing other smaller children has been good for him and their play therapist is brilliant – in fact, all the staff are. It's worth every penny, even though it takes quite a chunk out of our budget.'

'I can tell she's enjoying work,' Celine said to Max. She turned to Jenny. 'I love hearing you talk about how you help your patients, now you're back at it – see, what goes around, comes around. You help in your specialist field, and the play therapist helps Jacob.'

'Ah, that's a nice way of looking at it. Makes me feel less guilty about leaving him,' Jenny said.

'Careful Issy, mind he doesn't fall off.' Celine jumped up

to rescue Jacob, who the girls had lifted up onto a dining chair. 'I think they've forgotten he's so much younger than them. Now he's toddling about and trying to climb, he's one of the gang.'

'I bet the girls are missing their playground at the big house,' Max said. 'When will that be in use again?'

'Oh, everything is taking far longer than we thought. The priorities keep shifting, and Oliver is constantly moaning about listed building consent being needed at each step of the renovation work.'

'Max misses taking his runs on the estate, don't you, love? I don't think the municipal park gives quite the same feeling of freedom. But as you know, we decided we needed a bit of distance after all that's happened,' Jenny commented.

'I can't say I blame you,' Celine said.

'But we're glad you come over here to see us and keep us informed about Lawn House,' Max said.

'The go-between?' Celine said.

'No, as a friend,' Jenny said. 'Don't feel you have to tell tales. It's not like that.'

'It's fine, not a problem. Oliver likes to know what's happening with you lot, too, but you know how busy he is. He gets a bit bothered about chit-chat in the village, of course, but you and Max are regarded as part of the family.'

***

It was Celine who told them that Oliver wanted to formally acknowledge John Jacob's existence. The police were still taking their time deciding whether Arthur could be posthumously charged with the illegal activity surrounding the baby's burial, and a formal hearing would be needed at some stage; but meanwhile, Oliver and Gus wanted their half-brother buried properly, and as soon as possible. Mrs Hall allowed them to make the arrangements so long as they kept her informed. She was busy looking after Reg, who was getting more muddled by the day. Sandra helped out if Mrs Hall had to go somewhere, but that didn't happen often because the older woman was more anxious than Oliver about the local gossips. Max noticed Celine's forced smile, when she told them Sandra and Gus seemed much closer these days. She must have had to let go any unlikely ideas she ever had about Sandra – all the trouble had brought her and Gus together, not driven them apart as it could have done.

'If she's taken him back, he's a lucky man,' Max said.

'How about you, though? Are you alright, not running yourself ragged looking out for other people all the time?' Jenny asked tactfully.

'I'm fine, don't worry about me,' Celine replied with a blush and a smile. 'Actually, I don't want to say too much, but I have a new friend.'

'Do you want me to leave so you women can talk more freely?' Max offered.

'No, don't worry. There's not much to tell yet,' Celine said.

'Yet? This is sounding interesting,' said Jenny.

Celine didn't need much encouragement to say more. And once she'd started she couldn't stop.

'She's called Lynn and I met her on a one of the park walks – Gus and his men have tidied it up enough for the walking group, and fenced off any dangerous areas left over from the storm. We walk the estate and the fields and woods around us, once a week on a Wednesday morning. We set off from the garden centre and walk briskly for an hour. It warms you up a treat on a winter morning. I'm sure it's doing me so much good.'

'I want to know about Lynn, not the flipping park,' Jenny said.

'Okay, Lynn does me good too,' Celine replied.

'I can tell!' Jenny laughed.

'You should come and join us,' Celine said. 'Lynn's a bit

younger than me, and much fitter, but I'm catching up.'

'Yes, why don't you, Jenny?' Max said, thinking he'd never seen Celine so animated.

'Shame I work Wednesdays,' Jenny said. 'Still, I get my exercise chasing Jacob.'

'Sandra can't come either, because of work. Oliver's given her responsibility for the re-launch of the swanky new garden centre. She's had a new sign painted and it's now called The Lodge Garden Centre, and she's converting the barn next to it into a gift shop and café. I'm really pleased for her,' Celine said.

'That's a lot of work,' Jenny said.

'She's got a couple of village girls helping out,' Celine said.

When Jenny and Max talked about this later he said he hoped the new staff had signed the Official Secrets Act. Jenny ignored him and went on to discuss how the twins had been asked to name the café. It was to be called The Treehouse Café, and a special tree logo had apparently been commissioned from a graphic designer to head the menus. Max loved the idea that a photograph of the twins' treehouse had been printed on a large canvas to go behind the serving area. He thought how proud Alexis would have been.

Max did, however, query where the money had come from for all this

'Not our problem,' Jenny said. 'Remember we're trying to keep a little distance.'

'Maybe the insurance has paid out,' Max said. 'I hope Oliver's not getting himself into debt.'

'Stop it, Max. It's up to Oliver, just leave him to it,' Jenny said sternly.

Of course, that was easier said than done. The local paper had run some articles about Lawn House trying to recover from the storm, and they'd done a fair amount of digging for information about the baby in the attic. There were some inevitable nasty comments, and a few made-up details, but the household at Lawn House tried not to react too much.

Shortly after Christmas, however, Oliver turned up unexpectedly on the Brown's doorstep. Max and Jenny were still in their pyjamas and Oliver either didn't notice, or was too polite to comment.

'I got the papers in town, couldn't face the village shop this morning. I knew from social media something bad was coming. Have you seen it?' he said, standing on the doorstep with a great pile of papers in his arms. 'The Sunday papers have got hold of it and done a huge exposé.'

'Come in and I'll make a pot of coffee,' Jenny said.

She parked Jacob in front of a Thomas the Tank Engine DVD and Max made room for the papers on the table. Every one of them from The Sun to The Sunday Times carried the story on their front page. The headlines varied from fake concern to downright cruelty:

"SUFFOLK STORM SCANDAL"; "STATELY HOME STORY"; "BODY FOUND IN LOFT"; "WHOSE BABY?"; "HOW THE OTHER HALF LOVE"; "MANOR HOUSE MAYHEM"; "A DISASTROUS AFFAIR", and, finally, in one there was a picture of Oliver with the label, "TOFF'S COMEUPPANCE".

Jenny returned with a tray of coffee. Oliver was opening one of the papers to show something to Max.

'There's something else, I'm afraid, and I'm so sorry,' he said. 'This is why I came straight here ... I had to show you this.'

It was a photograph of Max going through the gates to the estate, taken the morning after the storm when he was "papped". Beneath the picture was an article stating how

Maxwell Brown was seen visiting the house, where nearly a year ago his baby son had been attacked by a dangerous spider. They described it as, "The house where no baby is safe", and gave graphic details of Jacob's injury and progress.

'Oh my god,' Max said.

Jenny spilled the coffee. 'Shit! Why now? Where did they get this information?'

'I know, it's awful. This isn't news, it's invasion of privacy. Your story has nothing to do with the storm.'

'It's pretty bad for your family, Oliver, and the Halls, though,' Jenny said.

'Yes, not great, but after what Arthur got up to, I'm not so surprised. Throw a Tory MP into the mix and the press were bound to get over-excited. I'm surprised it took so long – perhaps the Christmas holidays delayed things. I'm a bit worried the girls will get some flack when they go back to school, but the rest of us will cope.'

'I think you're being very calm about it,' Max said.

'By not reacting it might make it go away quicker. That's been my theory from the start of this mess. I'll try to persuade Celine and the Halls to do the same.'

'Good luck with Gus,' Max said.

'Ha, I'll manage. No choice really. You, however, have a case to be answered, and you need to shut down this uncalled-for attention on Jacob. I think you should call your solicitor and seek legal advice. It could help Lawn House too if you do.'

'On a Sunday? Do solicitors work on Sundays?' Max said.

'Tomorrow will do, but you really don't have to put up with this,' Oliver said.

Jenny passed Jacob a toy train to play with. He took it in both hands and Jenny smiled, noticing his rapidly improving dexterity.

Oliver started folding up the papers. 'It does make me wonder where the journalists get their information,' he said, and then the phone rang.

'Oh heavens! That'll be one of our parents. They'll all have seen the papers this morning. I'll get it. I'll put it on loudspeaker so you can hear,' Max said.

His face fell when he picked up and heard the familiar voice on the other end of the line: 'Hi, Max. It's me, Tricia. I just phoned to see how you are. I heard about the storm. I've been looking at the paper this morning and saw the article about Jacob. Nice picture by the way.'

'Oh ... hello. Thanks. We're all right. And you? Where are you?' Max pulled a face at Jenny, who shook her head and made a cut-throat sign across her neck.

'I'm as well as can be expected after all I've been through. I'm in Manchester.'

'What, at your mother's?' Max said, still pulling faces at Jenny as if pleading for help.

'No way. I'm trying to make a new life for myself,' she said.

'Look, Tricia, can I call you back? It's not very convenient to talk at the moment. Give me your number.'

'Yes, I expect you've been trying to reach me, I've changed my phone. Make sure you call. Give Jakey a hug from me.'

'Thanks, I will. Take care.' Max scribbled the number down and put the phone on its cradle quickly, as if it was burning his fingers.

'Wow, that was interesting timing,' Oliver said. 'She's all we need at the moment.'

'I do wish she wouldn't call him Jakey,' Jenny said. 'What do you think she wants?'

'Heaven knows. I really wasn't up to talking to her right now, as you could tell,' Max said.

'Trust her to pop up out of the woodwork on a day like this. Highly suspicious if you ask me. And why phone us? She could have called Celine if she wanted to make contact. The woman is tricky, Max, so just be careful when you phone her back,' Jenny warned.

'I might put it off for a while,' Max said.

'You'll have to call her now, she's expecting it. Besides, it would be good to find out where she is in Manchester,' Oliver said. 'There are still unanswered questions about what she might have got up to when she was with us. Look, sorry, but I'd better go now and face the music at Lawn House.'

<hr />

Max phoned his solicitor the next morning and asked for Frances Freeman. She was busy but soon called them back. She'd already had a quick look at yesterday's papers, put in front of her by her secretary, and Max was able to give her a neat summary of the situation.

'I think you have a case here. This is blatant invasion of privacy,' Miss Freeman said. 'We can get an injunction taken out on the newspaper and stop this pretty sharpish. First though, I'll talk to the paper's editor and we'll take it from there. Can you come in to see me this afternoon and we'll talk more?'

'Fine, I'm working from home today but I can work around a two o'clock appointment,' Max agreed.

'Meanwhile, please don't talk to anyone, especially not the press. They'll be trying to find out more about the affairs of Lawn House. It's easy to get sucked in and find yourself saying the wrong thing. My advice is to lie low for a few days,' Miss Freeman said.

Jenny switched on the answerphone to field any incoming calls. They planned to go into hiding for a day or two, at least while the solicitor did her magic and made the problem disappear. Jenny wanted to go with Max to the appointment, but felt she couldn't even ask anyone to look after Jacob.

'We should be able to manage him between us,' Max said. 'I'd like you to be there.'

The three of them got to the office in Ipswich in good time. The secretary was delighted to meet Jacob, having heard all about him and now, unfortunately, read about him too. She offered to mind him while Max and Jenny talked with Miss Freeman.

'I'm sure that's not in your job description,' Jenny said.

'I'm Girl Friday around here. I'll be just next-door if you need me,' she said, and scooped Jacob up, along with the bag of toys Jenny had packed to keep him occupied.

'Don't forget his giraffe,' Jenny called out. 'Giraffe has to go everywhere with us at the moment.'

Frances Freeman didn't mess about. 'I've spoken to the newspaper involved and they've told me their informer was a woman called Tricia Bird, who says she was Jacob's nanny.'

'We know Tricia Bird all too well, and that makes sense,' Max said.

'Oh, I'd hoped it was just someone from the village wanted to make a quick buck,' Jenny said.

'No, Tricia Bird asked for money in return for information, and said there was a lot more to tell if the price was right. She demanded a significant sum, and a reporter is planning to go to Manchester to meet her tomorrow at a hotel called St Margaret's. She plans to negotiate a final fee before they get the rest of her story.'

'Goodness, can we stop her in time? This won't just be about Jacob, it'll be about the house too. How long does an injunction take?' Max asked.

'It'll be a push to get one for tomorrow. We might be better off thinking outside the box,' Miss Freeman said.

'What does that mean? We haven't the money to pay her off ourselves?' Max said.

'Oh, nothing as crude as that Mr Brown, I'm sure that

won't be necessary. We can settle this just as we settled the Dr Grey episode. I presume you heard no more from him once the spectacles were paid for?'

'No, all quiet there, thanks,' Max said, not daring to catch Jenny's eye. Jenny didn't like to be reminded of the little glitch this had caused in their relationship.

'I think Miss Bird will burn her own boat by demanding too much money. I'm planning to work with the editor to make sure of that, anyway. I'll also be able to convince him to accept that she's an unreliable witness and not worth the money.'

'Isn't that a risk? Perhaps she'll be angry you haven't phoned her back yet, Max? You know what she's like, she could say anything to the reporter, money or not. We know she has a history of making things up to suit herself. I don't think it's just money that's driving her, she enjoys causing trouble,' Jenny said.

'Do you have another suggestion, Mrs Brown?'

'I'd rather just phone her and talk her down myself. I suppose I could even say that Jacob's problem was of her making and we might sue her for damages ... but that'd make me as devious as her, wouldn't it? No, I won't do that, but I could just play the "hurt mother" card,' Jenny said.

'That would be quicker and cheaper than a gagging order,' Miss Freeman agreed. 'You'll have to be careful what you say, however. Let's prepare a script for you and give it a try.'

Jenny phoned Tricia's mobile number and it went to voicemail. She emitted an exasperated huff then, with great composure, left a very normal-sounding message, asking Tricia to call back.

A minute or two later Jenny's mobile phone rang. She put it on speakerphone.

'Hello, Tricia, thanks for calling back. Max is awfully busy at work so I thought I'd phone you.'

'Hi, Jenny. I'd rather talk to you, anyway. Men are so hopeless on the phone: they pass on secret messages and tell me to do bad things. Jesus Christ phoned me himself yesterday and told me to cut myself.'

'Oh dear, does he phone often?' Jenny asked. Max and Frances Freeman frowned at each other – she was already straying from the script.

'Most days, and do you know he sometimes comes into my room at night?'

'What, your hotel room, that must be very disturbing?' Jenny said.

Tricia gave out an awful laugh; it leapt from the phone and bounced round the solicitor's office, making Max cringe. 'It's not a hotel, it's a clinic in a grand house, like Lawn House but with more servants. I have a very nice room, and there's a lock on the door, but men still get in. They want my body, I expect. They all do.'

Miss Freeman's eyebrows jumped up to reach for her hairline. Max shook his head. The reporter wouldn't have got far looking for St Margaret's Hotel and it was no wonder they couldn't find it when they Googled it either – a hospital, not a hotel! – it was starting to make sense. Jenny however remained in control.

'Do you want me to try and stop them? I know how to stop things like that. Tell me the address where your room is and I'll speak to someone.'

'Look, it's called St Margaret's and it's near the station in Manchester.'

'What road is that?'

'Oh, I'm not sure. Got to go, Jenny, there's someone at the door. Hope it's not another man. No, it's just the maid bringing tea.'

'Can I speak to the maid? I can tell her how to stop your unwanted visitor. She might know the name of the road too,' Jenny said.

'You are so kind, Jenny. I'll pass the phone to her. Make sure you call back soon.'

A voice with a northern accent took over. 'Hello, who is this?'

'My name's Jenny Brown and I'm a friend of Tricia's. I'd like to visit her if possible. Can you tell me the address?' Jenny said.

Miss Freeman gave her the thumbs up, making Max smile proudly at his clever wife.

'St Margaret's Hospital, Cheshire Street, Manchester. Visiting times are two 'til four. Please report to the desk on arrival.'

'Two 'til four. Got it, thanks. Goodbye.'

'Brilliant,' said Miss Freeman. 'Calm, in control, great powers of detection and flexibility – do you want a job?'

'Thanks, but I have one,' Jenny said.

Max had already Googled St Margaret's Hospital. 'It's a psychiatric hospital with rehab facilities,' he announced.

'Good. Plan A and B now seem irrelevant. We won't need an injunction and we don't need to pay her off. All we need is Plan C, and I don't think you'll even need the "hurt mother" card,' Miss Freeman said.

'Is there a Plan C?' Max asked.

'There is now,' Miss Freeman said. 'I'll speak to the consultant in charge of Tricia's case and ask him or her to refuse admission to any reporters who might turn up. That'll sort things out in the short term. Then I'll speak to the newspaper editor and, without breaking any confidentiality issues, get the message across that she's unwell.'

'Could you ask if the hospital have a next of kin on record? If it's Celine, that could be helpful,' Jenny said.

'I like working with you two – what a pair!' Miss Freeman said jovially. 'Perhaps you'd better collect your son, now, or Miss Lee won't get any work done.'

When they went to collect Jacob, he was playing happily and loath to leave.

'Miss Lee's done so well with Jacob, perhaps we should offer *her* a job,' Max said.

When Miss Freeman reported back to Max and Jenny a few days later, she was pleased with her work. The consultant was a good listener, even if he couldn't say much, and had reassured the solicitor that all guests had to sign in and the reporter would not have been allowed in. He even offered to speak to the newspaper editor himself to say Miss Bird was unwell and would be unable to speak to them again for the foreseeable future.

'Can he do that?' Jenny asked. 'Won't that make the editor more suspicious and make him dig deeper?'

'That's possible, but the psychiatrist seemed to know what he was doing. He'll be doing it to "protect his vulnerable patient from public scrutiny",' Miss Freeman said. 'I presume that works for you and you don't actually want to sue her for damages.'

Max was beginning to accept the word vulnerable was right: Tricia was ill; it was just a shame so many people got caught in her slipstream.

'No, of course we don't. We just want to protect Jacob's privacy,' he said.

'And ours, and Oliver's too,' Jenny added. 'That's what all this is about. I guess we'll leave it in the doctor's capable hands. At least we can tell Celine where her sister is now,' Jenny said.

Max thought Gus might be grateful to know too, but decided not to mention him to Miss Freeman.

'That's up to you. You've discovered Tricia's whereabouts on your own as far as I'm concerned, so you can use the information as you wish. Now, I have another appointment, so I'll show you out.'

· ══◄◊►══ ·

Celine was upset when they told her they'd found Tricia's whereabouts. She said she'd tried so hard to be a good big sister and was sad it had all gone wrong. The fact that Tricia was mentally ill didn't help, as it only added to the guilt at not having picked up on it. Celine made a dutiful phone call to the hospital in Manchester, offering her name as next of kin, but apparently, they already had their mother's details on file. Max noticed Celine did not rush to visit.

Gus, by contrast, was quietly delighted. He thought the fact that Tricia was psychologically ill meant no one would believe her if she said she'd been raped. Max considered that wasn't a correct line of thought, but let it drop, knowing full well Gus hadn't raped her anyway and the dates confirmed that.

· ══◄◊►══ ·

A few days later the postman made a larger than usual delivery to the cottage in Stowmarket. Top of the pile of letters to be opened were two utility bills.

'We must get these put on direct debit,' said Jenny.

An invoice for Jacob's nursery was next to be opened, then two separate invoices from Smith & Son, Solicitors. The first was a minor one for the Dr Grey Debacle, signed off by F. Freeman, and the second, for a slightly larger amount and signed off by again by F. Freeman, was for sorting out the newspapers.

'Frances with an e turned out to be a very expensive new friend,' Max said.

'She's not our friend, Max, and we don't want to be meeting her again any time soon,' Jenny said.

'All I can say is how grateful we should be to Ed for his generous contribution.'

Jenny's phone then rang and the screen said, 'Tricia calling'. She let it ring and go to Voicemail, then blocked the contact.

36

CERTIFICATION

Celine told Jenny and Max about her one and only visit to the psychiatric ward in Manchester. She reported that Tricia sounded less disturbed, which was good. Max could tell they'd found it hard to feel the sisterly love both women had once hoped for, but at least it seemed they'd managed some polite communication. Tricia had told Celine she would soon be discharged from in-patient care, but agreed to have further treatment in a supported, halfway house, and it might be some months before she was really well; then she randomly added that their mum had been to visit, but hadn't stayed for long.

'That's good,' Celine had said. 'How was she?'

'Okay. Said she missed us both.'

'I find that hard to believe. Is she still with the same bloke, or has she moved on to some other poor soul?' Celine asked.

'She's on her own. I might be able to go and stay with her once I'm ready. '

'Did she actually say that?' Celine asked.

'Not really, but I could, couldn't I?'

'Take it steady, Tricia, one step at a time.'

'It's been so boring in here. There's no one to have fun with and they watch my every move. The only decent thing is the art therapy.'

'I guess keeping an eye on you is the whole point, isn't it? You're so much better, Tricia, don't get impatient and mess it up,' Celine said.

'Are you going to see Mum while you're here?'

'Don't think so. I've only got a few hours. I'm getting the six o'clock train back.'

Celine didn't add that her new partner, Lynn, was meeting her at the station, or that she'd only gone to Manchester because Lynn persuaded her it was the right thing to do. She said she was pleased to have seen Tricia and it brought some closure to their troubled time together in Suffolk, but she realised she felt not one jot of regret at not seeing their mother.

<hr />

Jenny and Max noted that Lynn was proving to be useful on all sorts of levels, and not just decorating Celine's new cottage on the estate. Oliver, Issy and Willow stayed on in Oak Lodge and Sandra moved in permanently with Gus, into his old childhood bedroom at Chestnut Cottage.

'I think Sandra finds it easier to be Celine's friend now Lynn's around. I reckon they'll be moving in together soon,' Jenny said one night in bed.

'Oh, you're such a matchmaker,' Max said.

Jenny looked up at the paintwork in her own bedroom. 'I wish I'd married a decorator,' she said.

'You can't have everything. I wish I'd married a masseuse,' Max said.

'You did, you fool. Roll over and I'll give you a back massage.'

'Now you're talking.' He sighed as she spread aromatic oil across his back. *Physio, aromatherapist, masseuse, who's quibbling?* he thought.

<hr />

Next time he went running, Max came upon Gus supervising a team of workmen mending fences. Max smiled at the thought that until quite recently Gus would have been doing the mending himself.

'How's life?' Max asked. 'Working hard?'

'No need to sound sarcastic, I am actually. I've not had a day off since the storm, and nor has Oliver. It's one thing after another, and today it's very important they get this fence right.'

'I know, don't worry. The old place is gradually getting back to normal,' Max said.

'Even better than before, I'd say. The upheaval made us deal with stuff we've neglected. I just wonder if we'll ever get finished,' Gus said.

'Things okay at Chestnut Cottage? You can't have much time to help with your dad.'

'Sandra's making all the difference. Mum loves having her around – enjoys her company more than mine I think,' Gus admitted.

'Isn't it strange being back in your childhood home? I mean it's a bit inhibiting having your parents in the next room,' Max said.

'We cope. Anyway, I think they're going deaf,' Gus chortled. 'No seriously, Dad's been a bit more settled since they put him on tablets, so we're managing quite well for now. They confirmed it is Alzheimer's, which is shit, but at least we know what we're dealing with.'

'I'm really sorry,' Max said.

'It's Mum I feel bad for. I've calmed myself down a bit, you know, rationalised the whole John Jacob thing. I realise it's old Arthur I should be cross with, not Mum and Dad.'

'Whatever's come over you?' Max said.

'Sandra and I did some counselling with Relate. Bloody marvellous. It's helped me a lot.'

'Well, I am truly astonished, but well done, mate,' Max said.

'Thanks, and the best thing is we've heard nothing else from Tricia.' Gus grinned.

'I'd better let you get on with this fence. Is Oliver around?'

'Dashing about somewhere, probably in the big house. He seems to have got a new lease of life. Can't stop the man working on his new projects.'

Max continued his run and, on his way round the back of the house, found Oliver in the boarded-up conservatory, surrounded by papers and plans.

'Hi, Max, come and look at these samples. The conservatory will be finished soon and I've got to decide on the floor tiles,' he said.

'Heavens, don't ask me. I thought you had your own art advisor?' Max said.

'I suppose I have, but she's in London and I need a final decision today,' Oliver said, without rising to the bait.

'I'd say that darker one, then, but you could double-check with Celine's Lynn. So, fill me in on your trips to London – all going well?'

'Good idea. I'll ask Lynn to pop in. London's pretty good, thanks,' he said. 'Charlotte's helping me sell off some of the Cornish ancestor portraits and we're restoring some of the nicer paintings to go back in the house. I want to make everything just right and absolve the house from its horrible past.'

'You realise we haven't met Charlotte yet,' Max said.

'All in good time, my friend,' he replied. 'I need to sort out a few more things before I can tempt her to be a permanent part of this place.'

'God, it's serious then?'

'Yep. It might never be that we'll live together in this house, but I think we'll be together somewhere. I've got really mixed feelings about Lawn House now. I've rather enjoyed living in the lodge, even if it is small.'

'What about the girls?' Max asked.

'Here they are now. Let's just ask them?'

'Daddy, Celine's made tea. Daddy, are you coming over? You too, Uncle Max!' shouted Issy.

The kitchen at Oak Lodge was a smaller gathering place than the kitchen at the manor house but they all managed to sit round the table for afternoon tea.

'What cake do we have today?' Max asked. 'Did you girls make it?'

'Yes. It's carrot cake,' Willow announced. 'I did the icing.'

'Girls,' said Oliver once the cake was cut. 'I want to ask you something, you too Celine.'

'This sounds worrying,' Celine said as she handed out the plates.

'Just a simple question – you know how much we've enjoyed living over here, well how would you feel if we didn't move back to the big house? I was wondering if we might look for a new family home, somewhere we could make our own?'

'I don't mind, as long as we live with you, Daddy. Could we still see Gus and Sandra?' Willow said.

'And I don't want to change schools, and I want to be able to see Jacob,' Issy said.

'What about Celine? She'd have to come with us wherever it is,' Willow said.

'And we'd want to see Mrs Hall for our baking lessons,' Issy said.

'Celine, what do you think?' Oliver asked.

'I can see the advantages of somewhere more manageable, as long as it's not far away. I wouldn't really want to leave my cottage, not now Lynn's joined me.'

Max pricked his ears up.

'But the girls are growing up so I needn't be a live-in nanny,' she continued. 'I could still look after them, we could just change the arrangements.'

'Right, so no one minds leaving the big house, but we

all want to have everyone we love nearby. That could work. Leave it with me,' Oliver said.

Oliver walked Max back to his car after tea.

'That went well, I think,' he announced.

'Are you seriously planning to sell Lawn House?' Max asked.

'Thinking about it, but the reality could be the problem. I've got some ideas to work on, but who'd want to buy it? Of course, I can't do anything until the police and the CPS have finished with Mrs Hall and Arthur's mess – and heavens, they're taking ages to wrap that up. They've had a special court hearing, in private, and I'm taking Mrs Hall for a final meeting with the coroner next week. At least they've sorted out the wretched MP's documents; they turned out to be less interesting than your average spy novel.'

'And I gather the press have backed off, as you hoped they would, so you're gradually getting there,' Max said. 'Phone us when the coroner closes the case. Jenny's been worrying about Mrs Hall, but doesn't feel she can do or say much until the legalities are sorted.'

Oliver turned up on the doorstep a few days later, just as Max and Jacob arrived back from an outing to the local park.

'Too much to say on the phone and I fancied an outing,' Oliver said. 'Am I interrupting anything?'

'No, in you come, there's a lasagne in the oven,' Jenny said. 'Max and Jacob just need to wash their hands. Poor child, he'll have him doing marathons soon.'

'Don't forget to put the oven timer on this time,' Oliver said.

Jenny hugged him boisterously.

'Is it all over?' she asked.

'I think so.'

'Look at these two, father and son in their tracksuits. I see what you mean, Jenny.'

Oliver and Jenny were laughing as Max lifted Jacob out of his buggy.

'What's the joke?' said Max, heading to the cloakroom. 'Jacob's been in the sand pit – filthy place.'

The three adults sat at the table to eat lasagne. Jacob listened to the adult talk from his high chair as if he understood every word.

Oliver confirmed the DNA sample from the baby in the suitcase gave positive matches with the stains on the hanky from Della Hall's tin. It also matched DNA from Gus and Oliver. All the information the police could gather confirmed Mrs Hall's story, but there was no imperative to charge Arthur with anything of significance. Nothing would be achieved by a posthumous conviction for concealing a body.

'Bridget, the young maid, took a bit of tracing. She married twice and moved around a lot, before she died from breast cancer, as we know, somewhere in Galway,' Oliver said. 'It's so sad, because she'd have been the best person to talk to about January 1965.'

'Tragic,' Jenny said. 'So, there were no remaining witnesses?'

'Only Reg,' Max said.

'He wasn't even able to understand the questions. His memory was totally unreliable,' Oliver said. 'In the end they've issued a birth certificate for John Jacob Trelawney-Smythe and a death certificate dated the same day, 23rd January 1965.'

'Goodness, I suppose that's what you wanted, Oliver?' Jenny said. 'Did they put a cause of death?'

'It said "respiratory failure" as the primary cause and, secondly, they put "premature birth".'

'Does that mean you can give John Jacob a proper burial?' Jenny asked.

'Yes, we've arranged a private ceremony, just me, Gus and Mrs Hall, and we're burying his remains beneath Alexis's oak tree. He'll have a brass plaque next to hers simply bearing the name John Jacob. We've decided no other details are necessary.'

'What if you leave the house and move away?' Max said.

Jenny suddenly looked alarmed. 'He won't do that,' she said firmly.

'He could,' Max said.

'I might,' Oliver said. 'I've been thinking it could be for the best. You know I've always found the house difficult.'

'But then you'll be leaving Alexis and John Jacob.' She suddenly turned on Max. 'You knew, didn't you?'

'Not really, Oliver just mentioned in passing last time I was there. He was just looking at his options, I didn't think he meant it,' Max said.

'Well, I'm astonished. I wish you'd warned me.'

'There really was nothing to warn you about,' Max said.

'Look, calm down you two, nothing's sorted yet,' Oliver said. 'Even if I could sell the house, the arboretum would have to be retained – there's a preservation order on several of the older trees including the big oak. My solicitor has been checking it out for me because I wouldn't want to move Alexis's ashes. She so loved that place.'

'Where would you go?' Jenny said. She still sounded upset at the thought. 'What about the girls?'

'We wouldn't go far. I'd like somewhere smaller, and a simpler life. That house has brought me enough heartache.'

'Oh, Oliver, there's so much to consider,' Jenny said.

Jacob started to grumble and Max helped him down from the table and set up his little plastic train track.

'I know, but I've decided I want a new life with Charlotte. I can't expect her to just slot into place in Lawn House. We've got some other ideas.'

'Oh my god, you mean it, don't you? Charlotte is your future and we haven't even met her yet,' Jenny said.

'You will soon, and you'll love her as much as the girls do. Now we know there will be no prosecutions, we can get on with a bit of normality and we'll see what happens. I must be off home soon, though. I'm going to London early tomorrow and I need to see the girls before bed.'

'Seeing Charlotte in London?' Max said.

'Of course. We're off to the auctions to see what some of Mum's silverware and jewellery will make, and before you panic, Jenny, I'm not selling off the family jewels, just the sparkly trinkets William Du Bois gave her.' Oliver smiled to reassure her.

Max was amused at the word "trinkets". They were probably the finest diamonds and sapphires, knowing what he did of Oliver's mum.

After Oliver had gone, Jenny crashed around in the kitchen doing the washing-up, while Max played with Jacob then read him a story before bedtime.

'Want drums,' Jacob said.

'No, darling. Mummy wants some quiet time, I think. You can play drums tomorrow.'

Two stories later and after a good splash in the bath, Jacob went to bed.

'You all right?' Max asked when Jenny finally came and sat down.

'I just feel unsettled. I'm relieved the investigation is over and people can move forward, but it sounds as if there are major changes ahead.'

'Nothing stays the same. Think of the positives. It's good that Oliver's fallen in love again, and he can plan a future. The girls are growing up just fine and they could probably do with a more normal lifestyle too.'

'You're right. It just came as a bit of a shock. Oliver's put so much into the renovation of the house,' Jenny said.

'He didn't have much choice,' Max said.

'I suppose not. It's cost him a lot – I mean money as well as effort and stress. Perhaps there's something to be said for a simpler life, after all.' Jenny at last relaxed into a smile

'Apparently Arthur was a canny old man. When you were in the loo, Oliver told me his father had some mighty effective insurance policies in place – which is weird considering his tax situation was such a mess when he died. The Inland Revenue's bills were settled by the sale of the art, and the insurance is paying for much of the restoration, along with a grant from some heritage fund Lynn told him about.'

'I knew about that. Celine was awfully proud to tell me. What a gem Lynn's turned out to be,' Jenny said.

'Who on earth would want to buy a huge manor house, though, even if it's been beautifully restored?' Max asked.

'What you mean is, who could afford it? A film star or a rich businessman, probably someone famous,' Jenny said.

'It won't sell quickly. One thing's for sure, you'll have plenty of time to get used to the idea of Oliver's gang moving.'

37

ARBOUR GARDENS

September 2015

Max heard Jenny on the phone to Celine.

'Mr Hall's in hospital. He had a fall a few days ago,' Jenny whispered to Max, covering the mouthpiece. 'Oh dear, anything broken?' he heard her ask, and signalled for her to put it on loudspeaker.

'No, just badly bruised, but more confused than ever. They've asked Gus to persuade his mother that the old boy needs to be in a nursing home,' Celine's telephone voice echoed across the room.

'I know it's been a struggle for some time. I gather he really can't be left alone now,' Jenny said.

'These decisions are so difficult. You know a bit about things like this – perhaps you could have a word with Della. Gus and Sandra would appreciate it,' Celine asked.

'Are you all right, Celine? You don't sound your normal self. Is there something else? It's not Tricia, is it?' Jenny asked.

'No, it's Oliver. He's been to view a house. This move might happen sooner than I thought and I've only just settled into my cottage. It'll be very disrupting for the girls. Everything's changing, Jenny.'

'I know, but don't worry too much, change can be good. He still hasn't sold the big house, and that'll take forever. Look, I think I'll come over next week to see everyone. I can't manage it sooner. Max's parents are coming to visit for a few days for Jacob's second birthday. I'll phone Mrs Hall in the meantime.'

Jenny arranged to take Jacob over to Chestnut Cottage a week later. She told Max how shocked she was when the door opened and she saw Mrs Hall looking thin and drawn. Despite her own worries, though, she still had a birthday present and a card waiting inside for Jacob.

'It was so kind of her to remember,' she told Max later. 'Look at these little dinosaurs she gave him. Jacob played with them the whole time we talked.'

'How's she coping?' Max asked.

'I think it'd be okay if she could sleep. She hasn't slept properly for weeks. Now she feels guilty at the thought of putting Reg in a nursing home, even though it's the right thing. They've found him a bed at Arbour Gardens, and he's moving in a few days.'

'So soon?' Max said.

'Yes, I helped her start to pack some personal bits and pieces for his room, so it'll feel more familiar. That's what the matron suggested when she assessed him.'

'That's nice, it's good you could help her,' Max said

'Yes, I thought photographs would give the nurses something to talk to him about. I found an amazing one of Reg and Arthur as young men, standing with their arms on each other's shoulders. Arthur was surprisingly handsome in his day.'

'He must have had something, to get away with what he got up to,' Max said. 'Both Reg and Della had this great attachment to him.'

'Yes, she had the photo reframed this year, after they buried John Jacob. It's all made her rethink the past, and she spontaneously told me she did love Arthur, and she grew to love Reg too. When she described them as "quite a pair", she actually chuckled. Do you know, Max, I realised then just how willingly she'd given her life to these two men. One has gone, and the other is on his way.'

'Your little visit has made you thoughtful about the past, too, hasn't it?' Max put his arms round his wife. 'I do love you,' he said.

'Ah, thanks. We don't say it enough, do we? I love you too.'

Jacob tottered over to them where they were sitting on the sofa and tried to climb up and join in the hug.

'Hello, little man, show me your dinosaurs,' Max said. 'I wonder what Mrs Hall will do with herself? Will she stay at the cottage?'

'If Oliver sells up, she thinks that'll be her sign to leave. She's got her eye on a bungalow near Arbour Gardens and seems quite resigned to the idea. Do you think Oliver might help her buy it?' Jenny said. 'I wonder if it'll ever really happen?'

'I've heard there's someone interested Lawn House,' Max said.

'Really? Any idea who?' Jenny asked.

'It's top secret, apparently,' Max said.

'Oh, go on, Oliver must have given you a clue. I can't imagine who on earth would want to buy it – must be someone flipping rich,' Jenny said.

'That's all I know at the moment. You'll just have to be patient, my darling,' Max replied and gave her a kiss.

'Okay, but if you've been talking to Oliver, have you heard any more about Charlotte – is she the one?' Jenny couldn't resist probing. 'Mrs Hall's met her and says she's lovely.'

'Mmm! I've been talking to Gus, too, and he says while Oliver's in London this weekend he's in charge, and he's offered to show you the renovated interiors at Lawn House. It's nearly all done.'

'Seriously? I'd love that, but as long as Oliver's okay with it,' Jenny said. 'Don't you want to come too?'

'I've seen some of it already, but I suppose we could both go tomorrow if Celine can look after Jacob for half an hour.'

Jenny and Max met Gus in the entrance hall. Jenny gasped at the changes.

'Not bad, eh?' Gus said as he greeted them. 'I can't show you everything, but I'll show you what I can downstairs. The paint's still wet upstairs.'

Beautifully polished oak had been used to repair the main staircase with its carved newel posts. The curved-topped window frames across the front of the house had been replaced with the same wood. The afternoon light scattered in with patterned rays through small leaded lights above the oak front door, playing off the new parquet floor that had just been laid. Burgundy drapes, tied back at the windows, were the same colour as a big round rug in the centre of the hallway. It looked so rich Jenny bent to feel the deep, wool pile.

'Oh, feel that, Max, it's so thick. This all this looks wonderful, Gus.'

They drifted through the plush reception rooms, then inspected the brand-new kitchen and scullery. Jenny looked more impressed with every step she took.

'Just wait until you see the conservatory,' Gus told her. 'It's all been done to comply with the regulations of the heritage people and it's better than ever.'

'Wow. I wouldn't want to clean all this glass. Oh, and the chandeliers are wonderful. I wonder if Ed will ever have chance for another performance here? Wouldn't that be perfect!'

'That all depends on the new buyer, I suppose. There's someone in the wings I've heard, but it's hush-hush,' Gus said.

At the end of the downstairs tour, Jenny surprised both men by asking one last question. 'About upstairs, is the blue bedroom still blue?'

Gus hesitated, unsure what answer she expected.

'I asked Oliver to change the colour. I hope you agree. It's now ivory, with green drapes. He says there will no longer be a blue bedroom in the house.'

Jenny didn't say anything, but Max detected a gentle smile of acknowledgement.

———

They were both quiet on the drive back to Stowmarket. Jacob had fallen asleep so Jenny stayed in the car while Max went into the supermarket for a bottle of wine. When they got home there was an answerphone message waiting for them: *Call me back. I have news,* Ed's voice said.

'He sounds excited. Do you think he's asked Lucy to marry him?' was Jenny's first thought.

'Or she's pregnant?' Max said.

'Whatever, it sounds like good news,' Jenny replied. 'Phone him back. Loudspeaker please.'

Jacob joined in. 'Nucle Ned-Ned.'

'Jacob, it's Ed not Ned. Try to say Ed like you say *egg* ... *Ed*,' Jenny said happily.

'Egg-egg,' Jacob said with a grin.

'Well done,' Max said, picking up the phone.

'Hi, guys,' Ed's voice boomed out.

'What's happening?' Max asked.

'I know a secret. Who do you think wants to buy Lawn House?'

'You?' Max said.

'No, idiot! Steve! Steve Cain!' Ed announced, as if he was declaring a lottery winner.

'Heavens above! But he's American,' Jenny said so Ed could hear her.

'He's also very rich. He wants to split his time between LA and London, and fancies trying life as a country squire.'

'I suppose it's less than 100 miles from London, and that's

no distance for a guy from California,' Max said. 'It's a good idea. You sound pleased, Ed.'

'Yes, it's cool. It'll certainly keep the recording studio on the map,' Ed said. 'It sounds as if not all Oliver's meetings in London were with Charlotte. Oliver and Steve have been in talks for months.'

'So, all that stuff about "it might never happen" and "just exploring the options", was just a load of guff while he did his sales pitch,' Max said.

'Do you think Steve's contributed to some of the renovations?' Jenny added.

'Shush, Jenny. Stop interrupting or we won't get the picture,' Max said.

'I never thought of that,' Ed replied. 'I wouldn't be at all surprised.'

'Oliver's been going on about art sales, diamonds and insurance policies, but they were probably just smoke screens. We might never know the whole story,' Max said.

'Well, I must say I'm intrigued,' Jenny said in hushed tones, quite unable to stop interrupting.

'Me too. Steve's coming up to Lawn House soon with his advisors to have a big site meeting with Oliver and Gus,' Max said.

'Gus?' Jenny said.

'Yes quite!' Ed said. 'They want to talk about the land that goes with the house and do more surveys, but I've got to go away. Max, I wonder if you might be able to take a coincidental run on the day of the visit – thought you could drop in all casual, like, and put some feelers out,' Ed said.

'You want me to be your eyes and ears?' Max said.

'Exactly. You're the man for the job, Max. What do you think?'

'Love it. Count me in. Just let me know the time and date.'

38

FORTY ACRES

October 2015

When Max appeared at the end of his run, Steve Cain and Oliver, dressed in matching Barbours, were talking in front of the house. Max, in his therma-cool running gear, with a red face from running in the cool air of autumn, wished he had a fleece to put on after his exercise.

'Hi there. Max, isn't it? Good to see you.' Steve shook Max's hand with a grip worthy of Superman, and peered at him over the top of what looked like expensive tortoiseshell glasses – Max was an expert at identifying such items. He tried not to react as his hand was released, or feel intimidated as Steve looked him up and down.

'Of course, you two have met before, in California. It must have been years ago, when Max was travelling with Ed,' Oliver said. 'He often comes running on the estate.'

'So I see,' Steve said, looking doubtful.

'Oh, it's a great place to run, four acres of space and fresh air,' Max declared cheerily.

Steve frowned and turned to Oliver. 'He means forty, doesn't he?'

'Well, yes, if you include our surrounding fields,' Oliver said.

'F-forty acres?' Max spluttered.

'The garden, the park and the arboretum make about

four acres. The rest of the land is rented out to neighbouring farmers. You know I'm no farmer, Max,' Oliver said calmly.

'I was just saying I love what he's done to this place. It was looking pretty shabby last time I was here, but wow, what a difference a year makes,' Steve said.

'Yes, a year ... and a storm,' Max added.

'I'd heard a while ago Oliver might want to sell, so we've been talking. My guys are giving it the once-over right now. We've seen the floor plans, and next we're going to walk round your little park, Maxwell, before attacking the studios.' Steve smirked rather than smiled and Max decided not to correct his name.

'You set off, Steve, get the feel of the land, and I'll join you by the arboretum shortly. I'll just see Max off before he catches a chill,' Oliver said.

When Steve was out of earshot Oliver said, 'I think he likes it, Max. This could be it. I don't want to get too carried away, but it all fits.'

'I can't believe it. I'm still boggling about the fields. I always thought I was trespassing when I went over the far boundary. You're a dark horse.' Max couldn't quite believe these Trelawneys and their love of secrets.

'I thought you knew? Everyone round here knows. He's fussing that there's no pool – he obviously hasn't given much thought to the British weather!'

'Have you talked about how he'll run the estate yet? Will he make big changes?'

'No, he says he'd like to keep it much as it is, and the garden centre is to remain too. He thinks it's quaint! All the staff will be employed for the first year and then he'll reassess,' Oliver said.

'I suppose that's fair. So Gus and Sandra will be okay. Can Celine stay on in her cottage?'

'It's early days in the negotiations, but I hope so. He'll need reliable tenants. He has suggested in the future he might want to add a fine-dining restaurant to what's on offer as well. That would bring in more employment for the area.'

'Dare I ask what he says about the arboretum? He won't be able to touch the oak tree, will he?' Max said cautiously.

'That's next on the agenda. I'd better get over there. I need to explain a few things to him.'

'Good luck,' Max said. It seemed Oliver was standing on the edge of something big, and Max unexpectedly leaned forward and gave him a hug and a pat on the back.

When Max told Jenny all he'd discovered, she was quick to analyse the situation.

'It will all change, but it has to in order to survive. Sustainability is key. I can imagine him turning it into a hotel one day, or one of those restaurants with boutique rooms. He'd be able to charge a fortune.'

'We could go and stay there and be pampered?' Max suggested.

'I don't think so! God, I hope he doesn't attract the huntin' and shootin' brigade. I might have to get up a petition and demonstrate if he does.'

'Behave,' Max said. 'No, he'll attract the musicians and arty types. He'll want to make more of the association with the studio.'

'Whatever. By then it'll be nothing to do with us. Did Oliver say where he'll move to?'

'No. He's still saying it'll take ages for contracts to be drawn, even if Steve makes an offer. He seems to think he has plenty of time. I did ask him to keep us informed.'

Having kept radio silence for months, the phone calls

once again buzzed regularly between Lawn House and Stowmarket. At long last Oliver invited Max and Jenny to come and meet Charlotte over dinner at a nearby country pub that did great food.

'Get a babysitter and arrange a taxi. We're having champagne,' he said.

'What are we celebrating?' Max asked.

'It's Jenny's birthday soon. Let's call it an early birthday party,' Oliver said.

'We'll get a babysitter,' Max said.

It was a place they'd not been to before, and when the taxi dropped them off Jenny commented it looked smarter than she'd expected for a pub.

'Gastro-pub,' said Max. 'I looked at the menu online and I don't think we'll be disappointed.'

'Make sure you leave your mobile on in case Jacob needs us,' Jenny said. She was pleased she'd put on a decent dress and not turned up in her jeans when she saw the tall blonde woman, elegantly, albeit casually, dressed in black, standing at Oliver's side at the bar.

'Jenny, Max, this is Charlotte.'

'How lovely to meet you at last,' Jenny said. 'We've not been here before, have you? It looks very nice.'

'We've been a couple of times,' Charlotte said. Jenny bridled slightly at the thought they'd never met this woman, even though she'd obviously been in the area enough times. She looked at Max, who was smiling like an idiot.

'It's become one of our favourites, that's why we wanted to bring you here,' Oliver said tactfully.

'The food's great, especially the steak and ale pie. Oh, and the brown bread ice cream is to die for,' Charlotte added, and that simple statement made Jenny relax and realise they would be fine.

Oliver ordered champagne while they waited for their food.

'What are we celebrating?' Max asked.

'Just tell them, Oliver,' Charlotte said, and for her directness, Jenny liked her even more.

'We have a deal. I've accepted Steve's offer and we're selling Lawn House. Contracts are signed and we can exchange once the funds are released, which should take just a few weeks,' Oliver announced.

'Congratulations!' Jenny and Max said in unison, and everyone clinked glasses. Jenny anticipated that word would be used a lot that night.

'Tell them the rest of it,' Charlotte said. 'Then I want to hear all about Jacob.'

'We've found a house. It's called The Drift House,' Oliver said.

'Oh, nice name,' Jenny said.

'And it's halfway between Stowmarket and Lawn House, and easy distance from the girls' school,' Charlotte added.

'Sounds great,' Max said, and he raised his glass again for another round of clinks.

'It was built in the eighties, next to a lane called The Drift, and has five bedrooms, three bathrooms, three reception rooms and an annexe,' Oliver said.

'Oh, a normal house, then,' Jenny said, and they all laughed. 'What about the garden?'

'Big enough, but manageable,' said Charlotte. 'We took the girls to see it this afternoon and they loved it.'

'Willow was a bit worried where they'd put the treehouse,' Oliver said. 'I'll have to consult Gus about that. Celine can travel over daily from her cottage to look after the girls, or she can stay in the annexe if we are away or in London.'

'She's still going to be a part of our family,' Charlotte said.

Max saw Jenny's eyebrows raise, at the ease with which she said "our".

'Charlotte will keep her flat in London to begin with, then gradually shift her work up here, won't you, darling?' Oliver said, then added, 'Not too gradually, I hope.'

Jenny thrilled inside at the obvious and contagious romance in the air. She looked happily at Max as he tucked into his steak and ale pie.

'Now, tell me about Jacob, I can't wait to meet him. He sounds quite a character,' Charlotte said.

There was nothing Jenny liked better than talking about Jacob with an appreciative audience. As the conversation continued, Max slipped his hand under the table to stroke Jenny's.

39

THE DRIFT HOUSE

May 2016

One weekend, in late spring, a garden party was held at The Drift House. The main event was to be the unveiling of the redesigned treehouse. Gus and his men had moved it with great difficulty from Lawn House, now jokingly named "Cain Castle" by the locals.

'Nightmare,' Gus informed the Browns as he greeted them in the drive.

'Your fault for making it so solid,' Max told him.

'There wasn't a tree substantial enough, so we had to chop off the post-Disneyland extension,' Gus said. 'Steve doesn't want what's left, so we wondered if Jacob would like it as a playhouse?'

'We don't have any big trees, but it could sit at ground level,' Max said.

'Would that be good, Jacob?' Gus asked.

'Yes! Yes!' Jacob replied.

'A playhouse, Jacob, aren't you lucky. What do you say?'

'Tankoo.' Jacob pointed beyond Gus.

'There are Issy and Willow. You can go and play with them if you're careful,' Jenny said. 'It's all right, Daddy and I will follow.'

Jacob scampered over to the girls who were swinging

on a wrought iron side gate, guarding the entrance to the back garden.

'I got a certificate for my writing at school this week,' Issy announced before anyone could even say hello. 'I'm going to be a famous writer.'

'I thought you were going to be an explorer?' Max said.

'I'll explore, then I'll write about it, silly,' she replied.

'I got a prize for drawing,' Willow said.

'Well done, both of you. Jacob got a prize for music at pre-school, didn't you, darling?' Jenny said. 'He's a great drummer these days.'

Issy took Jenny's hand and pulled her into the garden. The others followed them round the side of the house.

'You have got a bit fat, Aunty Jenny. Is that a baby in your tummy?' Issy asked.

'How did you guess that?' Jenny laughed.

'I just know about these things,' Issy said seriously. 'Is it a boy or a girl?'

'It's a secret,' Jenny said. 'You'll have to wait and see.'

'I do hope it's a girl,' Willow said.

'Me too!' Jacob announced and Max chuckled.

'Hey, we've made you a welcome card for your treehouse,' Max said. 'Jacob wants to deliver it himself.'

'Me too!' Jacob said.

'Yes, you too. He means he helped make it too. It's his new phrase! Everything is "me too" at the moment,' Max explained.

'Just look at this,' Jenny said, when they reached the back garden. 'It's about ten times bigger than our garden, Jacob. Aren't they lucky girls? Who put all this bunting up, I wonder?'

'I did.' Oliver leapt forward and swept Jacob off his feet, stopping him on his way to the treehouse. He swung the squealing Jacob round and round. 'You'll have to wait for the ribbon to be cut, young man,' he announced.

Celine and Lynn were pouring out glasses of lemonade and iced tea, while Sandra and Charlotte balanced cupcakes on a fancy cake rack. Mrs Hall seemed to be supervising at a side table, laid out with paper plates and sandwiches, while Gus was making final checks on the all-important treehouse. Wooden benches and deckchairs had been strategically placed with clear views of the play area.

'Looks like we're the guests of honour, and last to arrive. Aren't Ed and Lucy coming?' Jenny whispered.

'No, they're working in London this weekend,' Max whispered back as Charlotte approached. He caught sight of something move behind the hedge near the serving table and heard the scattering sound of birds taking flight.

'Hi, lovely to see you. You do look well, Jenny. Isn't this great?' Charlotte said. She slipped her hand into Oliver's and leaned comfortably against him.

There was a squeal from Willow at the food table as Issy poked her finger into a pink cupcake. Max saw Mrs Hall raise her hand and feared a reprimand but instead she swatted away a giant hornet. 'Things are hotting up,' he said.

'Yes, let's get started before we all get overexcited,' Oliver said.

'Me too!' said Jacob.

'Yes, you too, Jacob. Come on kids, let's cut the ribbon!'

Oliver and the children escorted Mrs Hall to the red ribbon tied across the steps to the treehouse. Like the Queen launching a ship, Mrs Hall gave a little speech, then cut the ribbon.

'Where's the champagne bottle?' Charlotte said, and everyone laughed as the girls scurried like squirrels up the stepladder to their new playhouse. Jacob followed them and tried to climb the ladder, with one hand still holding the card. He squawked when Max tried to take it from him, explaining it would be easier to climb with two hands. Eventually a compromise was reached and Jacob allowed the card to be tucked into the top of his shorts. Then with huge determination he climbed, alternate hands, one rung at a time. Max hovered behind him, just in case, but could hardly conceal the pride he had in his son. Progress was slow, however, and eventually Celine took over supervising so Max could go back to Jenny.

'Charlotte's been telling me she's selling her flat in Islington and moving in here permanently,' Jenny said.

Oliver joined them. "Have you told them?' he asked Charlotte.

'I thought you'd want to,' she said and a look passed between them like a pair of excited teenagers.

'What?' asked Max.

'Okay, so ... we're going into business together.' Oliver put his arm round Charlotte. 'Charlotte's quitting her job and we're opening a gallery in Snape.'

'That's wonderful news!' Jenny said.

'Yes, about time you got yourself a proper job,' Max teased. 'And I'm sure you couldn't have found a better business partner.'

Oliver grinned benignly. 'Nor a better life partner,' he said.

'He's full of romance, isn't he? Can't we find a better term than life partner?' Charlotte said.

'Okay, girlfriend, or how about future fiancée?' he said.

'That'll do nicely, but no rush.' Charlotte kissed Oliver.

Jenny suddenly let out a cry and put her hand to her bump. 'Sorry, it's an active little thing.'

'Maybe a footballer, or a drummer like Jacob?' Oliver suggested.

'Or a dancer,' said Charlotte.

'Whatever it is, it's dancing on my bladder. I'll just pop to the loo.'

'It's in the hall to the left of the front door. Can you manage?' Oliver said.

'Yes, of course,' Jenny said, thinking she'd enjoy a little peep inside the house.

Max thought she seemed gone a long time. When she got back to the garden Jenny looked pale. She grabbed Max's forearm.

'Do you need to sit down?' he said, turning to get a garden chair. Jenny held him back.

'I'm okay,' she said, 'but I've just seen something through the cloakroom window. It was so warm in there I felt a bit queasy, so I opened the window for some air. I saw something move behind the garden hedge, so I waited and watched for a while. I'm sure someone was peering in through the hedge. I thought I might faint. I splashed my face and looked again and what or whoever it was had gone.' Jenny swayed and closed her eyes.

'You should have called for help. Sit down before you fall down. I'll fetch a glass of water. It would just be a walker in the lane. I'll ask Gus to go and check. Sit!'

'No, not Gus. Ask Oliver or Celine. Oh God, I feel faint again.' Jenny bent forward over her bump with some difficulty, and briefly hung her head while Max tried to stop her toppling from the chair. He fanned her with his handkerchief.

'Can I get some help here?' Max called. Celine came running across the garden.

Jenny lifted her head and grabbed Celine's hand. 'I saw who it was. It was Tricia, and I think she was watching Jacob.'

'Where is Jacob?' Max yelled.

40

THE TALE END

They found Jacob, hiding with Willow in some shrubbery, with a plastic dinosaur he had brought from home. She said they were making a dinosaur den. Once the minor panic was over, Charlotte took Jenny inside to lie down and rest, while Max, Celine and Lynn played with the children. By now Oliver had disappeared on his own, to look down the lane, and Max suspected he only went to satisfy Jenny.

It seemed an awfully long time before Oliver reappeared, and when he did, he was followed by Tricia and a tall, handsome man whom Max didn't know. Oliver showed them into the garden, whereupon the party fell silent, apart from a gasp from Sandra. Max saw Gus go pale, as if his blood was being rapidly diluted. Jacob ran to Max and clung on to one of his legs and Max realised the toddler didn't even remember Tricia, but must have sensed the change in atmosphere.

'Hello, everyone,' Tricia said. 'This is James, my boyfriend.'

'Good afternoon. We're so sorry to crash your party. We won't stay long. Patricia just wanted to say hi to Celine as we were in the area,' James said with a confident voice.

'Don't tell me that's Jacob!' Tricia said. 'And just look at these grown-up girls. It's so good to see you all.'

'Now you know we mustn't stay long, Patricia,' James

said. He took her by the elbow, and Max thought she flinched slightly. He watched her closely as her eyes swept round, taking in the view of the garden and the people gathered there. Apart from the flinch, she looked well.

'You can have something to drink, then you can go,' Celine said abruptly. She took them over to Mrs Hall's refreshment table for an iced tea and Max left them to it. He slipped indoors to see if Jenny was all right and found her fast asleep. He sat awhile and seeing her peaceful face, decided not to disturb her.

Celine caught him in the hallway on his way back out to the garden. Max pulled a quizzical face.

'Don't worry, James is driving her back to Manchester tonight. They live together now and it appears she'll do whatever he says,' Celine said calmly. 'She's just off-loading some of her nonsense on poor Mrs Hall, with Oliver standing guard. I'm still not sure we can trust a word she says, though.'

'I really don't want to get involved in a long conversation with her. How's Gus dealing with it?'

'He and Sandra have disappeared into the kitchen to do the washing-up. It's all right, Charlotte and Lynn have the children under control. Look, Max, I think Mrs Hall's had enough, would you be able to run her home, it's not far, and then come back for Jenny and Jacob? I can keep an eye on him for you.'

'Course, no problem.'

Mrs Hall was exhausted, but at the same time too revved up to go and be at home on her own. Once in the car she asked Max to drop her off at Arbour Gardens instead of her new bungalow.

'It's on the way to my place so it'll be easier for you. I want to be with Reg awhile and then I'll get a taxi home.'

'I'll come in with you for a few minutes, if that's okay. I haven't seen Reg for ages,' Max told her.

'He won't know who you are.'

'That doesn't matter.'

Mrs Hall rang the bell and the residence manager unlocked the front door for them, then tapped the key code lock on the entrance to Reg's unit.

'How's he been today?' Della asked, after introducing Max to the woman.

'Quiet today,' said the manager. 'He wouldn't come to the dining room for lunch, and he's been lying on his bed all afternoon. Didn't even want the telly on. We've just persuaded him to have a cup of tea and a piece of cake. Would you like something?'

'No, thanks, we'll just go and sit with him awhile.'

Reg was lying on top of his bed, fully clothed, with his slippers on. Max noticed a stain down the front of his jumper where some part of a previous meal must have missed its target. Mrs Hall tried to scratch it away, then got a clean jumper out of his drawer. Reg opened his eyes.

'Hello, love, it's me, it's Dell. How are you today? Look who's here. It's Max.' She brushed some crumbs off the bedcover as she leaned to kiss his cheek. 'You've not had a shave, Reg, and I can smell coconut. Did you have coconut cake for tea today? Was it nice?'

Reg grunted quietly. Max thought how sad it was to see him so depleted. Della sat in the easy chair by his bedside, rearranged the cushions for comfort, and took his hand. Max noticed Reg gave it a little squeeze and she smiled.

'I'm on my way back from the garden party at The Drift House. It's looking lovely, but I'm not sure the garden's up to your standard yet. Still, the twins have got their treehouse in place, so they're happy. Our Gus has done a good job. Young Jacob even managed to climb up to it. He's come along so well, considering. Max says he's enjoying pre-school. That's good, isn't it, especially as Jenny and Max here are expecting another soon? I told you that last week, didn't I?'

Della knew not to expect much response from Reg but

liked to keep him informed about the outside world. Max thought it amazing she still had so much consideration for her husband after all these years, and even though he seemed an empty shell. He wondered if he and Jenny might one day be like this.

'Anyway, Gus and Sandra send their love, they seemed happy enough, and Mr Oliver had his nice new girlfriend with him. They'll be married soon, you mark my words. Even Celine had her girlfriend with her. I was the only one there on my own, Reg. I did miss you.'

Della pulled a hanky from her cardigan sleeve and blew her nose. Max wanted to leave now, but Della Hall was on a roll and didn't stop talking long enough for him to say his goodbyes.

'There was a bit of excitement at the end of the party, though. Are you still listening, Reg? Guess who turned up, out of the blue? That woman Tricia, that's who. Calls herself Patricia now. I know she was never one of your favourites, but she looked really well. She's quietened down, put on a bit of weight, and it suits her, that and a nice new hairstyle – she's somehow got those curls under control. Her new boyfriend drove her down. She wanted to see Lawn House one more time. She saw something on the internet about the renovations and just turned up, apparently. She's always had a nerve that one. Even she was shocked when it wasn't Mr Oliver but that American man who opened the door. He told her Oliver had moved and gave them the address for The Drift House.'

'So, they drove over to the new house, just to have a look, said she wasn't going to come in, just wanted to see where it was. Miss Jenny spotted her in the drive and it gave the poor love quite a turn. Oliver went to investigate and, in the end, he asked Tricia and her fella into the garden to see everyone. There she was, making out she's a changed woman.'

Della stuffed her hanky up her sleeve and poured a cup

of water from a plastic jug on the side table. Max stood up, ready to leave but Della started again.

'Do you want a sip, Reg? No, okay. So, Tricia met her new boyfriend in rehab – James, he's called, handsome man, older than her, said he was an art therapist. They live together now in Manchester, and she's got a job in a shop now – thank God it's not with children, eh?'

'I really should be getting back to Jenny and Jacob, Mrs Hall. Will you be staying?' Max managed to squeeze in.

'Yes, love. You'd best be getting back. I'll get a taxi from here. We'll be fine, won't we, Reg? Look at us, still going strong after nearly fifty-two years.'

She was still talking when Max left. He stood outside the door and listened for a while longer.

'Of course, Celine was cross her sister hadn't made contact or warned them she was coming, but Tricia said she didn't dare after all the trouble she'd caused. It seems James wanted to know more about her bad times in Suffolk. He was very talkative. Told me he thought it would be good for her to face up to her past, and helpful for him to understand her better. That's kind, isn't it?'

'She said it was you who vandalised the tree and Arthur's grave, Reg. Said it was you who blew up the electrics too. She admitted she'd given you the idea, and a few nudges, but it was you who did it. I just don't know want to believe, Reg. James said it was all in the past now and best to let it go. I don't know what to think, but that James was very convincing – seemed a bit of a charmer, actually. He reminded me a bit of our Arthur in the old days. Anyway, he kept a close eye on her, and did most of the talking come to think of it. You'd have said he was a bit full of himself, Reg, like you used to say about Arthur when he was in a bossy mood. Perhaps James might keep her on the straight and narrow – she needs a strong man that one. Anyway, they've been planning a trip to Suffolk for months, but it got delayed because at last she's found out who her real father is. You remember her father isn't the same as Celine's? James said Tricia's been trying to find her dad for years and that having no father in her life was one of her main problems. He said she had identity issues. Huh!'

'Would you believe it, her dad's name is Arthur, too, and he's a retired plumber from Brentwood? When his wife died he started looking for his ex – Tricia's mother – but never even knew he had a daughter, apparently, so he must have got a shock. When they met he told Tricia he'd never forgotten the waitress he'd had a fling with on his stag night in a bar in Manchester.'

Max heard Della sigh and take a breather.

'I don't think you ever had a stag night, did you, Reg? Good thing, too, if you ask me – waste of money and more trouble than it's worth. I never had a hen night, either. Still, like I just told Mr Max in the car, we've managed all these years, and we've both made mistakes, but we've not done too badly.'

Reg suddenly snorted a loud snore, and Max could imagine Della smiling and her eyes closing, probably ready for a nap too.

30751651R00176

Printed in Poland
by Amazon Fulfillment
Poland Sp. z o.o., Wrocław